PATTERSON

PATTERSON

A WESTERN DUO

LAURAN PAINE

FIVE STAR
A part of Gale, Cengage Learning

Detroit • New York • San Francisco • New Haven, Conn • Waterville, Maine • London

LIBRARY OF CONGRESS CATALOGING-IN-PUBLICATION DATA

Paine, Lauran.
 [Dead men in a row]
 Patterson : a western duo / by Lauran Paine. — 1st ed.
  p. cm. — (A Five Star western)
 ISBN-13: 978-1-59414-687-9 (alk. paper)
 ISBN-10: 1-59414-687-X (alk. paper)
 1. Western stories. I. Paine, Lauran. Patterson. II. Title.
PS3566.A34D43 2008
813'.54—dc22   2008010696

First Edition. First Printing: July 2008.

Published in 2008 in conjunction with Golden West Literary Agency.

Printed in the United States of America
1 2 3 4 5 6 7 12 11 10 09 08

CONTENTS

DEAD MEN IN A ROW 7

PATTERSON 123

★ ★ ★ ★ ★

DEAD MEN IN A ROW

★ ★ ★ ★ ★

I

They called it "Custer's luck", and Sheriff Ackroyd was thinking of that when he leaned over the wagon side to look at the
dead men, three of them. But they had simply been shot. There
was no indication of anything else having been done to them,
and Ackroyd noted this, as he straightened around when a light
hand fell upon his shoulder. The man who had strolled over was
Paul Beaman, owner of the wagon the bodies were lying in,
owner, too, of the stage, freight, and mail company in Cedarville. Paul was a burly, graying, smiling man with dark brows
and black eyes. He leaned, looked, pulled back, and said: "The
driver explained it to me. Why would someone shoot three men,
then lay them out like cordwood at the side of the road where
they were sure to be found?"

Jim Ackroyd had no answer. He had wondered the same thing
when the driver had left his rig out front of the Cedarville jailhouse and gone back to the corral yard to tell Paul Beaman
what he had found on his way home after delivering block salt
to the foothill cow camp of the Dagger Ranch.

Beaman looked in again, then firmly turned his back. The
three dead men were not pleasant to see. "Indians," he told Jim
Ackroyd. "But it's been a long time, Jim. Must be at least fifteen
years since we've had strong hearts in the territory."

Jim Ackroyd leaned his durable, burly body against the wagon
side and considered the heavier and older man from pale eyes.
"Why Indians, Paul?"

"Well, look at them." Beaman scratched as he considered Sheriff Ackroyd. "Be better if you blamed it on Indians, Jim."

"Why?"

"Because from the looks of those men they've been dead several days, and, if it was outlaws shot them, by now they're out of the country and folks will say you were too slow, or too lazy, to catch them. Indians . . . hell, they ducked back onto the reservation. Folks would accept that."

Ackroyd gazed dispassionately at Beaman, who had already made more money than he ever would, and the sheriff was still young. "Paul," he told Beaman, "I'm not running for office. I don't care what people say. As for those three corpses, look at it another way. Anyone who would kill three men would kill you or me, or anyone else who went up the road from Cedarville, and anyone who would line up those corpses for travelers to see did that in defiance, as a challenge. If it was Indians, which I doubt like hell, I'll find out which ones. If it wasn't . . . I'll find him, too. Or maybe two or three killers, but they've got to be found, unless you don't care about someone . . . maybe your wife . . . riding a northbound stage which might get stopped, and her shot."

Beaman was not impressed. He was a thorough realist, a man whose humanitarianism burned very low, and whose sense of success burned very high. He waved a hand. "I'll send someone for the rig, if you'll get them out of it."

Ackroyd nodded, then watched the portly older man walk away.

He took the rig around back, unloaded the bodies in his shed across the alley, returned the wagon and hitch to his jailhouse rack, and left it tied there while he took all the personal things he had removed from the bodies inside to spread out atop his desk.

Murder was not uncommon. Probably in Sheriff Jim Ackroyd's county it was much more common than people thought, because most murderers hid their victims, and northern Wyoming was a very large, sparsely settled, insular world.

Ackroyd tipped back his hat, sat down at the desk, and studied what he had—three clasp knives, some folding money and some silver money, sulphur matches from the third corpse, along with handkerchiefs and some smoking tobacco. There was no clue about the identity of the corpses. He guessed that, if there was a clue, it was probably in the saddlebags that no doubt had been on the saddles of the horses those three men had been riding, and of which there had been no sign at the place where the bodies had been lined out, according to the teamster who had brought the bodies to Cedarville.

If it had been murder for money, why hadn't the gunman taken what Ackroyd had found in the pockets of the corpses? If it had been some kind of personal feud, or if Indians had indeed done it, why had they left the bodies to be found in plain view? And finally, if it had been murder to obtain three saddle animals, then at least Ackroyd could understand something about the affair, but he had a feeling that three riderless horses were going to turn up. Not because he doubted that the corpses had been left lying beside the road because some outlaws needed fresh animals, but because of late this was how Jim Ackroyd's luck had been running.

He swept the nondescript items from the corpses into an empty desk drawer and went out back to stand in the rickety old shed gazing at the bodies. One of them was an older man, perhaps in his late forties. The other two were younger. All three men were dressed as range riders, but this did not mean much; even preachers and saloon men dressed that way; it was the custom of the territory.

He guessed the older man had been the nonsmoker. He also guessed that, despite appearances, these were not range men.

What, exactly, they really were, Ackroyd had no idea, but there were small details others might have missed altogether, which told Ackroyd, who had started out riding ranges, that these three men had not been professional riders. They had been lying beside the stage road about six miles north of Cedarville. They had probably been heading southward, probably with some notion of sleeping at the Cedarville rooming house overnight before going on. If there were bedrolls and saddlebags, these were still on the missing saddles.

Ackroyd had the feeling these dead men had been traveling through. He had no logical reason to think this, but he had a hunch, and, for lack of anything to displace it, he continued to speculate that the three dead men had been nothing more than travelers. Why, then—excepting a need for their horses—had someone shot all three of them? Of course, it could have been someone who had been on their trail, someone whose grim resolve had been nurtured elsewhere, and who had taken his time following the three travelers. When everything seemed right, he had shot them.

Ackroyd grumbled under his breath. It was late springtime; fish were feeding off May flies at the mountain lakes. He had intended to vacation in the northward mountains for a couple of weeks. Now, some damned fools had got themselves shot in his county, and because there were three of them, and also because by this evening it would be all over town, and perhaps out as far as the cow outfits, too, that Jim Ackroyd was finally going to have to earn his wages, the mountain trip would have to be postponed, at least for a while. If something did not come along to help Ackroyd very soon, by the time he got to the mountain lakes the fish would be so well fed and fat on May flies, his bacon-rind bait would not accomplish a damned thing.

He walked up to Dr. Campbell's place, told him what he had in the shed across the alley behind the jailhouse, then went over to Donovan's saloon for a couple of drinks.

John Donovan had already heard. He put out a bottle and glass, then said: "What does it look like to you, Jim?"

Ackroyd was filling the jolt glass when he replied: "They were shot from in front, John. They had their guns in holsters. Not a gun had been fired." Ackroyd paused to down the drink and dash at the water that sprang to his eyes. "What does that sound like?"

"Shot from ambush," stated the florid, paunchy saloon man in a tone of intransigent conviction.

Ackroyd was pouring his second jolt when he said: "Maybe. Maybe not. If you and I were talking, like we are right now, you could shoot me. I wouldn't be expecting it."

Donovan's low, broad brow got two deep furrows across it. "Someone they knew, a friend maybe?"

"Yeah. Maybe. John, this is green whiskey."

Donovan didn't look at the bottle. "That feller who brought them to town said they looked like they'd been dead a couple of days. By now the feller who shot them is likely halfway up across Colorado."

Ackroyd wiped his eyes again, and this time pushed both the bottle and glass farther away. "Maybe. I hope he is. I can't be blamed for something I can't help, can I? Where did you get that whiskey, John?"

Donovan snorted, finally glancing at the bottle. "I got it from the same old gaffer who lives in the mountains I usually get it from, and you never complained before."

"Yeah, but look at it. It's got no color, hardly any color anyway. He didn't age the stuff."

Donovan sighed, leaned on the bar eyeing Sheriff Ackroyd, and finally said: "This is how I know summer's arrived. You always start getting cranky when the weather warms up."

II

James Campbell had been a physician since he had been twenty-eight—back in New Hampshire. He had also been a drinker back in those days, and somewhere between then and now, between New Hampshire and Wyoming, things had happened that had changed him. But he had probably never been a man of much humor, and he had probably always been an individual of bluntness. Those were things people said came with the New England milieu.

He sat in Jim Ackroyd's jailhouse office, legs extended, blue eyes fixed, and said: "What caliber would you say?"

Ackroyd hunched thick shoulders as he examined three misshapen lead bullets on his desk top. "Not what I expected," he answered, and picked up the least flattened of the slugs. "Small caliber, Jim."

"Very small caliber. They would be small caliber even for a belly gun, wouldn't you say?"

Sheriff Ackroyd put the slug down and looked across the room. "No, I wouldn't say that. I've seen a lot of small caliber hide-out and vest-pocket guns." He leaned a little, and smiled. "But generally they're larger than this. What's on your mind, Doctor?"

"A woman's weapon."

Ackroyd continued to lean and gaze across the room. He'd had no suspicions because there had been nothing to base suspicions upon, but this stopped him cold. "A woman's weapon . . . All right, maybe. But I don't see some lady lining up three fellers and killing them face to face . . . even from ambush. And them armed. After the first shot . . ." Ackroyd leaned far back and shook his head.

Dr. Campbell's face remained unreadable. Most of the time it was that way. "All right." He fished in a pocket, brought forth

14

a balled-up piece of cloth, and pitched it atop the desk. "Smell the collar."

Ackroyd sniffed, considered the worn flannel shirt, sniffed again, and put the shirt aside.

Campbell's stony features showed nothing. "What did that smell of, Sheriff?"

"Perfume."

"I thought so, too," stated the medical practitioner dryly. "You've probably known more range men than I have . . . or freighters . . . or horsemen. . . ."

Ackroyd sighed. "All right. I've never known any to wear perfume."

"Or carry a piddling little gun that shot bullets the size of a small pea."

Ackroyd nodded. He knew his guest very well. After seven years Jim Ackroyd knew all the permanent residents of Cedarville very well. Dr. Campbell was one of those people who was not satisfied with just being right; he also had to wring confessions from others about how right he had been.

"Where is she?" Ackroyd asked, and Dr. Campbell sighed and shoved up to his feet before replying. He was a man of average height, possibly an inch above average height, and lean, slightly stooped, one of those men who had always looked older than he was.

"That's your job," he told Sheriff Ackroyd. Then he also said: "You went up there. Wasn't there anything at all?"

Ackroyd had not only gone up there to fetch the corpses back, he had also gone back up there on horseback and had scoured the area for a couple of miles in all directions. He had found horse tracks, about fifty or sixty head's worth, all barefoot, someone's loose stock being driven from the range southward in the direction of one of the cattle outfits. Otherwise, he had found absolutely nothing.

He considered Dr. Campbell. "Yeah, there was something. Not a single mark anywhere close."

Campbell's saturnine eyes widened slightly. "That's something?"

"Yeah . . . They weren't shot up there, Doctor. They were stretched out on the ground up there, next to the road so's someone would sure as hell find them, but they were not killed up there. Why would someone go to all that trouble?"

Campbell turned thoughtful. "I'd have to ponder that," he said, as the sheriff arose from the desk. "I had some idea it might have been because someone, perhaps outlaws on the move, needed three fresh horses."

Ackroyd went to the door and courteously held it open as an invitation for his guest to depart. Almost without thinking, Dr. Campbell strolled past to the sidewalk before speaking again. "Why?"

Ackroyd smiled. "It's something to think about, isn't it?" he replied, nodded, and gently eased the door closed.

Dr. Campbell went up to John Donovan's saloon, which was nearly empty in the mid-morning, had a shot of Irish whiskey, and mentioned what was uppermost in his thoughts to Donovan.

"Sometimes Jim Ackroyd acts like a damned sphinx."

Donovan knew his patron. He was neither fond nor unfond of Dr. Campbell. As far as he was concerned, Campbell was a dour, poker-faced individual without humor, probably without imagination as well, who could set bones and roll pills and do a good job of cutting and sewing. Donovan himself was a man of quick interest, lively humanitarianism, rough humor, and great curiosity, so perhaps it was both natural and inevitable that he found Dr. James Campbell a difficult man to care very much for. As for the doctor's statement about Sheriff Ackroyd, who John Donovan liked, in rebuttal he simply said: "That's his job . . . to act like a sphinx."

Campbell raised his glass, downed its contents, then put a steady, pale gaze upon the saloon man. "Sure," he said dryly, paid up, and departed.

On his way northward and across the dirty roadway he encountered Sheriff Ackroyd, riding out of town. They nodded and Ackroyd said: "When you get around to it, Jim, I'd like the rest of their clothing and what-not brought to the office."

Campbell was agreeable, and, after Ackroyd had passed the limits of town on the north stage road, and looped the reins so he'd have both hands free to roll a smoke, he wagged his head. Campbell's visit to the jailhouse with those little bullets had given Ackroyd a real riddle. He did not believe a woman had killed those three men. He did not have a very clear idea about who the killer was, but he had been a lawman a long time—fifteen years—and had yet to meet a female who would line up three men and deliberately murder them. From ambush or any other way.

He lit the cigarette and trickled smoke. There were such women; he was satisfied about that, but not in Wyoming, certainly not within a ride of a day or two of his county. He would bet everything he owned on *that*.

He left the road riding northwesterly and continued angling off in that direction for several miles. As for perfume on that shirt collar—those dead men had looked to Jim Ackroyd like range men. Every town of any size he had ever been in had dance-hall ladies and saloon ladies. Range men patronized places where there were such women as often as they could afford to do it.

He halted where a large, scaly old volcanic rock stood about a mile west of the winding roadway, dismounted, tied his horse to a lodgepole pine nearby, went over to the tall, finger-like thick old scabrous rock, went around back where the prehistoric carved steps were, and without difficulty climbed the plinth. There was a place on top barely large enough for a man to sit. Around the base of this rock were stone chips where centuries ago, and maybe more recently, Indian watchers had sat, making arrowheads to relieve boredom while they kept a vigil. It was near the boundary of the Dagger cow outfit. About a mile closer to the mountains was the Dagger cow camp the freighter had been hauling rock salt to when he had found the dead men.

Jim Ackroyd did not know when those dead men had been laid out, but he had an idea that it had not been during broad daylight. The north-south stage road was well traveled. In fact it was the only route through the northward mountains heading southward to the Cedarville country of Pawnee Valley. One thing he *did* know was that the corpses had not been brought down there on pack horses, because there had been no tracks. They had come by wheeled vehicle, had been laid out, and the wheeled vehicle had gone on, and right now it was the vehicle he was interested in.

Having satisfied himself the Dagger range men up at the cow camp would have been able to hear a wagon in the night, he climbed down from the rock and rode northward into the wide, rolling belt of foothills. The log shack was east of the plinth, a little closer to the road, and sat on the lee side of a grassy side hill where it would be protected from both the north and east winds. It had a sod roof with clumps of bunchgrass sprouting up there, chinked walls made of logs as thick as a man's body, one recessed, glassless window, and a low door with some rat-gnawed wapiti horns above it. Out back there was a pole corral and a horse shed, and from the center of the corral two bay horses were as motionless as stones watching Jim Ackroyd ride in.

The cowboy leaned in the doorway, also watching. He was an older man, round-shouldered, leggy, with black eyes and enough beard stubble and unkempt hair of the same color to make him look part Indian. He spat amber, shifted his cud, and called ahead: "Beans are on . . . with pone, Sheriff! There's hay in the shed out back." Then the cowboy went inside, closed the door, and did not reappear.

Ackroyd cared for his horse, strolled around front, ducked to enter, and smelled food. The cowboy grinned from the stove. His name was Hudd Sawyer. He had been with the Dagger outfit eighteen years. He and Ackroyd had known one another about that long, but intermittently because Hudd Sawyer was a rare range man—he did not visit town unless he absolutely had to. He was what Dagger's range boss had once told Ackroyd he was: a solitary, taciturn man who was absolutely reliable and did not have a close friend on this earth.

Hudd pointed toward the dented wash basin. Ackroyd sluiced off, toweled dry, and went over to accept the mug of black coffee Hudd held out to him. He smiled and said: "It's been a while, Hudd."

The cowboy was expertly turning his golden corn pone when he replied. "Yeah. I was thinking that when I seen you coming. Maybe a year or two, Sheriff. How's the java?"

"Good."

Hudd nodded. "You hit it right. I washed out the pot yestiddy and put in fresh grounds this morning." He filled two plates, took them to the worn-smooth old table, and kicked a chair around as he said: "Set, Sheriff. Nice time of the year to be out riding, ain't it?"

Ackroyd eased down, put the cup aside, and picked up the only utensil, a large old dented spoon. "For a fact. I always like late springtime the best, Hudd."

The black eyes lifted. "What you doin', Sheriff?"

Ackroyd tried the beans; they were hot enough to melt a brass monkey. So was the corn pone, but it had been cooked by a master. He savored several mouthfuls before replying.

"Snooping around."

Hudd laughed suddenly. "I figured as much. Well, hell, you got to do that to make your wages, I guess."

Ackroyd smiled. "Yeah. Were you up here a few days back?"

"Yeah. I been up here since late February. Four straight years now they been puttin' me up here with traps and poison to thin out varmints before the cattle is drove in for the first grass."

"You sleep here every night, Hudd?"

"Yes. What's on your mind, Sheriff?"

"Maybe three days back, at night, did you hear the late stagecoach pass southward?"

"I listen for it every night. Seems to me years back, before that new feller bought 'em out . . . what's his name?"

"Paul Beaman."

"Yeah. Beaman. Years back before he bought 'em out down in Cedarville, you could almost set your watch by them night stages." Hudd spooned in some beans before continuing. "Now . . . hell . . . they go past any time." He spooned in some pone with butter on it. "People don't have no pride in how they do things any more, Sheriff. We get riders nowadays who can't heel a calf the first three times. Sometimes I wonder what things are coming to."

"After you heard the coach go through three nights back, Hudd, did you hear another rig pass southward?"

Hudd drained his cup and went to the stove to refill it, then brought the pot over to top Ackroyd's cup before answering. "Yes. As a matter of fact I did. Light wagon. You interested in it?"

"Yeah."

"More beans?"

"No thanks. I'm full."

Hudd sat down again. "Maybe an hour after the stage went

by. Not many rigs are still movin' through after dark. They used to, when I first come to work for Dagger, lots of freighters drove at night because of the Indians and what-not. Nowadays folks got things easier. They carry along big quilts and all and bed down plumb safe."

"You didn't see that rig, did you, Hudd?"

"No. I was readyin' for bed. It warn't all that unusual anyway. Now and again a wagon'll come through in the dark. Anyway, I thought it was maybe one of our wagons, or maybe belonged to one of the other outfits. . . ." Hudd finished his beans, finished his pone, shoved the plate and bowl away, and snagged up the dented coffee cup. "I went outside to pee before beddin' down. Was a fine night, clear as glass with stars right out there so's a man could touch 'em, and quiet. That wagon stopped down yonder a ways, maybe a half mile or such from the old Indian rock." Hudd got more comfortable in his chair. "Thought they was maybe goin' to make a camp down there. I was headin' back inside when I heard it start up again."

Ackroyd pulled out his tobacco sack and went to work. "Heading toward town?"

"Well, no, Sheriff, that's what made me think it must have been a rig from one of the cow outfits. It cut southwesterly across the range."

Ackroyd lit up, shoved the makings toward his host, and eyed Hudd Sawyer steadily. He had ridden that whole country down there and all he'd found was sign where someone had driven a remuda through, no tire tracks at all, not even old ones.

"You sure of that, Hudd?"

The black eyes puckered toward Sheriff Ackroyd. "I got to believe what my hearin' told me, don't I? Yes, I'm sure of it. Southwesterly out over the range like it was makin' for one of the ranches. Go down there an' look. There'll be tracks." Hudd lit up, blew smoke, and eyed his visitor. "You already done that, ain't you?"

"Yeah. Couple of days ago. And there were no tracks of any kind."

Hudd tipped ash to the floor and reached inside his shirt to scratch. He was quiet a long while, right up to the moment Jim Ackroyd leaned to arise, then he said: "What's it about?"

"Three dead men laid out beside the road down about where you heard the rig stop."

Hudd's Adam's apple bobbled. He forgot to draw on his smoke and the thing went out. "Who was they?"

"Strangers, Hudd." Ackroyd went after his hat, dumped it on, and turned to consider his host. "I'm obliged. You make better pone than anyone I ever run across. I'm not bulling you, that's a fact."

Hudd went outside and trooped in Ackroyd's wake to the place where Ackroyd's horse was finishing up his flake of meadow hay. He did not say a word until the sheriff had flung up the left stirrup to tug up the cinch, then Hudd leaned on the corral wearing a frown. "There's got to be more to it. Don't make any sense to just fetch three fellers in the back of rig down through here, lay 'em out alongside the road like that, then cut overland."

Ackroyd smiled. "Dragging sacks or something behind the tailgate to wipe out tire marks, Hudd."

As Ackroyd turned his horse, then stepped across it Hudd scowled. "I know what I heard, Sheriff. Tell you what. I'll scout around."

Ackroyd leaned on the horn, looking down. "Do me one favor. Don't mention this to anyone. Not even to your friends or the range boss at the home place."

Hudd showed irritability. "I'm not goin' to. Why should I mention it to anyone? Anyway, they won't be any of 'em comin' up here for a couple more weeks. Sheriff, by God, I know what I heard!"

Ackroyd evened up his reins. "Be careful, Hudd."

The line-camp rider was not listening. Slowly his annoyance had been building up. "There *was* a wagon, and, by God, I heard it, an' I know it cut inland from down where it stopped below the Indian rock. Somewhere, Sheriff, he had to take off whatever he was draggin' to brush out his tracks."

Ackroyd rode back the way he had come, satisfied with what he had learned, but worried over what their discussion had done to Hudd Sawyer. Before he got back to Cedarville, however, he was assuring himself that, if any range man would be wary, it would be old Hudd Sawyer, one of the few still left around who had ridden back in the days when a man out in grass country by himself never got home at night unless he had an eye in the back of his head.

III

The clothing from those three corpses was atop Ackroyd's desk when he lit the lamp in his jailhouse office. He went over them, found no more scent of perfume, and was disappointed but not really surprised when he found no letters, papers of any kind, no wallets, nothing that would have identified the dead men.

He rolled a smoke, put the clothing back in the box, and placed the box in a corner behind his desk. Then he considered the speckled blue-ware coffee pot atop the cold wood stove, decided he'd go to Donovan's instead, and arose to pick up his hat, and the door opened to admit Dr. Campbell. Ackroyd sighed inwardly but still dumped the hat on the back of his head and remained standing.

Campbell took a chair, ignoring the clear signs that Ackroyd had been about to depart. He said: "Find anything?"

Jim Ackroyd shook his head without speaking. Campbell

knew it had never been the sheriff's habit to discuss things like that.

Campbell leaned. "I did," he said, and tossed a small metal object onto the desk top, then watched as Ackroyd lifted the object to examine it. Campbell's dour expression showed a trace of saturnity when he spoke again. "That's a fifty-dollar gold piece."

Ackroyd turned the coin over, still without speaking.

"It was in the boot of the feller with the perfume on his collar. I'd have left it in the boot when I put their stuff in that box, except that I thought you might not find it. Looks new, Sheriff."

Ackroyd finally sat down. The coin was indeed new. Gold coins did not seem to wear as well as silver ones; when they were only a year or two old, they showed wear. This coin was as fresh as though it had either been minted very recently, or had not been used. By date it was six years old. Ackroyd put the coin down and leaned on his desk. "Anything else?"

Campbell wagged his head. "No. Would you care to hear my theory?"

Ackroyd woodenly nodded.

"The coin was in a vault, or maybe a coffee can under someone's bed, or maybe in a hidden cache somewhere."

Ackroyd could believe that. He smiled. "Where?"

Campbell's expression changed a little. "How would I know? I'm a physician, not a lawman. But it shouldn't be hard to find out if a bank or maybe a ranch has been robbed lately."

Ackroyd continued to smile a little. "I sent out letters of inquiry the day I brought those fellers to town, Doctor. The trouble is, those men probably didn't come from anywhere close by. Still, I won't know that or much else until I can identify them, and where they'd been hanging out."

Dr. Campbell arose to depart. He had not had supper yet and the café man closed up right at 7:00 p.m. week nights.

"Good luck," he said, without sounding as though he meant it, and departed.

Ackroyd leaned back to reëxamine the gold coin, then he put it in the same drawer that held the holstered six-guns taken off the three dead men, and locked up for the night.

Up at Donovan's place there were only a handful of customers. Week-night business was seldom very brisk. Donovan saw Ackroyd enter and went after a bottle and glass. They met near the empty lower end of the bar where Donovan set up the glass and said: " 'Evening. Nice night."

Jim Ackroyd smiled. "How would you know?"

Donovan grinned. "Well, sometimes I go to the door and look out." He watched Ackroyd fill the glass and push the bottle aside. "You got a bad one with those three strangers, eh?"

Ackroyd downed the jolt before replying. "Yeah. But it's always something, John. Did the newspapers reach town today?"

"If they did, no one's fetched 'em over from the stage office, which is not exactly unusual. They read 'em first." Donovan reached for the bottle, but Ackroyd wagged his head.

"I'll be out of town tomorrow," he told the barman. "There's something you could do for me while I'm gone, John."

"Sure."

"If the papers come, look through 'em for anything about a bullion robbery."

"Gold?"

"Yeah."

Donovan nodded with his eyes fixed on the sheriff's face. "I guess you aren't ready to talk about it yet."

Ackroyd smiled. "I don't know anything, John. Look through those papers for me, will you?"

"Sure. Be glad to."

Ackroyd paid up, and strolled out into the night on his way to the rooming house where he and most of the other unmarried men in Cedarville lived.

It was a bell-clear night. As Hudd had said about a previous night, the stars were so distinct they seemed within arm's reach.

He was not a worrier or he might have remained awake in the dark of his room wondering about those three dead men. He did briefly wonder about something else—the woman named Eloise Henrichson who was staying at the Dagger outfit, and who was rumored around town to be the sister of the owner's wife. They had met briefly, last month when Catherine Morrell had driven to town with her husband to meet Eloise Henrichson at the stage office, and, when gruff, graying Andy Morrell had introduced his wife's sister to Ackroyd, the sheriff had forgotten to smile. He had been startled to see so much beauty in one person.

Six or seven days later he had manufactured a plausible excuse to make the long ride to Dagger headquarters—and Andy Morrell, with a wise and steady look, had informed Jim Ackroyd that his wife and her sister had gone riding in the foothills. Then, perhaps as a consolation, Andy Morrell had taken Ackroyd inside the main house to eat and have a shot of pure Irish whiskey.

He closed his eyes after telling himself he was reaching pretty darned far afield for his suspect.

In the morning he was the first one to eat at the café, and the first one to rig out a saddle animal at the livery barn. The sun did not rise until he had been on the trail about an hour. By then he had just about convinced himself that what he was doing had nothing to do with the mystery. It made him feel guilty to be using a desire to see the beautiful woman as an excuse for making an official visit to Dagger.

Then, with the sun about an hour above the horizon, he saw a solitary horseman watching him from the northwest. It did not have to mean anything, and the horseman had made no attempt to be sly about what he was doing. Still, it was the custom when a man saw someone on the range, to ride down and talk a little.

Ackroyd watched the distant horseman but did not change course as he did so. Finally, then, the rider moved out on an intercepting route, and Ackroyd's curiosity grew a little. It was early; Dagger riders would perhaps be on the range about sunup, but ordinarily not so far out so early.

Ackroyd recognized the horseman from better than a half mile out, aimed for a little bosque of white oaks in a green swale, drew rein, and, when Hudd Sawyer raised a gloved right hand, palm forward, Jim Ackroyd did the same. Then he swung off and waited.

The unshaven, unshorn old range rider came on up, stepped solemnly to earth, and, trailing reins, came forward to nod as he said: "I thought it looked like you."

Ackroyd did not smile. Hudd was a long distance from his foothill line shack, and in order to get down this far he'd have had to roll out, saddle up, and strike out in the dark. Dryly Sheriff Ackroyd said: "Pretty hard to see wolves and what-not in the dark, Hudd."

The older man hunkered down. "Wasn't lookin' for 'em." He waited until Ackroyd had also gotten into palavering position on the ground before also saying: "In fact, I been down here since yestiddy evening." The solemn black eyes did not leave Ackroyd's face as Sawyer raised a gloved hand to gesture. "Bedded down yonder in an arroyo. My stuff's still over there."

Ackroyd knew what he was supposed to say, so he said it: "Why?"

"Wagon tracks," stated the old range man, and dropped his gloved hand to his lap. For a moment they regarded each other before Sawyer continued. "I told you . . . a man's got to believe what he hears. An' they didn't do much of a job brushin' out their sign once they got off the grass and onto some alkali here an' there."

"This close to headquarters, Hudd, maybe it was. . . ."

"Sheriff, there's no reason for anyone from Dagger to drag out their tracks."

That was true enough. "All right. Where did they lead?"

"Within a mile of the yard, down in a swale, then away from there toward the westerly foothills." Hudd spat aside. "One of 'em stayed with the rig, in that swale. He left enough cigarette butts there to make it look to me like they was maybe an hour or two in that place."

"Two of them?"

Hudd cleared his throat, and for the first time his eyes shifted away. "Well, it's grassy down there. I'm not as good at readin' sign as I was twenty years back." Hudd cleared his throat again, clearly chagrined. "Maybe two. Sure as hell one of 'em walked from the swale to the yard in the dark. There was most likely two of 'em . . . but there could have been three. The damned grass had sprung up again . . . and all those butts. I'd say two sure as hell and maybe three, Sheriff."

Ackroyd understood the old range man's embarrassment and spoke to alleviate it. "Hell, this time of year even Indians can't read sign better than that, Hudd. Dew and new grass and all."

Hudd eyed Ackroyd stonily, then changed the subject. "I rode around in the dark. This is open country, y'know. They'd have seen me sure as hell in daylight. In the dark you got to rely on your horse. I think I know where they got a camp." He gestured again with his right hand. "But if you go up there today, they're goin' to see you long before you even get close." Hudd spat again, and shifted his cud. "Sheriff, I'm satisfied I was right about that damned rig. And I'm satisfied there's somethin' sly goin' on. An' I never run from anythin' in my life . . .

but a man had ought to have some idea of what he's gettin' into, don't you agree?"

Ackroyd smiled. "Sure. Only it isn't your worry, Hudd."

"Yes, it is. I been on Dagger longer'n I ever rode for anyone. I was here when Andy taken over from his pa. I know some folks got no use for Andy Morrell, but he's been good as gold to me. You understand?"

Ackroyd understood. Moreover, while he had not anticipated anything serious out here, and certainly not today, he was here, and broad daylight or not he wanted to find that rig, and the men with it, and the best way to do this was to have someone like Hudd Sawyer along, because if there was a Dagger range man around who knew every yard of Dagger cow country, it was Hudd. He said: "Is there a way to get up there without having to ride across open country all the way?"

Hudd nodded. "Sure." His black eyes narrowed slightly. "You goin' to the ranch?"

"Yes. I was going to ask questions, but right now I think it'd be better if I just made it look like a social call."

Hudd nodded. "All right." He twisted to point. "That swale's about two, maybe three miles west an' a little north. I'll ride down in there and wait." He shifted his chewing tobacco again. "Whatever is goin' on, Andy won't know anything about it."

Ackroyd believed that. He arose, flexed both knees to winnow out some stiffness, and turned to mount up. "I got no idea how long I'll be over there."

Hudd was a lifelong range man. Time meant as little to him as it had meant to the Indians who had once owned all this country. "Don't make much difference," he replied, and waited until the sheriff had ridden away from the rendezvous before also stepping over leather to ride in a different direction.

Ackroyd rolled and lit a smoke, watched new day sunlight bounce off rooftops on ahead where the tree-shaded yard with its scattering of outbuildings was, and blew out a long sigh. It probably did not mean a damned thing, anyway; Catherine Morrell and Eloise Henrichson had ridden into the foothills a couple of weeks before those dead men had turned up—and that long, too, before the mysterious light wagon had gone up there. But nagging little doubts lingered and telling himself they were nothing more than the result of his having learned to be skeptical and suspicious did not make them go away. But, like Hudd Sawyer, he could not believe Andy Morrell would have a hand in any of this. If there was one obvious thing about Morrell, it was that his entire existence centered around Dagger. He had been born here, had grown up here, had been his father's top hand, and finally his father's range boss, before his father had died and Andy had inherited everything.

As Hudd had said, and as Ackroyd knew without being told, Andy Morrell, while respected throughout the Pawnee Valley country, never would have won a popularity contest. He was too forthright, too gruff and blunt and unwilling to yield on issues he thought were not negotiable, such as open-range boundaries, Dagger's prior right to certain water holes and creeks, and matters that were, in Morrell's view, unchallengeable.

As Jim Ackroyd came down into the yard, and a dog barked somewhere out behind the big old log barn, he decided that Andy Morrell and Dr. Campbell were a lot alike, their biggest difference being that Campbell was a cow country physician who lived in a small cottage in Cedarville, while Andy Morrell was a wealthy cowman with six steady riders including a range boss, owned thousands of acres of prime range land, and had more cattle than any other cow rancher in Pawnee Valley.

IV

Probably in response to the dog having announced that someone had ridden into the yard, two men strolled from the shade out behind the big barn where the log corrals were, and eyed Sheriff Ackroyd with interest as the lawman tied up to the rack in front of the barn.

One of those two men was paunchy with thin, lank hair and puffy eyes. He was chewing an unlighted stub of a thick cigar. He nodded to Ackroyd, hesitated briefly, then nodded again, and walked eastward in the direction of the big cook shack upon the far side of the yard. The second man was about medium height, but thickly, powerfully put together. He had a lined, weathered face with a hard cast to his features. He, too, was chewing an unlighted cigar. He had doeskin, roping gloves hooked over a hand-carved, expensive gun belt, and his Colt had ivory grips. He was probably not as old as he looked, and, when he stepped into barn shade and said—"You don't give up easy, do you?"—his hint of a tough smile made him look a little younger.

Ackroyd grinned. "I just never saw a woman that pretty before," he said, and leaned on the tie rack, eyeing the thicker and older man.

Andy Morrell removed the cigar and dropped it. He had dark eyes that were shrewd and probing. He was not a man to be easily fooled. "You're luckier this time, Jim. She's at the house with my wife." Morrell paused, still watching Ackroyd with his dark, hard gaze. "Something else is on your mind," he said.

Ackroyd did not try to slide around it. "A few days back I picked up three dead range men lying side-by-side up the north roadway below the Indian rock. Shot to death. Had their guns holstered and hadn't been fired. Shot in the chest from in front. I've got no idea who they were. I've been going around trying to find someone who might have seen something."

Morrell stepped to the rack and leaned down upon it, eyeing his visitor. If he was shocked, it did not show. But he took a long moment to say anything, and then it was a simple question. "Why Dagger, Jim?"

"Like I just told you, I've been goin' around trying to find someone who might have seen something. That's all."

Morrell's gaze drifted to the distant main house in its setting of soft tree shade, then back again. "The riders are out. If you want to hang around, they'll likely be in about noon." Then Morrell wagged his head. "But I doubt that they'll know anything. We've been moving cattle for the past few weeks, taking them over to the west range up near the foothills, so's when the grass is a little stronger we can drift 'em through up there. The men wouldn't have been anywhere near the road, Jim."

Ackroyd accepted this judgment with an agreeable nod of his head. When he did not speak for a moment, Andy Morrell pushed up off the rack and said: "Come on around back. We brought in some colts yesterday. That's where I was when you rode in."

The colts were orry-eyed and snorty. They had gotten over their first fear, though, and, while they remained as far as they could get from the two men and never took their eyes off the men, they did not offer to mill or spook.

Ackroyd had been a range man years earlier. Between then and now like all men of his kind he had never stopped being a horseman. "Good quality," he told Morrell as they leaned on peeled-pole stringers, looking in.

Morrell fished around until he found another cigar. He mouthed it but made no attempt to light it. Like many range men who had chewed right up until they got married, then had to devise a way to continue chewing tobacco without seeming to, Andy Morrell almost never lit a stogie.

"Big and stout," he averred, looking thoughtfully in at the

colts. "It makes my back ache to think of riding them the first week or so."

Ackroyd turned in surprise. "You're not goin' to break them, are you?"

Morrell grinned, showing square, large white teeth. "No. But years ago . . . that's what I was thinking about." Then he said: "I've got to drive to Cedarville tomorrow for the mail and other things. . . ." Whatever else he might have said to provide a reason for saying that much was left unsaid as two women came around the side of the barn into Morrell's sight. The woman with black hair showing gray over the ears was Morrell's wife. She was a handsome, friendly woman. The other woman was Eloise Henrichson. They looked alike, with perhaps ten years' difference in age separating them.

Ackroyd touched the brim of his hat and smiled. He did not notice Catherine Morrell and her husband exchange a look, because he was gazing at the younger, tall woman as she strolled up to lean and also to look in at the snorty, big, green colts. With a smile and without looking at Sheriff Ackroyd she said: "I like that blazed-faced sorrel." Then she turned her very clear and very dark blue eyes. "Do you, Mister Ackroyd?"

He did not look at the blazed-faced sorrel. "Yes'm. He's a good animal."

The very dark blue eyes twinkled. "He is a filly, Mister Ackroyd."

Morrell removed his cigar, looked from his wife to the horses, replaced the cigar, and said: "She wants to break that one."

Catherine Morrell began shaking her head immediately. Ackroyd got the impression this was an issue they had discussed before. He had no intention of getting in the middle, so he murmured an easy comment: "It'll be a strong animal."

Eloise Henrichson turned back toward the horses, giving Ackroyd an opportunity to study her profile at close range. It was flawless. He saw Catherine Morrell watching, and turned toward the horses. They visited a little longer, then Ackroyd said he had to be getting along. Morrell strolled back to the tie rack with him; the women remained by the corral. As he was un-looping his reins, Andy Morrell finished what he had been saying earlier.

"I've got to go to town tomorrow. Eloise has a trunk comin' on the morning stage from Laramie."

Ackroyd was interested. A trunk meant she was going to stay more than a few days. "She's Pawnee Valley's gain," he said, turning to swing up.

Andy Morrell looked straight at Ackroyd. "Yeah. I expect her husband thinks so. Well, I'll ask the men when they come in if any of them saw anything over by the Indian rock the last week or so."

Jim Ackroyd rode out of the yard feeling somehow betrayed, or double-crossed. She did not wear a wedding ring. He rode with that feeling all the way to the swale where Hudd was drowsing in the grass with his grimy old hat over his face. When Hudd lifted the hat to see who was arriving, Ackroyd swung down with a question on his lips.

"I didn't know Eloise Henrichson was married."

Hudd sat up, then stood up. He beat grass off with his old hat. "Couldn't really say. I only met her once . . . that was the day she arrived. I was down gettin' some salt that day." Hudd dumped on the old hat and went after his horse. Beautiful women were something that had never bothered him very much, and even less the last ten or so years.

He led off in the direction of his line shack. If Ackroyd had been thinking much about this, he would have deduced what course Hudd had in mind and it was going to use up a lot of daylight.

They had the sun nearly overhead when Ackroyd mentioned

Eloise Henrichson again, and this time Hudd turned slowly and steadily regarded his companion over a long interval of quiet. Then he said: "I'll tell you somethin' I learned when I was a little shy of twenty. If a man makes his livin' off a saddle, he's got no business thinkin' serious about a woman. Unless of course he figures to quit, move to town, and take up blacksmithing or something like that. Well, I couldn't do it. I tried once, a long time ago, but me . . . I can't stand towns much. Anyway, I never was smart enough to make a decent livin' for two people. You're likely smart enough, Sheriff. The question is do you want to trade off a lot of things for a ball and chain?"

That was the longest bit of conversation Jim Ackroyd had ever heard come out of Hudd Sawyer, and he did not comment upon it as he squinted at the sun for the time of day, then took more interest in where they were. As though women had not been mentioned, he said: "You think we can get through the hills to their camp before sundown, Hudd?"

Sawyer was confident of that. "Sure. Sheriff, I've been making trails up through those hills a long time. I'll show you."

He did, but not until they were well beyond visibility and the distant mountains were much closer, huge, hulking, and forested, with a faint bluish tinge to their long slopes and distance-hazed rims, then Hudd turned off almost due west, put his bay horse to a steady little lope, and did not slacken off until they were just about on a line with the Dagger yard but miles north of it.

Hudd got a fresh cud pouched into his cheek, riding on a slack rein, and lifted his old hat to use a soiled cuff to mop off sweat. As he replaced the hat, he said: "You see that spit of big timber yonder a few miles? Well, that's where I expect we'll find those fellers. It's got the only meadow and water for a hell of a distance east an' west."

Ackroyd studied the immense, distant fir trees. He knew the

area. He had buck hunted up through there a few times. In fact, he knew all the westerly foothill country, but not as well as his companion knew it.

Hudd broke across Ackroyd's thoughts with a question. "Why the hell . . . will you explain it to me . . . would anyone in their right mind leave three dead men beside a road where they was bound to be found?"

Ackroyd had no idea why that had been done, and he had asked himself the same question a number of times. "All I'm sure of, Hudd, is that, if someone did a thing like that, they sure as hell knew what they were doing."

Hudd tartly said—"Well, I sure don't."—and did not offer to speak again until he picked up a needle-covered game trail heading deeper through the foothills on a northward angle, and took it.

Now, they were riding into stands of big timber well north of the lower foothills, closer to the genuine mountains farther northward.

Hudd halted finally, where a noisy, deep, white-water creek ran crookedly from something like northwest to northeast, and downcountry. He nodded as though Ackroyd knew where they were, dismounted, tied his bay, and waited for the sheriff to do the same, then Hudd spat, wiped his lips, and said: "What we got to be careful of is that they don't have someone back up through here somewhere watching. Would they likely do that, Sheriff? What exactly might they be wanted for? You never told me."

"I don't know whether they're wanted or not."

Hudd planted his big-booted feet widely, facing Sheriff Ackroyd. "Partner," he said in a crisp, hard voice, "I'm all for helpin' a man." That was all he said, but the black-eyed stare he put upon Ackroyd made the rest of it clear enough.

"If they are the ones who planted those three dead men,"

Ackroyd growled, "then they've got to know how those men died and who killed them. If it was murder, Hudd, and if these are the same men, then maybe we're goin' to be looking for kill-ers. As for who they are or what they've done, or why they planted those corpses, your guess is as good as mine."

Hudd tugged loose the tie down over his holstered colt and turned to gaze southward without saying another word. For a moment he stood like that, perhaps going over in his mind the safest way to get down into the area where he thought the wagon camp was, then he started walking without haste but purpose-fully.

Ackroyd followed. They did not make any noise; this entire area was spongy from layers of needles. It also had a musty and aromatic scent of tree sap, but not nearly as noticeably as the area would have it in another month or two when hot weather reached this territory.

Ackroyd picked up the wood smoke scent before Hudd did and reached to tap the range man's shoulder. Hudd sniffed, wrinkled his nose, nodded, and turned off to their right where the trees were thicker. He did not move any slower, though. He did not appear to believe they were in any danger yet.

The last time they halted it was when the solid, measured blows of an axe against wood came up to them. Hudd smiled a little. The sounds of camp noises fixed for him the exact loca-tion he was seeking. He looked around and said: "Sheriff, if we got killers down there, they ain't goin' to hold still for us to just walk in and tell 'em it's a nice day."

Ackroyd jutted his jaw in the direction of the unseen wood chopper. "We'll get closer. In six-gun range. Then we'll tell 'em it's a pretty day. Hudd, be damned careful."

Hudd took one long onward step when the gunshot came. He went down like a pole-axed steer, rolled once, then flopped onto his face, and did not move again.

Ackroyd hurled himself behind a big fir tree, palming his six-gun as he moved. The invisible gunman was not using a six-gun. The muzzle blast had been sharper and higher in sound. The man had a carbine, which was bad enough, but he was also invisible. Ackroyd could not make up his mind whether the shot had come from on down the slope southerly, in the direction of the camp, or from over eastward. One thing was clear enough, whoever that gunman was, he was not using the customary black powder bullets. There was not even as much as a hint of burned powder in any direction.

Ackroyd had sweat running under his shirt. It was also oozing past the sweatband of his hat and trickling down his forehead. He raised a cuff to skim it off, then sank to one knee to peer around his tree, and, when he leaned to look, a voice as cold as ice hit him between the shoulder blades. *The gunman was behind him.*

"Drop that gun an' stand up with your hands shoved out behind. Do it!"

V

Jim Ackroyd did not see his captor until after the man had come in close and had lifted away Ackroyd's gun, shoved it down his front waistband, then stepped back as he said: "Face around."

Ackroyd turned slowly. The man was half a head shorter and about fifty pounds lighter than Ackroyd; he was a wiry, weathered individual with one of those droopy dragoon mustaches and chalk-like, pale-blue eyes. He was holding his cocked carbine in one hand. The six-gun on his right hip had a carved walnut stock, but otherwise the man looked faded and worn, and, when his very pale eyes saw the badge on Ackroyd's vest, they widened just a trifle, then rose slowly to Ackroyd's face.

"A lawman," the sinewy man said. "I didn't figure that. I thought you was sneakin' damned skulkin' horse thieves. A god-damned lawman." The sinewy man regarded Ackroyd a long time before speaking again. "From that town yonder, on over east of here?"

Ackroyd nodded. "Cedarville. My bailiwick is all of Pawnee Valley. I'd like to look after my friend yonder."

"Naw," retorted the sinewy man. "He's dead. He don't need no help. But you sure as hell do."

"Maybe he's not dead. Maybe I can. . . ."

"All right, Sheriff, go over there and look." The sinewy man gestured with his cocked saddle gun. "Be careful."

Ackroyd was kneeling beside inert Hudd Sawyer when a second man appeared. This one was bushy-headed and full-bearded. He was powerfully built, and his attire, too, looked faded and worse for wear. When he saw Ackroyd kneeling, he stopped in his tracks, watched as Ackroyd gently eased Hudd over, then the burly man said: "Christ, Marv, you said you was going after a deer."

Ackroyd paid no attention to their crisp exchange. He leaned, saw the bluish little puckery hole an inch above Hudd's eyes and squarely between them, and slumped where he was kneeling. Hudd Sawyer had been dead before he had stopped rolling.

From back where the two strangers were, the killer called Marv said: "Toss his Colt back here, an' you'll want to be almighty careful. Toss it!"

Ackroyd did not obey at once. Dead men were not something he had not seen before, but this time it had happened in such a way, so fast and with such unexpected finality, that he was stunned.

The bear-built bearded man growled in a rumbling way: "Fling the gun back here . . . or I'm goin' to break your neck with my hands."

Ackroyd reared back, drew Hudd's old six-gun, and pitched it over his shoulder, then he arose and slowly turned as the burly man bent to retrieve Hudd's old gun. He looked steadily at the sinewy man, and got back a mirthless, crooked smile. "I told you he was dead, Sheriff. I ain't missed since I was a button." Marv gestured. "Pull up your pants legs."

Ackroyd obeyed. He did not carry a boot knife nor a hideout gun. As he was straightening up again, the burly man finished examining Hudd's gun and sneered. "Worn out," he said, and hurled the gun away. "Never saw a range man in my life who owned a decent weapon." He jerked his head. "Walk, lawman."

The light wagon was parked in fragrant forest shade, and to the west, where the brawling creek ran past, southward down through the trees to the less-forested foothill grassland, two good-looking, big, young, seal-brown horses were peacefully grazing along in hobbles.

They had established a good camp. Ackroyd walked past the stone fire ring, stopped where some harness had been draped from high fir limbs to protect it from salt-hungry varmints, and turned.

Marv went to the tailgate and put his Winchester inside, then strolled back where the burly man was watching their prisoner. Marv started to make a smoke, and Ackroyd did not see the third man until he stepped around the wagon from the shadows. He was carrying two buckets of water from the creek, had his sleeves rolled to the elbows, and his shirt open part way down from the throat. He was as old as the other two. Ackroyd guessed they were all in their forties. But the man putting down the buckets and looking across in mild surprise had sharper, narrower features than his companions, and was clean-shaven.

He said: "That's not camp meat, Marv."

The sinewy man laughed. "Never got that far back. There

was these two sneakin' down on us from behind. The sheriff here an' his friend."

"Where's his friend?"

"Dead, Ryan. It was a good shot. The son-of-a-bitch took a forward step as I was squeezin' it off. I had to correct my aim in maybe half a second."

Ryan's eyes were tawny tan. His coloring was light tan, and not entirely from exposure. He was a well-built, easy-moving man with a tied-down right-side hip holster worn so that it tipped back just a little. Ackroyd classified him as they were looking at each other. Ryan was a competent and experienced gunman.

The burly man began wagging his head, as though the killing and capture were just now finally sinking in. He turned a little. "He's the law from that town east of here down the stage road. This is a god-damned mess, Ryan. I was set to loaf for a couple weeks anyway."

Ryan came closer and studied Jim Ackroyd. His attitude, once the surprise passed, was calm and interested. Like Marv, he appeared to be an individual who did not become very agitated, but the burly, bearded man seemed to be. He spoke again, his growly voice showing irritation and disgust. "It had to be the damned local sheriff, for Christ's sake."

Marv turned. "No matter who they was, they would have come down behind us, Chet."

Chet was not placated. He turned broad shoulders, stamped to the wagon, and fished among their supplies upon the tailgate until he found the bottle, and took two long pulls off it, then remained over there, glowering.

Ryan sighed, dug out his makings, and began working up a cigarette. He was thoughtfully silent until he had the thing lighted, then he said: "Sheriff, how'd you know we was in here?"

Ackroyd had known this question was coming and had

41

worked out an answer they could not prove was untrue, and it was not entirely untrue, but it was certainly unverifiable. "Hudd, that man this feller killed, saw you come up in here. He's . . . he was . . . the line-shack rider for Dagger Ranch. They own all this country. He'd been in the hills since February, thinning out varmints before they put cattle up here."

Ryan inhaled, exhaled, then looked at Marv. "Like Chet said, we got a mess on our hands."

Marv became defensive again with Ryan as he had with Chet. "I was up there and saw somethin' makin' blurry movement. I figured it was maybe a deer. It was these two. The dead one yanked loose his tie down. I seen him do that when they moved among some trees. I wasn't goin' to give 'em a chance, not two to one, and that dead one ready to fight."

Ryan finished his smoke and ground it underfoot. "Well, Sheriff, who else come up here with you and that other feller?"

"No one."

"Who knew you fellers was comin' up here?"

Ackroyd had expected this question, too. "The owner of the ranch where we're standing."

Ryan's close-spaced ferret eyes grew still. "Morrell?"

Ackroyd nodded, not surprised that Ryan knew who owned Dagger Ranch.

From over by the tailgate Chet growled again. "God-damned mess. We can't wait now."

Ryan considered that, then said: "Take care of this son-of-a-bitch, Chet, then let's eat."

Ryan turned to stroll back toward the wagon, his concern now directed to other things, but Marv remained a few yards from Jim Ackroyd, sinewy arms crossed over his chest, grinning widely. He knew what was going to happen now. So did Ackroyd when he saw the bearded, bear-built man start toward him from the tailgate.

Chet was one of those individuals who had matured early, and fully, and as a result of that had become a natural bully. He had shoulders like a gorilla, a thick barrel-like chest, and massively muscular legs. He had almost no neck, but what there was of it was the same size as his head. Chet had beaten and bloodied other men all his life. His initial reaction to any kind of opposition was to smash it and stamp it out of existence.

Ackroyd watched Chet's rolling, bear-like approach. He felt cold. He had done his share of battling, too, had in fact met a few like Chet, but this time he was going to lose even if he could stop Chet. That was why Marv was standing nearby, arms crossed and grinning. Marv was armed and he was an almost casual murderer.

Chet hauled up fifteen feet away and balefully regarded Jim Ackroyd, who was a little taller and perhaps fifty pounds lighter. He was also a little younger but that made no difference. Chet tossed down his hat, his hair, in tight, natural wiry curls, stood out in all directions.

Ackroyd expected words but Chet started ahead without making a sound. He had made his appraisal, had decided how this was to be done in his small, savage mind, and was now moving to do it.

The clearing was not very large, perhaps 100 feet in either direction. It was pleasantly shaded by big trees, and the creek made a busy sound off to the west. Ackroyd saw everything more sharply as he stood waiting, powerful arms at his side.

Chet slowed to a shuffle and brought up both oaken arms. He did not smile, did not show any expression at all except around his little eyes; they were squeezed up in total concentration.

Ackroyd still waited, breathing deeply. Then, when Chet hunched his mighty shoulders to launch his attack exactly as Ackroyd had thought he would, charging ahead to sweep everything before him, Ackroyd balanced on the balls of his feet and moved in a blur. This was the only real advantage he possessed; he could move faster and maneuver better. Chet's eyes abruptly widened and his powerful arms moved—too late. Ackroyd's left fist went through the upraised guard and struck Chet over the heart with a dull, muted sound that reached to the wagon where Ryan turned in surprise. His right, cocked shoulder high, tore upward alongside Chet's bearded cheek to his temple, then Ackroyd sank away to Chet's left, expecting Chet to whirl after him. Instead, Chet's arms half dropped, all his weight came down on both feet, and his eyes showed a hint of glaze.

Marv squawked something unintelligible and Ryan faced fully around, back by the wagon, as Chet finally cleared his head and, roaring like a wounded bear, started flat-footedly after the lawman.

Ackroyd knew something now; for all his massive brute power, Chet could be hurt in the head. He could be stunned. He kept trading ground to the left and right, yielding space while awaiting a second opening. But Chet had both forearms up high now, little murderous eyes barely visible over his guard as he moved to force Ackroyd to stand.

Marv was no longer grinning. He had his right hand on the saw handle of a holstered Colt as he twisted to call shrilly to Ryan: "I'll shoot the son-of-a-bitch! I'll kill . . . !"

Chet roared and lunged. Ackroyd shuffled to get away, felt a rotten tree limb underfoot, and had to waste a second feeling for better footing. Chet came at him head down, big hands bent like talons, found cloth and lunged for a handhold as Ackroyd fired his cocked right fist again. But this time the blow was slipped upward over the raised arms and missed Chet's head. He came up beneath with his left, and missed that time, too, because Chet had him wrenched off balance.

Marv was weaving in and out and screaming. Ryan leaned on a distant wagon wheel watching, perfectly calm but very interested. This was something he had clearly never witnessed before; his bearded companion having to earn everything he got from an adversary, and, when Ackroyd finally steadied up and struck with all his weight behind two blows into Chet's unprotected middle, Ryan straightened up off the wheel when Chet's knees wobbled.

But he clung to Ackroyd's shirt. The cloth tore and Ackroyd tried to tear loose by throwing himself backward. It did not work; Chet's huge arms got half around Ackroyd's straining body. Chet buried his face against the lawman's chest, blew air like a surfacing whale, took all the abuse Ackroyd gave him, got his huge hands locked behind the sheriff's back, then began rearing backward as he set himself for the rib-breaking crush.

Ackroyd got both palms beneath Chet's jaw to exert all his strength. It might have worked if Chet had had a neck. With his lungs burning like fire and little blue explosions before his eyes, Ackroyd tried a desperate blow to Chet's exposed face, then a hot sensation flooded him and he lost consciousness.

Marvin ran in yelling and clawing. "Leave him go, Chet! Leave the bastard fall! I'll finish him!"

Chet roared, flung one huge arm savagely sideward to knock Marv sprawling, then he let Ackroyd fall, and stepped back to aim a kick. The inert man on the ground rolled under impact, and Chet kicked twice more before turning away, one bruised big paw over a wide gash in his left cheek that was pouring blood.

VI

It was dark, the camp was quiet, a fragrant low little blue-flame fire was burning, and three squatting men over there floated hazily into Jim Ackroyd's vision where he was lying. Each breath hurt, his stomach was queasy, and he had to wait a long time before his vision cleared.

It was not a cold night. In fact, it was a pleasant, pine-scented night with two-thirds of an old rusty moon showing down across the Dagger Ranch's sloping foothills and beyond.

Ackroyd eased a cramped leg and straightened a bent arm. He flexed his hands and they also hurt. He lay back, trying to minimize the pain from breathing by taking down shallow breaths. He did not know why his chest and midriff hurt; he had lost consciousness before Chet had put the boots to him, but by the time his mind was clear, he could make a guess at that. He was probably lucky to be alive. He knew for a fact that the sinewy man with the droopy mustache was a killer, and Chet, sitting over there with a clumsy, soiled bandage across one cheek, would not hesitate, either, particularly after the shellacking he had taken from Ackroyd.

Ryan's calm, spaced words crossed the intervening distance. "Well, like Marv said, we can wait until tomorrow night. We got to do something else, too."

Chet growled, still in a vile mood, but it probably did not take much to make Chet like that. "Quit foolin' around, Ryan. We went in down there, and nothin' happened. We can do it again the same way. We *got* to do it now."

Ryan and Marv fell silent. Ackroyd turned his head a little to watch them. They were sitting hunched, like men in despair. Marv suddenly said: "What about them horses? Those two must have left 'em tied somewhere around."

Chet started to growl a negative reply, but Ryan cut across, saying: "See if you can find them, Marv." The sulphurous look Ryan got from Chet prompted him to add a little more. "Make sure they don't get loose. Nothin' roils folks up like finding riderless saddle horses."

After Marv went out into the darkness of the trees, carbine

cradled, Ryan said: "We got to get rid of those two. The one Marv shot and the sheriff."

Chet agreed. "There's plenty of cañons back yonder to dump them down." He yawned, and gingerly felt his split cheek, then reverted to his early disgust. "If those lousy bastards hadn't come skulkin' along, we could have set up in here for a week or more." Chet spat into the little blue-flame fire. "Ryan, our luck ain't been runnin' too good lately."

The other man fixed Chet with his calm, steady gaze. "It's been runnin' better than it was last year. How much money you got in your belt, Chet?"

The burly man picked up a twig and tossed it inside the fire ring, then bridled a little. "Well, what I meant was, there's still twenty thousand we ain't got."

Ryan handed across the whiskey bottle, which Chet took but did not drink from. Ryan said: "She knows we're here."

Chet reconsidered and took a long pull from the bottle and handed it back. "I know that. Who the hell you think went in down there and scairt her so bad she almost fainted? Of course, she knows we're here . . . but she ain't rode out, has she? Once . . . all right . . . once she rode out with some other woman . . . but she never stayed out long enough for us to talk to her, an' now we got this other mess on our hands, so we can't wait around." Chet lifted his badly discolored and swollen face. "I'm goin' to kill that sheriff."

Ryan shrugged and said nothing as he also hoisted the bottle and drank deeply before putting it aside. Then his dry words fell into the forest silence calmly. "Kill the son-of-a-bitch. But first find out why they came sneakin' in from behind instead of riding right on up to our camp the way anyone else would do."

Chet considered that a long while before speaking. "You got some idea they know?"

Ryan shrugged again. "I can't answer that. All I wondered

about was why they came skulking when they ordinarily would have ridden up in plain sight and maybe helloed the camp, like anyone else would have done."

Chet sat hunched and bear-like a long while turning this over in his mind, and off in the darkness of trees where Ackroyd was lying, sorting through what he had heard, a dim and fragmentary picture was forming. He only stopped worrying it around inside his head when he heard Chet grunt as he pushed up to his feet.

Ackroyd turned his head. Chet, with his thick back to the little fire, his bearded face in sooty shadows, looked more menacing than he had looked in broad daylight. Ackroyd groped among the forest débris with his left hand, feeling for a big stone. Instead, he felt rough fir bark and curled his hand around a deadfall fir limb half as large as a man's wrist. The fact that the bark was still on it indicated that the piece of wood had not been lying on the ground very long, not long enough to be rotten. He lifted it a couple of inches; it was solidly heavy.

Ryan said—"Chet."—and held up his hand.

There was a whisper of sound to the north and east that became increasingly audible. Chet growled: "Marv. He found their horses."

Ryan nonetheless arose, stepped around to the far side of the wagon, and rested a saddle gun across wood around there. Chet sneered and remained in plain sight, waiting.

Chet was correct. Marv came down into the clearing leading a pair of animals with saddles and bridles still in place. He sang ahead to his companions. "We got us a pair of good using horses, from the looks of them."

Chet waited until the animals were led close, then squinted. Ryan walked over also to make an appraisal. Chet said: "Like hell, they're branded."

Ackroyd had not moved except to bring the three-foot scantling up close to his off side. Seeing his horse, and Hudd

Sawyer's Dagger-branded mount, depressed him. He'd had some unclear idea that if he could cold-cock Chet, or maybe Ryan, he could roll away, get clear of the camp, and go out to his horse. He did not speculate about whether his battered body would be able to do all that; he simply saw no alternative. They would kill him. If not right here tonight, then tomorrow, but he had heard enough during Marv's absence to know they would do it, and soon.

Now, as the three men stood discussing the saddled horses, Ackroyd's hope dwindled. Then Marv said: "Ryan, I been thinking. We don't have much time left, and tonight we could go down there, find that damned woman, and bring her back up here. By morning we could have it out of her . . . maybe break an ankle or shove a hand into the fire. . . ."

Chet, who usually did not comment quickly, did so this time. "He's right, Ryan. We got the whole damned night." Then Chet sneered. "If you want to stay here, Marv an' I'll go down there."

Ackroyd had noticed Chet's veiled contempt for Ryan once before.

For a while Ryan did not speak. He stood hip-shot, gazing at the horses, then eventually he said: "You were lucky last time, Chet. There are six men in the bunkhouse, and Morrell don't look like he'd be easy to work over."

Chet's scorn made his voice rough. "There was six fellers an' Morrell down there the other time, too. You stay here . . . maybe fix the sheriff while we're gone. Marv and I'll fetch her back."

As he finished speaking, Chet turned, took the reins from Marv of Hudd Sawyer's Dagger horse, turned the animal, snugged up the *cincha,* and turned the horse again. As he toed in to spring up, he said: "Leave that damned carbine, Marv."

As he leaned the saddle gun against their light wagon and faced around, Marv pointed westerly. "We got to water 'em. They have been all day without a drink."

Chet wrenched the Dagger horse around and snarled. "Get up, Marv. It's a long ways down an' back. Mount up!"

Marv did not argue. As he settled across Ackroyd's saddle, with the stirrups six inches too long, and leaned down one side to see if there was a buckle, he said: "Maybe you better dump that dead one, too, Ryan." Then he swore because the stirrup leathers were laced, not buckled. But Chet was already moving down out of the trees.

Ackroyd watched as long as he could without shifting his body, and afterward listened to the desultory, profane conversation between Chet and Marv as they headed down toward the southward foothills.

He shifted his attention to Ryan, watched the man take another long pull from the whiskey bottle, then lean on the tailgate over yonder while he rolled and lit a smoke. Ryan was an unhurried individual. He did not even glance in Ackroyd's direction. He went beyond the wagon and was busy over there out of sight for a while, then he came around the front, stepping high over the wagon tongue.

He was evidently in no hurry. He hunkered by the coals of that little deadwood fire for a while, smoking, then he finally glanced over in Ackroyd's direction, and pushed upright.

Ackroyd snugged the scantling in still closer to his right side where he hoped it would not be seen in the dark tree shadows, and, as Ryan started toward him, Ackroyd feebly said: "Water . . . water."

Ryan halted, gazed at the lumpy, battered man on the ground, then turned back. Ackroyd watched him retrieve a canteen from the tailgate, then also pick up the whiskey bottle before starting forward again. Ackroyd eased the scantling down where his leg would conceal it, but kept it at finger length.

He looked badly, even in the gloom; his face was pallid and greasy; his shirt had been torn; he breathed shallowly, and, when Ryan stood above, looking down, Ackroyd said: "Water . . ."

Ryan dropped the canteen and Ackroyd did not have to feign difficulty lifting it. He spilled water and drank with difficulty.

Ryan sank to one knee and held out the whiskey bottle without saying a word. Ackroyd had less difficulty here; the bottle was much lighter than the canteen. He swallowed three times, then Ryan took the bottle away from him, stoppered it, and said: "Sit up."

Ackroyd's answer was fading. "I can't. My ribs are busted. Something's busted in my guts, too."

Ryan relaxed and crossed his legs as he gazed at the sheriff. "You shouldn't have fought back. I've seen him beat 'em to a bloody mess, then kick 'em to death. You split his cheek. You're lucky to be alive."

Ackroyd closed his eyes. The whiskey was working subtly to make him feel much better, and much warmer. His mind was clear, but the whiskey seemed to heighten that, too. In a half whisper he said: "Where is he?"

"Chet? He's gone. Want some more water?"

"Can't hold the canteen."

Ryan made no offer to hold the canteen for Ackroyd. He hunkered there, gazing dispassionately at the lawman. "Why didn't you fellers ride down into camp? Why did you come sneakin' in on us?"

"Precaution. We didn't know anything about you. Just that you were up here."

"How did you know we was here?"

"Hudd . . . saw your rig up here day before yesterday."

"And went for the sheriff?"

"No. I was down there and met him. We've been friends a long time."

"Good," stated Ryan in a thin, bone-dry tone of voice,

"because you're goin' to meet him directly." Ackroyd lifted the whiskey bottle for a couple of swallows, then put it aside again. "What do you know about Morrell's ranch?"

Ackroyd opened his eyes. "What do I know about it? It's big. They run more cattle than anyone in the . . ."

"I don't care about that. Do they come up this way very often?"

"They'll turn cattle up here soon. They graze off the foothills first, each summer."

"You know Morrell?"

"Yeah. Not real well, but well enough I expect."

"You know his wife?"

Ackroyd considered his interrogator. "To speak to is all."

"Did you know she's got a woman down there visiting her?"

Ackroyd hung fire briefly before replying, but there would not be much point in denying that he had met Eloise Henrichson. "I met a tall, black-haired woman down there a few days back. That's all I know about her." He continued to study Ryan. "Is she why you fellers are here?"

Ryan did not answer. Instead, he listened to the sound of distant hobbled horses moving between the camp and the creek, then shoved back his hat, and went to work rolling a smoke. After lighting up, he said: "You're a lawman. Did you ever hear of a man called Charley Walton?"

The implication was that Ackroyd should have heard of someone by that name, but the fact was that he never had. "Not that I can recall right off hand. What about him?"

Ryan's bloodless slit of a mouth pulled wide and downward a little. "You must not have a telegraph office in your town, Sheriff."

"That's right, we don't. Who is Charley Walton?"

"He robbed three Denver banks in the same day. One, two, three, just like that. Charley had guts. He was a good planner, too, and good with weapons." Ryan leaned to punch out his cigarette. "Forty-eight thousand dollars." The cold eyes swept up to Ackroyd's face. "You got any idea how much money forty-eight thousand dollars is, Sheriff? It's enough for everyone who helped Charley rob them banks to live the rest of his damned life any way a man would want to live it."

Ackroyd was groping for things now. "Who Charley Walton *was . . . ?*"

"He's dead. Him and his two partners. I think they were his cousins or something like that. They got theirselves killed. Sheriff, if you ever have forty-eight thousand dollars, don't be a damned fool and trust anyone. Not even your best friend." Ryan's mirthless smile appeared again. "Least of all your best friend."

Ackroyd was watching Ryan closely. "You?"

Ryan's smile broadened. "You're not as dumb as I thought. Most cow town lawmen are dumb as hell. You figure things pretty well, Sheriff. I'm going to kill you. You know that, don't you?"

Jim Ackroyd said: "You killed all three of them, Walton and his two partners?"

For a moment Ryan sat there gazing at the lawman. Then he said: "You found 'em, eh?"

"Yeah. That's what I was riding around the country asking questions about. I needed someone who saw someone in a light wagon line them out beside the road. I had no idea who they were."

"Charley and his partners . . . or cousins . . . or whatever they were. There was six of us, Charley and them two, me and Marv and Chet . . . one, two, three. By God, I never saw so much money in my life, and we only got half of it at that."

"How did you get them off guard?"

"That wasn't any problem." Ryan pulled up a trouser leg to

reveal a nickel-plated little five-shooter in a doeskin holster inside the upper part of his boot. He showed that mirthless grin again. "One, two, three, Sheriff, just like the banks."

Ackroyd said: "Chet and Marv knew it was going to happen?"

"Yeah. Split forty-eight thousand dollars three ways, and you got dang' near sixteen thousand each." Ryan wagged his head. "By God, they never saw so much money before and neither did I . . . but there was one problem. When we rifled the bodies, it wasn't all there. That son-of-a-bitch Walton had went and mailed off almost half of it to his wife."

Ackroyd forgot and took down a big, stunning breath. The truth had hit him like the kick of a mule. Pain made him gasp and clench both fists until the spasm passed. Now he knew why Ryan was up here, and why he and his partners had tried to find Eloise Henrichson. He knew who Eloise Henrichson's husband was, too, even though their names were different.

Ryan, thinking Ackroyd's gasp and fist clenching was the result of his injuries, indifferently said: "You won't have to suffer much longer."

Ackroyd tried feebly to hoist himself to a sitting position and held out his left hand. "Help me," he whispered.

Perhaps instinctively Ryan reached with his right hand. As he leaned back to haul Jim Ackroyd into a sitting position, they were less than three feet apart. Ackroyd's right arm came up and over with every bit of strength the sheriff still had. Ryan may not have seen the club—it was sooty dark where they were—but whether he saw it or not, Ackroyd gripped the outlaw's gun hand hard. When the club came down, it broke across Ryan's skull. It forced the outlaw's hat down over his ears, and Ryan, already leaning off balance, went backward and sideward. As he fell, he made a wet, sobbing gasp deep in his throat.

VII

Ackroyd took a pull from the whiskey bottle, then hung there for a long time recovering. He had used up most of his reserve strength in swinging that club. Now he continued to breathe shallowly while he sat there, supported by one arm.

Ryan had blood trickling down his cheek. He was lying in a slightly curled, awkward-looking position. For a while Ackroyd did nothing. For almost a quarter of an hour he simply sat there, then he gingerly eased around until he could take the Colt from Ryan's hip holster. After another long wait he got the little nickel-plated hide-out gun as well. He sat a while examining the five-shooter, certain in his mind he was holding the gun that had killed those three men he had found up alongside the stage road.

There were upended saddles over near the fire. The distance was no more than fifty or sixty feet, but it required more than a half hour to get over there, remove one of the lass ropes, and go back where Ryan was feebly breathing. There was more blood on his face by this time. Ackroyd speculated that Ryan might have had a thin skull, in which case he would probably die from a crushed skull, but as Ackroyd worked at trussing the unconscious outlaw, he was more concerned with how he was going to get Ryan out of sight.

He used up another hour rolling the trussed man over and over, with frequent stops to rest, until he had Ryan beyond the fringe of trees and over into some buckbrush. There, still without making an examination of his victim, Ackroyd used Ryan's neckerchief to gag him effectively. Then he went back over to the coals and helped himself to a tin cupful of black coffee.

His stomach was sore, but the coffee did not increase his soreness, so he also ate some food while sitting beside the stone ring. Then he stood up and leaned upon the near side of the light wagon. That made his chest hurt. It also made him briefly light-headed, but he persevered.

Two hours later, with a hint of night chill arriving, Ackroyd felt almost human again. In fact, the soreness in his middle seemed to diminish after he had eaten. It was still there, but less so. His chest, however, hurt as much as it had when he had first regained consciousness. He minimized that by breathing in shallow, quick breaths. It did not help much, but it was much better than trying to breathe normally, which hurt like hell. He was satisfied that he had at least two broken ribs.

He had time, which was fortunate, because if he'd had to hurry, he would never have been able to locate all the weapons, unload each one, and rummage through the bedrolls and war bags as thoroughly as he did. He found extra cartons of bullets, some personal property like a change of clothing, some fishing equipment, even two old dog-eared letters that he could not read because of the poor light.

He also found three Wanted dodgers, and recognized the likenesses on each dodger. Chet, Ryan, and Marv were wanted for murder as well as robbery. The total in rewards amounted to $3,000. Ackroyd stuffed those papers in his pocket, went back for more coffee, felt strength returning to his lower body, and squinted skyward to estimate the time. After that, he guessed about how much time would be required for Chet and Marv to reach Dagger headquarters, and return with their hostage— providing they did not run into trouble down there, which he fervently hoped they would.

Eventually he went back over where he had left Ryan. The outlaw had flopped onto his back, but he was unable to focus his eyes or to speak when he was spoken to, so Ackroyd went back to camp, rearranged things in the wagon so that both sideboards had something behind them, and finally he finished the coffee.

When the cold arrived, he took a blanket from someone's

bedroll and stirred up the fire, then sat there with the blanket around his shoulders like a buck Indian.

Putting the scraps together was not difficult, not since Ryan had been so helpful. What bothered Ackroyd was the extent of Eloise Henrichson's knowledge. Had she known her husband had been an outlaw? Had she suspected that money he had sent her was stolen?

A pair of owls sat in treetops with 100 yards separating them, calling mournfully back and forth. Years earlier Ackroyd would have dived under the wagon. Now he listened, guessed about where each bird was, and went back to his private thoughts.

He was trying to protect Eloise Henrichson; he sensed that in himself but did not find it odd. He had met her once and had seen her twice. She was certainly involved with an outlaw—was clearly the widow of one. He wanted to smoke but knew better than to try it. Gradually his body seemed stronger, and eventually he went back over where he had left Ryan. He took the nearly depleted whiskey bottle with him.

He did better for the outlaw than Ryan had done for him; he supported the injured man while helping him down some liquor. Then he propped him against a tree, and they looked at each other. Ryan said: "I can't keep . . . my thoughts together."

Ackroyd had a suspicion that he had struck Ryan too hard. At the time he had swung the club he had been aware of what was going to happen to him whether he missed with the club or not. Now, with no sense of guilt, he said: "Did you know Charley Walton very well?"

Ryan blinked slowly without taking his glance off Ackroyd. He did not answer.

"Did you know his wife, Ryan?"

This time he got part of an answer. "I saw her a few times, with Charley. I . . . it's kind of red, isn't it?"

Ryan toppled sideways.

Ackroyd did not move for a long while. He did not have to look closer; he had seen death too many times not to recognize it now even in the semidarkness.

He went back to the fire, studied the sky, guessed about the time, and decided he would get ready. Taking the Winchester Chet had insisted Marv leave against the wagon, Ackroyd went over beyond the wagon, draped a blanket around his shoulders, and used up a little time trying to breathe a little more deeply with each fresh breath. The pain did not permit him to do this very long.

He thought he heard a steel horseshoe southward grind over stone. Evidently it was not a horseshoe because an hour later there was no sign of the returning killers.

He went down through the trees a short distance, down where he should have been able to see the bare foothills, but by now the rusty moon was gone.

Then he *did* hear riders. They were not moving fast and they were coming upland through the lower hills. He went back to his position on the west side of the light wagon, with the bedrolls and other articles lined up along the sideboards to stop bullets that would pass through the wood. He checked Marv's saddle gun, found it fully loaded, lifted out the six-gun he had taken from Ryan, and checked that, too. It had five slugs; the cylinder under the hammer was empty. Some range men carried their guns like that to minimize the possibility of an accident if a horse should fall with them. He punched out a shell from his own belt and filled that hole, then hefted Ryan's weapon. It was a good gun.

From a great distance northeasterly the high, long cry of a rutting wolf carried for miles. There was no answer. It was actually a little late for mating.

A horse blew its nose 100 or so yards south of the camp, and a deep, growly voice clearly said: "Sing out, Marv."

The answer was waspish. "What the hell for? Ain't no one up there but Ryan."

"Sing out anyway!"

Marv's slightly nasal voice rose in a short call. "Hey, Ryan, we got her! Kick up the fire!"

Ackroyd did not risk replying. He squinted, saw no one down through the trees, went quickly to the stone ring, pitched in several twigs, and kicked coals to make sparks rise, then he went back to the far side of the wagon and picked up the carbine. He had no intention of giving anyone a chance; he was not in physical condition for a hard fight; they had already taken everything from him they could. They thought he was dead, and, if either one of them had remained behind instead of Ryan, he probably would have been dead by now.

He eased the saddle gun over a sideboard, leaned down to snug it back, and wait.

They had seen the fire stir; evidently that satisfied them. Ackroyd saw Marv in the lead. Behind him was another horse, its rider not as roughly built, and hatless. Bringing up the rear was gorilla-shaped Chet. He had a carbine balanced across his lap, steadying it with his right hand while holding his reins in his left hand. Ackroyd did not remember Chet taking a carbine with him, and he certainly had not got one from the saddle he was riding, but that was not particularly important.

Ackroyd moved his carbine over wood with a grating sound. Marv came almost to the fire, then drew rein, and stepped down, stamped cold feet and flexed saddle-numbed legs.

Chet came down more ponderously, and, as he reached the ground, he snarled to the rider up ahead. "Get off and stand still!"

The lighting was not good enough for Ackroyd to make a positive identification but he was sure who that third rider was. Then Marv walked back to her and Ackroyd's finger eased up inside the trigger guard long enough for him to shift aim to Chet, but she was too close in this instance, too. Ackroyd was a good shot, but no one was good enough to take that kind of a risk in the night.

Chet came ahead leading his head-hung horse. He halted and pointed. "Go on up to the fire, lady, and set down. And don't make no moves until one of us tells you to."

She turned and walked ahead, flat-footedly as though she were weary to the bone, but Ackroyd guessed it was not tiredness that made her move like that.

He shifted the gun barrel slightly to cover the pair of outlaws. Chet sat, then shifted his hat, scratched, and replaced the hat as he said: "Ryan, you can come out now. It's us." In a rougher, quieter tone he said: "I told you Marv. I told you he didn't have no guts."

Ackroyd squeezed the trigger. Both the head-hung horses flung upright in abrupt panic, jerked free, turned, and fled back the way they had come. Black powder and gunsmoke hung in the air, invisible in the darkness but strongly acid to the nose.

Chet went down like a bear, and rolled, then floundered as Marv squawked in complete astonishment. Chet came up onto one knee with his Winchester rising. He bellowed something indistinguishable and slammed a shot in the direction of the wagon. Over the gun thunder he was cursing raggedly and fiercely.

Ackroyd did not flinch when the bullet struck wagon wood, but he had to straighten up slightly from a crouch in order to be able to depress his carbine muzzle. He had the roaring, half-kneeling, gorilla-like outlaw coming up the barrel to him past the buckhorn sights, when Marv fired from the hip. This time the slug was larger and it splintered wood. Ackroyd had to wait a moment, then he squeezed off his second shot, at the precise moment Chet fired again, too.

Chet's bullet broke a wheel spoke and split apart against the steel tire. Ackroyd levered up for his third shot. Chet leaned forward, far forward, tried to plant his butt plate upon the ground for support, failed, and fell forward with the slow, massive movement of a bull. He went down on his face, and did not move again.

Marv was running eastward, over in the direction where Ryan was lying dead, still tied. He whirled twice to slam shots in Ackroyd's direction and did not come close either time.

Ackroyd tried to track Marv, but he did not have much ground to cover before being among the yonder trees. Nevertheless, Ackroyd fired, and heard the bullet strike a tree, hard.

Silence settled, and it was deep and enduring. Ackroyd did not fear Marv's trying to get around him through the timber. He thought Marv would probably stumble over Ryan back in there, and that would provide all the answers Marv would need about the identity of the man who had shot Chet and who had tried to shoot him.

Over by the pencil-thin little rising flame Ackroyd saw the woman's shoulders heaving. He speculated on his chances, decided to try it, and went around the tailgate, left the carbine there, and went ahead without drawing his Colt. He saw her look up, saw her wilt in terror, and had no idea how he must have looked in his draped blanket with starlight on his stubbled, hollow-eyed face until she shrank back as he reached for her arm and said: "Get up. Run behind the wagon. Damn it, lady, *get up!*"

He wanted to pull her to her feet but the pain was bad again; he would not have enough strength. What finally got her to her feet was a random six-gun shot from the eastern timber. It was not very close, but the slug struck a stone and made a hair-raising *whine* as it spun off into space. She sprang up and ran.

Ackroyd turned to follow, half expecting another gunshot,

but there was none. He got back around the tailgate, picked up the saddle gun, and faced eastward. Marv was not going to run, after all. Probably he did not think he could get away on foot, and that reminded Ackroyd of the hobbled horses over toward the creek.

He turned and saw the beautiful woman staring at him, at his badge, then up at his sweat-shiny face with its deep pain lines. He handed her Ryan's six-gun and said: "Stay beside me. We've got to keep the wagon between us and him. He can't aim in the dark and from that distance a handgun's not likely to kill anyone . . . except with a lot of luck. Are you all right?"

She was holding the gun as though it were red hot. He leaned and pushed the barrel aside so that it was not aimed at him.

"Are you all right, Missus Henrichson?"

She nodded with a wooden up-down motion, then glanced in the direction from which Marv had fired at them.

Ackroyd reached, roughly patted her shoulder, and turned. "Stay with me. He's got to get a horse. You're safe for now. He'll be a half hour getting around here and even longer out where the horses are." He stopped and turned. "Can you make it?"

She released a big, ragged breath, then started over toward him. He forced a smile of encouragement, gathered the old blanket close, and started walking. He had felt no pain during the gunfight, and even now his lower body did not bother him, but the chest pains were still there, and were unrelentingly fierce.

VIII

The chill was increasing as this long night pressed toward its small hours. Ackroyd could see the hobbled horses from where he had decided he would await the arrival of the last of the outlaws. In fact, he had an excellent sighting of the horses, the entire small grassy place where they were dozing, and even of the creek on westward a fair distance. At his side the leggy, beautiful woman still held Ryan's six-shooter, but in a droopy manner as she hugged both knees and looked stonily out at the unsuspecting horses.

Ackroyd had trouble and leaned against a tree, holding the blanket close. She turned, studied him for a long while, then said: "Have you been shot?"

"No, last night I had a fight with Chet . . . that big one with the beard. I came off second best. I think I've got a couple of broken ribs."

She did not take her eyes off him. "That's all?"

He returned her look. "Do I look worse?"

"Yes."

"Well, I think I got a couple of kicks in the stomach after I passed out, but most of that pain has left." He smiled at her. "It could be worse, ma'am. It could be saddle horses out there instead of harness horses. I don't figure I'd get very far on top of a horse, but in the wagon I'll make it just fine."

She said: "I wish I had your confidence, Sheriff. Are you sure there were only three of them?"

"Yes." He paused in their quiet discussion to listen for a while, then picked up the conversation again by asking a question. "If you are Missus Henrichson, will you tell me why your husband's name was Walton?"

She seemed to stiffen slightly. Her regard of him underwent a subtle change, and, when she answered, it was in a guarded tone. "Have you been influenced by the money, Sheriff?"

He was a little surprised. "No ma'am. I'll try to get the money back. That's part of my job. That's my only interest in it. Are you Charley Walton's wife?"

She continued to regard him without wavering. "Yes. And you are looking for my husband?"

He had an answer to one of the questions in his mind. If she thought he was looking for her husband, she did not know that her husband was dead.

"Why Missus Henrichson instead of Missus Walton?"

"Walton is my husband's middle name. His last name is Henrichson."

"You knew he was an outlaw?"

She looked briefly away for the first time, then back again when she replied. "No. He was a cattle buyer. That's what he was when we were married six years ago. His business required him to be on the road a lot. Cattle buyers have to go where the . . ."

"I know about cattle buyers, Missus Henrichson. You didn't know he was an outlaw?"

Again her gaze sprang away from his face before she spoke. "I know it now, Sheriff. I didn't know it until a few weeks ago. We bought a house with some land around it in a little Wyoming town called Coulterville. There was no telegraph or newspaper, but a neighbor who got a newspaper from someone who passed through town on the stage had a story about what the news writer called the most spectacular series of robberies of the century. Three bank people gave the same description of the chief of the outlaws, and there was a drawing. . . ."

"Your husband?"

"Yes." She turned to gaze out where the dozing horses were. "And I received a packet from Charley, mailed from Denver, and a note telling me to put the packet in a safe hiding place, that he would explain when he got home. I opened the packet."

"Twenty-thousand dollars?"

"Yes. The notes were so new they were still crisp."

For a while neither of them spoke. Ackroyd was not as concerned over the stolen wealth as he was about how he was going to tell her that her husband was dead. Then she said: "I wrote my sister . . . Catherine Morrell. She wrote back for me to come down here at once."

"And you did."

"Yes."

"And you told her?"

"Yes." The beautiful woman turned back slowly to face Jim Ackroyd. "And her husband. I gave Andy the packet. That night I was asleep when a large man opened the bedroom window from outside. The noise awakened me. I sat up, but before I could cry out, he told me if I wanted to see Charley alive I would bring the money and ride toward the foothills the next day. I . . . did it. My sister came along. She got the packet from her husband's safe without letting him know. But no one met us."

Ackroyd dryly said: "Lady, you rode in the wrong direction. I was at the ranch that morning and Andy Morrell pointed in the direction you and Missus Morrell rode. These men were five miles almost due north from the route you took. Didn't he tell you which way to go?"

"No. Just to ride into the foothills. Then the dog began barking and he left."

She let go a long breath, and Ackroyd sat still for a while, listening. If Marv was out there in the northward timber, sneaking around to reach the horses, he was going to have to move into view shortly. Ackroyd speculated about this. Marv was not a fool; Ackroyd knew this from experience. To reach those horses, unhobble one of them, and mount it, Marv was going to have to appear in the treeless clearing. Marv knew Ackroyd—if he had not been shot—would be over here waiting. If Marv was reasoning well, he probably would not try to get a horse. On the other hand, he was a long way from a place where he could get another horse. He would also realize that being on foot with a lawman seeking him would almost certainly end up with him being run down.

There were other considerations, such as the woman. She could conceivably have already gone for help. For all the surviving outlaw knew, she could have caught one of the horses that had stampeded when the gunfight had erupted, and be halfway back to Dagger Ranch. Ackroyd tiredly wagged his head. *He* would try for a horse under these circumstances, but whether someone else would was an open question.

His final speculation left him satisfied to sit there. Whether Marv tried for the horse or not, come daylight, when it was safe to do so, Ackroyd would try to rig out one of the horses and send Eloise Henrichson back to the headquarters of her brother-in-law's outfit. Andy Morrell was a tough, hard, and unrelenting man. And he had six range men who knew these hills. If Marv tried to escape on foot . . . He said: "How did they get you off the ranch?"

"There wasn't a sound. I think they must have killed the dog somehow. I was asleep when someone shook my shoulder. It was the wiry man with the droopy mustache. He was standing beside the bed with a gun in his hand. When I opened my eyes, he put his hand over my mouth. . . ."

The other details were not important. She was here, so Chet and Marv had been successful. That mattered; the rest of it did not matter, for the time being anyway.

"Where is the money?"

"Andy put it back in his safe in the ranch office. He was . . . angry."

Ackroyd could believe that. Morrell had the reputation of being capable of fierce anger.

She said: "I don't know why they didn't try to get it."

"They had other plans," he said dryly, remembering Marv's suggestion about how to make her tell them where the money was. All he said was: "They were going to use you as a hostage.

They'd trade you for the money. Otherwise . . ." He shrugged, shifted position a little, felt a stab of pain in his upper body, and raised a soiled cuff to wipe his face. That motion caused pain, too.

He had never been particularly fond of Dr. Campbell, but right now he would have been pleased to see him.

"Sheriff?"

"Yes?"

"I . . . wonder about my husband. If he knew those men were after the money . . . ?"

Ackroyd debated with himself about explaining about her husband, and who the men were who were trying to use her to retrieve the stolen money.

He said—"He doesn't know, Missus Henrichson."—and would have left it like that, but she turned a slow, searching look toward him.

"They were with him in the robberies?"

"Yes'm."

"You are certain of that?"

"Plumb certain. One of them, a man named Ryan, told me the entire story. Ryan stayed up here to finish me off while his partners went down to get you."

She was looking straight at him. "And . . . ?"

He answered simply. "I killed Ryan with a tree limb. I didn't mean to kill him. I wanted at least one of them alive, but . . ." Ackroyd shrugged and returned her gaze without any sensation of regret.

"Sheriff . . . my husband?"

He looked out where the horses were standing. They were no longer dozing. One of them was grazing through the stirrup-high grass, selectively picking grain heads. The other horse was standing like a statue, his ears pointing, his head turned toward a distant northwesterly stand of trees that came down into the clearing for a few yards. The horse was not moving.

Ackroyd raised the saddle gun to plant it butt down at his side. He stared toward that distant spit of trees, too.

"Sheriff . . . ?"

He did not take his eyes off the distant trees. "Your husband had two men with him. Ryan said he thought they were his cousins . . . some kind of relatives. . . ."

"Yes. That would be Mike and Clancy Torrey. They actually were Charley's cousins."

"Well," murmured Ackroyd, watching both the horse and the far timber.

"Yes. What is it, Sheriff?"

"They are dead. All three of them. Chet, Marv, and Ryan somehow baited them, caught them off guard, and killed all three of them." Ackroyd still did not look at her face. "Somehow they knew you had come down here to Pawnee Valley. That's one of the things I wanted Ryan to tell me. But he's dead, too. They put your husband and his partners in a wagon, drove down here, and laid them out beside the road where I'd find them."

"Why did they do something like that, Sheriff?"

"Missus Henrichson, what I suspect they did not know was whether you had brought the packet of money with you or not . . . but they sure knew one way to convince you that they knew where you were, and they also knew how to convince you that unless you handed over the money, or told them where it was hidden, they would kill you." He looked briefly at her in the ghostly starlight. She looked white and rigid, but her steady stare at him was dry-eyed. Then he turned to continue his vigil of the trees.

That motionless horse had stopped staring in the direction of the trees. He was now picking grain heads as his companion was doing, but, as Jim Ackroyd watched, the horse would lift its head now and then and look toward the distant trees. Eventually the other horse also threw up its head, but to Ackroyd, the lifelong horseman, this second animal was not concerned with the distant trees; he was concerned with a scent, and that meant that Marv was not going to appear in the clearing standing up; he was crawling on all fours through the concealing grass.

Ackroyd softly said: "Don't move. Don't make a sound." They had timber at their backs and layers of long shadows around them. They would not be discernible to anyone at a distance, providing they did not make a sound or attract attention by movement.

She obeyed. She probably would have remained motionless anyway. What Sheriff Ackroyd had just told her had come as a stunning shock. He did not have to look at her to realize this. But right now he was only concerned with what had attracted the attention of those hobbled horses out yonder.

The cold had increased very noticeably. The stars were brilliant and the night had a scent of resin and unseen wildflowers to it. Distantly, over where the creek flowed, the sound was louder than it ordinarily would have been because of the great depth of silence in every direction.

For no particular reason Ackroyd thought of Hudd Sawyer. The man who had killed him was a good shot, even in the dark, and he was coming in Ackroyd's direction on all fours through the stirrup-high grass. In daylight he would have made grass stalks sway as he passed through on his way toward the horses. In the darkness there was nothing but the pair of horses for Jim Ackroyd to use as his gauge of the murderer's progress, and they were only generally reliable. Their interest would tell the sheriff about where the outlaw was, but not with sufficient closeness for Ackroyd to use his few remaining carbine bullets, and he had no intention of engaging Marv with a handgun. He wanted as much distance between them as possible when they fought. Anyone who could kill a moving man with one shot under the circumstances that had existed when Marv had killed Hudd Sawyer was not an adversary to get into a gunfight with at close range.

Eloise Henrichson was like stone. She, too, was watching the horses. Ackroyd was not concerned with her thoughts. There would—with luck—be time to explore something like that later. He whispered softly to her. "He's crawling, but when he gets close enough to remove the hobbles and get astride, he's going to have to stand up. That'll be our only chance. When he stands up, you roll to your left, away from me, and get behind a tree. You understand?"

She nodded her head without looking away from the horses.

Ackroyd forgot his pain. He did not move a hand to raise the old blanket that had fallen from his shoulders, but he gripped the carbine, and he waited. When trouble arrived, it was going to come fast, and he could not afford to miss, not entirely because Marv would spring atop the horse and sink in his heels, no doubt riding bent double to present as small a target as possible, but also because Ackroyd only had three cartridges in the carbine.

IX

Of the pair of horses, one was calm by temperament and the other one was a little snorty. He was not particularly young or green; he just had one of those spooky temperaments. It was the calm horse that had first watched the spit of trees, but it was the high-strung animal that finally began to suck back a little, to snort gently, and bob his head as though something he either saw or scented was getting closer than he liked. Ackroyd began very slowly to bring the carbine to his lap, still holding it upright. He'd had a choice: either do this slowly and surreptitiously, or wait until Marv stood up to spring aside, then yank the weapon up to his shoulder. Ackroyd was like that calm horse; he had had plenty of time to make his judgments in his calm manner.

Eloise Henrichson turned slightly to watch the lawman, but Ackroyd ignored her. He ignored everything, even the pain, which was less now that he had been resting for so long, still shallowly breathing.

The calm horse stood perfectly still with wisps of grass between his lips. Like his companion, he was intently watching something not very distant, but if he was poised to lift his hobbled front legs and whirl away, Ackroyd could see no sign of it. But the nervous horse was already shifting a little, shuffling his tethered legs to get into hopping position. A horse that knew about hobbles—which meant a horse that had been hobbled most of his life—could hobble a lot faster than a man could run. Some, in fact, could hop about as fast as an unhobbled horse could trot.

Ackroyd guessed the high-strung animal would know how to cover ground fast. He began losing interest in that animal. Marv would not try to outrun a horse tonight; he would, instead, try to reach the calm one. He probably knew both those horses very well. He and his partners had driven them a long way, had close handled them every night they had been on the road.

Finally the nervous animal reared slightly, whirled, and came down on his tethered front hoofs, then hopped. Not fast but without halting for a dozen or so yards, then he halted and looked back. The calm horse had not moved. He was looking downward at something close by in the tall grass. Ackroyd was confident the horse was looking at Marv, but until a faint sound of soft-spoken words came back to the area where Ackroyd and the woman were sitting, he was not sure. Not many creatures would crawl through grass directly toward a pair of horses, but there were some that would have, a badger for example, or a skunk.

Ackroyd whispered from the side of his mouth: "Be ready to roll."

The woman did not move or respond. She was staring intently out where the hobbled horse was moving its head gently up and down. Then she whispered: "Does he have a bridle?"

Ackroyd did not answer. He could have told her that Marv would probably not only not have a bridle, but would not use one if he had one; he wanted only to get astride that horse and run for it. Where the horse took him in a free run was much less important than that it would carry him well away from the clearing, his dead companions, and the lawman Marv knew was somewhere around in the darkness. It did not even matter whether the horse was broken to saddle or not, although most light harness horses were also combination animals. Ackroyd did not consider it likely that the horse would buck. That spooky horse probably would the moment someone landed astride its back, but the spooky animal was about six or eight yards distant, looking back, too distant for Marv to reach, even if the outlaw had wanted to.

Ackroyd freed his gun-gripping hand, slowly wiped sweat off the palm, then gripped the gun again. He shot a very brief look at Eloise Henrichson. She looked back, almost imperceptibly nodding her head as though in reply to what he was thinking. She would drop flat and roll.

Ackroyd squeezed his eyes tightly closed, then sprang them wide open. The horse was beginning to sidle a little; he was no longer hobbled. Ackroyd nearly stopped breathing. Then he saw the horse duck its head as a vague, blurry shadow came up out of the tall grass, barely visible upon the far side of the horse, and at that exact moment Ackroyd knew Marv had a fistful of mane.

Ackroyd swung the carbine easily to his shoulder. When Marv came flying upward on the horse's far side, Ackroyd cocked the carbine, took long aim, and fired.

What happened did not offer Ackroyd much of an idea of whether he had connected or not, but if he hadn't, then at least the unexpected gun roar, and perhaps the whistling bullet coming very close, accomplished what Ackroyd had not counted on. The bridleless horse gave a tremendous bound into the air, terror-stricken by the red-orange muzzle blast, the deafening sound of the shot, and the unexpectedness of everything that had occurred. He sunfished in mid-air. Marv, with one leg over the animal's back but still off balance, clung to the mane with desperation. He was fighting fiercely to get squared up on the animal. Ackroyd lowered his sights and levered up, then fired his second bullet. This time the slug tore into the grass and flinty soil less than a foot in front of the terror-stricken horse. It did not spring ahead, but sucked back with a violent movement, which was what Ackroyd had prayed would happen.

Marv, fighting to hold his balance, was leaning forward. The frightened horse simply sucked backward out from under him. There was no way for Marv to prevent what happened. The horse had its head down. Marv was catapulted forward, down the horse's neck and over his head. Then the horse wheeled and fled in a belly-down run. He passed the hobbled horse, his terror contagious, and the second animal went furiously hopping southward in the wake of the free-running animal. The only sound, now, was of the fleeing horses.

Ackroyd levered up his last cartridge and waited. There was a possibility that Marv had been injured in his over-the-head fall, but it was nothing to count on.

There was not a sound for a long while, and no movement. From fifteen feet distant over behind a red fir tree, Eloise Henrichson whispered.

"I think he was hit."

Ackroyd did not believe it. He lowered the carbine, ignored the beautiful woman, and gradually loosened his locked jaws. Those two gunshots had jarred his upper body and the pain, of which he had not been conscious before, was back again, stronger than ever.

Marv would be down on all fours again, scrambling back the way he had come. Ackroyd reached back, steadied himself against the tree he had been leaning against, pushed himself up into a standing position, and spoke without looking around. "Stay here. Don't leave this place."

He started walking back through the trees, wanting to hasten but unable to do so. He wanted to find Marv before he could get out of the clearing, back among the trees over yonder. It was the only thing he knew to do, but he was not hopeful until he was beginning to make the long curve in the direction of the distant spit of trees, and heard some large animal over there, probably frightened by the sudden gunfire, go crashing through some underbrush into the spit of trees. If Marv had reached the trees, the large animal would have detected the fresh man scent.

Ackroyd slowed his gait a little, even halted once to lean on a tree and catch his breath. The pain was steady. Back where he had been leaning upon the tree, it had only bothered him when he breathed, arriving in a spaced rhythm. Now it was constant.

He started forward again, slowly, making no noise because of layers of spongy needles underfoot. He had covered more than half the distance when he heard the large animal go crashing through the undergrowth again. Marv had either reached the trees or was close enough for the animal to have heard him.

Ackroyd kept walking. He had the trees clearly in sight, finally. The carbine seemed to weigh a ton. Ackroyd probably could have abandoned it. If he met the outlaw now, it was going to be within six-gun range. But he strode along with the

Winchester in his right fist.

The last time he halted he was close enough to make a half turn and see down through the spit of trees. They were not as dense as the timber was farther back. There was more undergrowth among them, though, and Ackroyd felt like swearing about that. He moved a little closer, stopped, and sank to one knee with his left shoulder against a rough-barked big old bull-pine.

It was a long wait, and during it he had a lot of doubts. There was no reason that he could think of for Marv to return the way he had traveled to get over here. He knew the sheriff was somewhere between him and the wagon camp. Ackroyd thought the outlaw would keep moving west, past the spit of trees and deeper into the timber. He was correct. He heard stealthy movement in the undergrowth, and gauged Marv's direction. The killer was indeed trying to work his way westerly.

Ackroyd's strength was ebbing. He could feel the weakness increasing as he started forward again. The specter of failure was galling his spirit but he knew he could not pursue the outlaw much farther.

When he by-passed the spit of trees, he heard a faint noise ahead then, without warning, the throaty growl of a bear. He stopped dead still and turned, striving to see around through the gloom, and for the first time noticed that there was more light; the night was ending and dawn was close.

The bear roared again. This time Ackroyd placed the animal as ahead of him, westerly, and slightly to his right, which was northward, which meant the bear had not caught Ackroyd's scent; it was growling at something up ahead, an enemy and an intruder. Ackroyd moved deeper among the trees and leaned there. He had reached his limit, was not even sure that he would be able to get back to the wagon camp.

Something was moving swiftly, in spurts, as though whoever

was making the sounds hastened for a few yards, then halted to look back or listen, before continuing toward Ackroyd, increasing the sounds as it evidently fled from the proximity of the aroused bear.

Ackroyd lifted the carbine, cocked it, and waited. Again his sensation of pain diminished as he concentrated—and hoped.

It was a man. Ackroyd heard leather boots scrape over bare stone. He saw a shadow, a bent-forward silhouette that seemed to be limping. Ahead, where star shine came earthward through sparse conifer tops, the man halted to strain rearward, and Ackroyd saw the taut, frightened face.

He raised the saddle gun. "Hold it," he called softly, "right where you are."

Marv jerked upright to his full height and started to twist toward the lawman he could not see among the trees. He did not have a carbine, only a holstered six-gun, and with bent fingers inches above the handle. He did not draw; he did not move at all, in fact. Split-second thinking told him that he could be seen, while he could not see anyone.

A second voice, softly feminine, spoke next, from ahead of Marv, eastward, and, when she spoke, she also cocked the six-gun she was holding with both hands, and that deadly little sound probably had more to do with Marv's sudden immobility than what she said.

"If you move, I'll shoot you!"

Ackroyd had a short, red flash of anger. He had told her not to follow him, to stay back where she had been. The anger passed almost as swiftly as it had arrived. He was watching the outlaw with the droopy mustache.

"Reach around with your left hand," he told the outlaw, "lift out that gun, and let it drop."

Marv gradually loosened. He did as Ackroyd had instructed him to do, dropped the weapon upon the spongy layers of needles, then wilted at the shoulders, and spoke for the first time. "Got a hurt leg."

Ackroyd had been out of sympathy for the last twenty-four hours. He said: "You're lucky. Eloise?"

"Yes."

"Step out where I can see you."

She did, and, as he looked, he felt an urge to grin. She was holding that six-gun straight ahead at arm's length, using both hands to do this.

"Move to one side. Marv, you walk ahead back toward the camp. You so much as *think* wrong and I'll kill you. Hands up behind your head and keep them there."

"Sheriff, listen, this hip is killing me. That god-damned horse . . ."

Ackroyd moved out of the darkness, past the trees, raised the carbine, and savagely jammed Marv in the back, forcing the man who had killed Hudd Sawyer to gasp and nearly fall as he began limping forward.

Not another word was said. Eloise Henrichson moved in beside Sheriff Ackroyd and leaned to look closely into his face. She said: "Can you make it?"

He pushed up a little grin and nodded. He would make it if he had to crawl. "I'll make it." His grin faded. He wanted to say something about the way she had disobeyed him, but because he understood why she had done it, he simply said: "You make a good partner when a man's in trouble."

Marv spoke in a whining tone of voice. "Yeah, she's a damned jinx is what she is."

He would have said more but Ackroyd poked him over the kidneys with the Winchester barrel again. "Keep your mouth closed."

Around them the first grayness of dawn was brightening, even among the stands of close-spaced timber. And it was cold.

Ackroyd put one foot ahead of the other one and willed himself to keep moving. It was a long walk back. Before they had the wagon in sight, Eloise Henrichson put her arm around his waist to lend support, and, as ill as he felt, he was surprised to feel the corded muscle in her arm. Maybe it was her closeness, her physical contact which gave Ackroyd the strength, but he made it back to the camp, and used up his remaining strength tying Marv with a lariat. Then he went over where the sun was finally shining with new day warmth, unrolled someone's bedroll with his foot, did not look back where Eloise or the bound killer were watching, sank down, and closed his eyes.

X

When Ackroyd opened his eyes, the sun was close to the meridian. He did not feel much better, just thirstier. He eased over very gently and met the beautiful woman's steady gaze. She was sitting in wagon shade. She had taken Marv's gun belt and buckled it around her waist. She had the six-gun holstered. Evidently she had been sitting there a long time. When she met his gaze, she reached for a tin cup, then went over to help him drink what he had thought would be creek water.

It was water, but it was also whiskey. He drained the cup and smiled at her. "How long have you been sitting there?"

She smiled back and offered an evasive reply. "You had a good, long rest." Then she also said: "I caught the horses and brought them back. Now that you're awake, I'll harness up and we can drive out of here."

He thought of the dead men, but mentioned only the live one. "Where is Marv?"

"Around by the near front wheel. He wheedled and even threatened, so I got tired of that and tied him to the running gear. I didn't know you had a companion when you came up here."

78

"Yeah. Hudd Sawyer. He worked for your brother-in-law. Marv shot him before we even knew who was around here."

"I knew Hudd," she said quietly. "He didn't like women but we got along very well. One night I beat him at poker."

She waited a while, and, when he stayed quiet, she finally arose to depart. He said: "I'll help you harness up."

She turned, having anticipated this offer, and gave him a stern stare. "You will lie where you are, and, if you try to get up and help me, I won't bring the horses in. Sheriff, they are light animals and the harness isn't heavy." She remained looking down at him for a moment longer, then smiled. "First, I'll cook some breakfast."

He watched her walk around the tailgate, sighed, and eased back down. The whiskey worked wonders. He had not eaten in a long while. It made him so drowsy he succumbed to the temptation and put his head back down. The morning had rising temperatures, but on the far side of the wagon the shade was fragrantly cool. He slept more soundly than he'd slept before, and did not hear Marv speak as Eloise Henrichson got busy upon the opposite side of the wagon.

Marv's hip bothered him. When the horse had wrenched back out from beneath him, he had catapulted ahead and had landed while his body was twisting in the air. The hip was not dislocated, obviously, or he would have been unable to walk back to the wagon camp, but by now it was achingly painful, and being unable to move either leg did not improve that condition. He asked Eloise Henrichson to free his ankles at least so that he could move his weight off the sore hip.

She ignored him and rummaged for things to make breakfast from. When she was kneeling at the stone ring to stir up a little breakfast fire, he eyed her closely, and finally said: "Lady, you know what the law's goin' to do to you for bein' an accessory to Charley's bank robberies?"

She replied indifferently: "I was not a part of it."

"Lady, you got almost half of the money. If that ain't bein' an accessory, I don't know what is."

She got the fire started, watched it briefly, pushed in another few twigs, then arose as she said: "Who killed my husband?"

Marv did not even hesitate. "That feller yonder in the bushes. Ryan. He met 'em. We all met, an', while he was tellin' Charley Walton how great he was, an' Charley was smilin' and relaxed, Ryan pulled out that little five-shot belly gun he carried, and commenced shooting. It was over in about a half a minute. Ryan was clever at somethin' like that. Lady, I'm tryin' to be helpful. If I could have my legs free, I could ease up on the sore side a little."

She stood regarding Marv for a long while in silence, then returned to the tailgate and started putting ingredients together for their breakfast.

Marv said: "You bitch, when I get loose, I'm going to make you wish to Christ you was never born."

Eloise Henrichson stopped moving. She picked up a wicked-bladed meat knife and walked purposefully up to where Marv was sitting in sunlight. He looked up, looked from the knife to her face, and seemed unable to breathe.

She knelt and pushed the knife against his soft parts, pushed until he gasped, then, with no expression showing, she said: "Apologize."

He did profusely, his weathered skin gray beneath the suntan, and with beads of sweat appearing on his forehead. She did not draw back. Her gaze was rock steady. "Who shot Charley?"

"I swear," he gasped. "I swear it, lady. Ryan did it. Chet and I was standin' there. I give you my word, lady, it happened just like I said."

She leaned very slightly and the knife-tip pierced flesh. "And Hudd . . . ?"

"Jesus," Marv panted, "I thought it was an animal of some kind."

From the corner of the tailgate a strong voice said: "You lying bastard."

Eloise Henrichson did not look up, but Marv did, jerked his head around, and stared at Sheriff Ackroyd.

Then Ackroyd said—"Come on, Eloise, I'm starving."—and turned toward the tailgate.

She withdrew the knife, arose, and went over where Ackroyd was waiting, put the meat knife down, and looked at him. But he was making biscuits with flour, baking powder, and water and ignored her until she spoke.

"Did you hear what he said about my husband?"

Instead of replying, Ackroyd dug in a pocket and produced the little nickel-plated revolver. "He told you the truth. This is the gun."

They went to the fire with meat and biscuit dough. She went to the creek for a coffee pot full of water, and, when she returned, Ackroyd had golden brown, feather-light biscuits on a tin plate. She smiled as he leaned to turn frying meat in a black-iron skillet. "You are very talented, Sheriff."

He was feeling better, hungry but stronger, and the pain seemed less. During her absence he had seen the horses, hobbled again and placidly cropping grass. As he dished up the food and without looking at her, he said: "I'd like to take Hudd back when we leave. The other two . . . I'll send someone up from town for them."

She nodded, and began to eat breakfast. The sun was on them, pleasantly warm, and except for the distantly visible lump that had been the outlaw named Chet, and the outlaw roped to the running gear, it was pleasant in the small clearing.

Food helped, too. When he was finished, Ackroyd felt like a smoke. He did not roll one; instead, he drank more coffee and studied the beautiful woman. She may have sensed this because she raised her eyes.

He grinned a little, and rubbed beard-stubbled cheeks. He knew he looked terrible, but she smiled at him. He wagged his head. "I'll remember coming up here."

She agreed. "I will, too, and I suspect that by now my brother-in-law will be on his way." She put the empty plate aside. "Tracks. This time of year the ground holds them well."

Ackroyd nodded about that. "Do you want to wait, or hitch up and head down there?"

She studied him before replying. "It would be easier if we waited. They should find us by midday."

He did not care either way, and said so, then watched her make up a plate for the outlaw, and take it over to him. She untied his arms but left his legs trussed and tethered to the running gear. Marv wolfed down the food and drank two cups of black coffee, then he rolled and lit a smoke, saw Ackroyd stonily watching him, and said: "All I did was go along."

Ackroyd sat still and did not speak.

Marv gestured with the quirley. "That friend of yours . . . that was an accident. I was huntin' for camp meat and thought . . ."

"You better shut your mouth," Ackroyd growled. "For two bits I'd leave you up here, hanging from a tree."

Marv went silent, submitted to the rope when Eloise retied him, and, when Ackroyd was not looking, Marv sent a venomous stare in the sheriff's direction.

The whiskey was almost gone. There were two more bottles beneath the seat but Ackroyd neither looked for them nor particularly cared that there might be more among the equipment of the outlaws. He waited until Eloise Henrichson was over at the tailgate, cleaning up after their meal, then walked southward, down where Chet was lying. He did not make a close inspection; he did not have to; the visible evidence where two bullets had struck the burly outlaw was enough. He retrieved Chet's six-gun and Winchester, went back, and flung them into the wagon.

Then he returned to the bedroll in the far-side shade and eased down carefully. Eloise came around there a while later and knelt. "I can bandage your ribs, Sheriff," she told him. "I've done it before."

He looked steadily at her, and ignored the offer when he said: "About your husband . . . ?"

She looked down. "I was stunned. More so when I found out what he had been doing, then over the fact that he was dead. Charley and I had been apart most of our married life. It was going to end . . . our marriage, I mean. I told him that last summer, but he rode off anyway." The violet eyes came up. "But the first year was wonderful. I'm sorry he is dead. Sheriff, you may doubt this, but I think you would have liked him. Men usually did. He never should have married. He was not a good husband. He was happiest with men." She eased back against a wheel in the shade. "And so . . ." She let it trail off into long silence, and Ackroyd changed the subject.

"Hudd heard the wagon. He went looking for tracks and found them. I guess, when something like this is over, you think of what you should have done instead of what you did. I shouldn't have stalked their camp. I should have gone back to town and rounded up a posse."

She said: "You didn't know."

That was correct; he hadn't known they would be murderers, but he *had* thought they had probably left those three dead men beside the stage road.

"Well . . . are you sure you know how to bandage busted ribs?"

Instead of replying, she arose, went to the side of the wagon, brought back some cloth, and knelt beside him again as she unbuttoned his shirt. As she worked, she told him a little about herself.

She and her sister had been raised on their father's ranch in southern Montana. They had lived thirty miles from a town. She and her sister had had to learn many different things and caring for broken bones had been one of them.

She helped him sit up, told him to put his arms out ahead, then she began bandaging his chest. She was deft at it. He was satisfied she had done it before. For as long as was required to finish the bandaging, she worked in silence, but when she told Ackroyd to lower his arms slowly, she watched his face, and, when he showed no pain, she smiled at him.

"Better, Sheriff?"

He cautiously tried a deep breath. It was better. He could not take as deep a breath as he might have, but when he tried, there was almost no pain. He smiled up at her. "I'll tell you something. The first time I saw you . . . that day in town . . . I thought I'd never seen a woman as handsome as you are. I never had any idea you'd be as good a doctor as Jim Campbell down there, and I sure never thought I'd see you pointing a cocked six-gun at someone."

She eased back into the shade, more relaxed, more at ease. "Have you noticed, Sheriff, that most of the time we do things during the day that we did not plan to do, and which by evening we can smile over?"

He regarded her thoughtfully. "I guess living alone makes people think more than they would do otherwise. No, I never figured out anything like that, but I'll tell you what I have thought about. If I don't get a shave and a bath soon, I'm goin' to start itching."

She almost laughed, then she pointed. "The creek isn't very far. We can find some soap in the wagon. Maybe a razor."

He had no intention of stripping naked to bathe in the creek. Not as long as she was with him. Dryly he said: "I'll wait." Then he switched the topic again. "There's reward money . . ."

Her mood changed at once. "I wouldn't touch a penny of it."

"You have to live."

She regarded him thoughtfully. "My father taught us to be self-reliant. I won't starve, Sheriff."

He had about half anticipated her reaction, and shrugged as he turned to look out where the horses were grazing. "Did you have trouble catching the loose one?"

"No. Horses that have been together a while aren't hard to catch, if you can get a rope on one of them. I didn't try to catch the snorty one, and the quiet one let me walk up and put a rope on him." She was also gazing out where the horses were. "Do you like horses, Sheriff?"

He gave a short, rueful little laugh. "I always have. I've got scars to prove it. If I'd been smarter when I quit range riding, I'd have gone to work in a store. Then I'd never have had to ride a horse in the rain or the wind, or scorching heat."

"Someday," she said musingly, "I'd like to own a few hundred acres, a good quality stud, and about fifteen or twenty good mares."

He turned that over in his mind for a while before saying: "I own twelve hundred acres south of Cedarville. Bought it a few years back from an old man who homesteaded it. The buildings aren't much . . . log barn and house and log corrals . . . but it's got fine grass and plenty of creek water."

"Do you live there, Sheriff?"

"No. I live at the rooming house in town, but someday I'll take a summer off, fix up the buildings, repair the fencing, and move down there. It's beautiful country, lots of trees and rolling plains."

She held up a hand. They were silent for a time, until he

heard the same sounds she had heard. There were horsemen coming upcountry from the foothills.

She lowered her hand and gazed at Jim Ackroyd. "Before Andy gets here, Sheriff . . . you kept them from killing me."

He recalled what they'd had in mind for her. Nothing had been said about killing her. "The only thing I did, ma'am, was keep them from using you as a hostage to get that twenty-thousand dollars."

She leaned to arise, and smiled directly into his eyes. "Would you like a swallow of whiskey before they get up here?"

"No, thanks."

"Then lie down and rest. It will be a hard trip back. I'll go meet them."

XI

There was trouble right from the beginning. When Andy Morrell and his unsmiling range men swung to the ground near the wagon and saw Marv, Morrell said—"Take down your rope, Pete."—and a perfectly willing cowboy turned to obey.

That happened before Eloise came up to greet her brother-in-law. He eyed her closely from a stone-set face. "Are you all right?"

She smiled. "Yes. I'm fine, Andy. Sheriff Ackroyd is behind the wagon. He's been hurt."

Morrell jerked a gloved thumb rearward. "Who is the big feller down yonder we rode past?"

"His name was Chet. The sheriff shot him last night. There is another one over through the trees to the east."

Morrell did not look down but he jerked his hand in Marv's direction. "Who is this one?"

"He shot Hudd and kidnapped me last night."

Hard-faced Andy Morrell turned from the waist looking over among the trees, and, if his sister-in-law thought he was interested in the dead outlaw over there, she was wrong. After a while he pointed to a particular tree. "That lower limb'll do, Pete." Then Morrell turned slowly to look at Marv.

The outlaw was sweating. He had been sweating in the sunlight before the Morrell riders appeared, but now the darkness increased on his shirtfront. He pushed out a torrent of words in a husky voice. "Mister, I shot that feller by mistake. I was supposed to find us some camp meat and seen movement and . . ."

Three of the riders tied their horses, shed their gloves, and moved in to untie Marv and lead him out of the clearing, over where the tree with the particular low limb was.

Eloise stood transfixed. Her brother-in-law had scarcely spoken to her, except to ascertain that she was uninjured, then he had methodically started to do what most range cattlemen would have done.

She said: "Andy, you can't do that."

Morrell turned his flinty eyes toward her. "Go around on the other side of the rig, Eloise."

Movement back near the tailgate of the wagon caught and held Morrell's attention. His eyes widened but he did not speak until Ackroyd growled at the Dagger range riders who were moving toward Marv.

"Leave him where he is. Stay away from him. There's not going to be any lynching!"

The riders hesitated and glanced toward their employer. Morrell stared steadily at the soiled, unshaven man with the torn shirt standing by the tailgate. In a cold tone he said: "I'm obliged that you kept her safe, Jim. An' you did a fine job with these bastards. But I lost a good man."

Ackroyd leaned. "Hanging one never brought back another one."

Morrell had a range man's stock reply to that: "No, but it

sure makes darned sure this one don't kill another one."

"That's what the law is for, Andy. If you want to be helpful, you'll help rig up the wagon and load the bodies so we can get down out of here."

Morrell was never very tractable. Now he stood considering Ackroyd. Finally he said: "How bad off are you?"

Ackroyd offered a cold smile. "Try me."

Morrell's eyes narrowed slightly. "What I meant was . . . Can you make the trip? Have you been shot? Maybe we can. . . ."

"Busted ribs is all," stated Sheriff Ackroyd.

Eloise interrupted. "He was beaten and kicked unconscious. I bandaged the ribs, but I don't think those were his only injuries. He needs medical attention."

Morrell flintily nodded his head and, without taking his eyes off Ackroyd, spoke to the range riders behind him. "You fellers bring in the horses and hitch 'em. Miz Henrichson will drive. We'll load the sheriff and the others into the rig. She can haul them down to town . . . we'll stay up here."

Ackroyd began wagging his head before Morrell had finished. He had guessed Morrell's intentions. "Marv goes with me in the wagon, Andy."

Again Morrell's eyes narrowed perceptibly. "We'll get rigged up first, Jim. Then we'll talk."

"No we won't, Andy, and none of your men is coming any closer to me than they are right now. That includes you. If you want to talk . . . do it . . . but you're not going to lynch a prisoner of mine."

Morrell's square-jawed, ruddy features settled doggedly into an unrelenting expression. He hung fire briefly before speaking. "Listen to me, Jim. Since my pa's time the range cattlemen had law. My pa leaned on a few hang ropes, and so have I. You know what the law is this far from any place."

"Range law, Andy," replied Sheriff Ackroyd. "That was all

right once. It isn't now and hasn't been for about twenty years, and you damned well know that. If you try to lynch that man, somebody's going to get shot. You or me . . . or some of your riders. Andy, he's not worth that."

Eloise turned and slowly paced back to halt beside Ackroyd. She did not make a sound; she simply stood there beside the sheriff, with that holstered six-gun at her waist.

Morrell's range boss, standing near the white-faced captive, quietly said: "Andy . . . ?"

Morrell answered sharply without taking his stare away from Jim Ackroyd: "What?"

"I quit."

Morrell's stare wavered. He seemed about to speak, then turned slowly in hard silence and stared at his range boss. Neither of them spoke, but the weathered, lean range boss was clearly not going to yield.

Finally an older man, standing back a short distance with a coiled lariat in his gloved hand, spoke out in a disgusted tone of voice. "What in the hell are we doing? Mister Morrell, he *ain't* worth it. An' I'm not goin' up against a lawman just so's we can do what the damned law is goin' to do anyway. He killed Hudd and the law'll kill him. I'm not goin' to shoot no lawman an' be a fugitive for the rest of my life just because you want to hang this son-of-a-bitch. The law'll hang him . . . that's good enough for me. And I quit, too."

Morrell's face darkened. He looked at the other motionless range men, and they looked straight back, but none of them spoke. They did not have to.

Finally the range boss said: "Cuff, you 'n' Al bring in those horses, let's get the rig hitched, and get the hell down out of here."

Morrell did not utter a sound as the older rider tossed his lariat aside and turned to accompany another cowboy out where the hobbled horses were dozing. He looked a long while at his obdurate range boss, then let his breath out in a long sigh and shook his head. He was beaten.

Jim Ackroyd broke the tension and the silence by saying: "They've all three got prices on their heads for murder and robbery. They worked with Charley Walton, Andy, he's dead."

Morrell turned sharply. "Dead?"

"Yeah. Him and his two cousins. They're the men I found up alongside the stage road a few days back. The ones I told you about."

Morrell was distracted by this unexpected revelation. "How . . . ?"

"There's a dead man over eastward in the timber. He shot the three of them, then he and these other two brought the bodies down here to be found."

"Why?"

"Because they knew Eloise had half the money they robbed from some banks up in Denver. They wanted her to know what had happened to her husband. They wanted her scairt so bad she'd hand over the twenty-thousand dollars."

Morrell stepped over to the wagon and leaned there. "That's why they kidnapped her?"

"Yes. To make you bring them the money before they would release her."

Morrell thought about that. "How did she know she brought the money with her?"

"I don't think they were sure of that, but they knew she'd come down here, and it was a safe bet she'd brought it with her." Ackroyd lowered his gaze to the bound outlaw. "Marv . . . ?"

The murderer bobbed his head up and down. "That's the whole story."

Morrell turned slowly to gaze at the outlaw, then faced toward

Ackroyd again. His expression showed surprise and wonderment. The stubborn, cold anger was gone. "Why . . . ?"

The sheriff shifted his weight before replying. "There was forty-eight thousand dollars, Andy. The twenty in your safe was less than half of it. Ask Marv. These three wanted it all."

Morrell's surprise was heightened. "Forty-eight thousand dollars?"

"From three banks all robbed the same day by the same six men. Marv, there, is the only one still alive."

Morrell turned again to stare at the perspiring outlaw.

The horses were brought in. The men who had been listening turned to go help with the harnessing and hitching. They related in quiet tones of voice what Sheriff Ackroyd had just told their employer.

Eloise turned to begin putting things inside the wagon so the tailgate could be closed and chained into place. Ackroyd watched briefly, then went to help. Andy Morrell turned for the last time to stare at Marv, and the wiry outlaw with the droopy mustache was wringing wet when he attempted to make a weak and uncertain smile. He had recognized Andy Morrell as his greatest danger. He was not altogether convinced Morrell's grim determination to kill him had been nullified. He said: "Mister, the sheriff told you the truth. But it wasn't me as shot Charley nor his partners. Ryan done that. He's over yonder like the sheriff said. Me, I was along because I couldn't find no work and . . ."

Morrell snarled and stepped past. "You worthless son-of-a-bitch!"

The horses were harnessed and backed onto the pole with a minimum of conversation, then Ackroyd took Morrell over where Ryan was lying. The men picked him up, and Morrell turned a puzzled gaze upon Ackroyd. "I thought someone said you shot him."

"No. He was supposed to execute me after Chet and Marv rode down to Dagger to abduct Eloise. We sat and talked. I had a little club. When he was close enough, I hit him over the head. I didn't mean to crush his skull, but . . ."

"He told you about Charley Walton?"

"Yes. And now you can tell me something, too. Did you know Eloise was married to Charley Walton the outlaw?"

Morrell waited until the men had lugged the corpse ahead before answering. "I knew Charley Henrichson's middle name was Walton, and I knew about an outlaw named Charley Walton. I never tried to figure it out." Morrell raised hard eyes. "You want to make out I knew who he was and charge me?"

Ackroyd was annoyed. "I'm not trying to make anything more out of this damned mess than there already is. I just wanted to know."

They started back side-by-side. Southward, two other range men were grunting under the weight of Chet. Finally the cowman said: "Eloise told us the night she arrived. So I knew who her husband was, but not until then. When she turned up missing . . ."

"Yeah, you tracked their horses. Did you know she rode out that day with your wife to find the outlaws and give them that damned money?"

Morrell covered another few yards before offering a reluctant answer. "I discovered the money was gone before they got back. She hadn't told my wife, but when I stopped her in the parlor . . . she admitted she'd taken the money, and why."

"Andy, that was *after* I rode in to talk to you."

Morrell cleared his throat and shot a look over where his men were loading the wagon. "Well, all right. The day you rode in, I knew she had been followed down here and . . ."

"Yes."

"And I was figuring to wait until they contacted her again,

then I was going to send her out to hand over the money. And I was going to be out there, too, with my riders."

Ackroyd looked around, then wagged his head. "I'm glad it didn't happen, Andy. If you ever get a notion to lynch someone again, I'm goin' to ride your damned butt all the way to the state penitentiary, and make sure you spend the rest of your life there. How would that work out for your wife, your ranch, everything else you have?"

Morrell did not speak.

Eloise had been to the creek, evidently, because her hair was in place and her cheeks shone in the morning sunlight where she stood near the wagon watching Sheriff Ackroyd and her brother-in-law approaching.

The riders brought up their horses and stood, slouched and waiting. Morrell accepted the reins to his animal, and finally remembered something. "We found your horse and Hudd's animal down near the ranch, grazing. We yanked the outfits and left the horses loose. We can make a sashay past and pick up the saddles."

He was brisk again, fully in charge as always, when he swung up. The riders swung up, too, and Ackroyd stepped from the hub to the wagon seat. From behind, Marv, still trussed with his arms in back, said: "I'm dyin' of thirst."

Ackroyd answered as Eloise climbed up beside him: "That's a lot slower than dyin' with a rope around your damned neck."

The riders headed southward toward the bare foothills and Ackroyd talked up the team. Eloise looked at him. "I can drive, Sheriff."

He smiled at her. "I'm fine." Then his grin deepened. "But I'm beginnin' to itch."

Behind, in the wagon bed, three dead men were concealed beneath bedroll tarpaulins, and Marv was sitting in a corner, gray, worn down, and willing to say nothing more. He had recovered from his near brush with a hang rope and was disconsolately considering his future. It was not at all promising.

Eloise cocked her head as they bumped across the clearing, heading downcountry behind the cavalcade of range men, then, without a word, she leaned down and groped beneath the seat. Ackroyd watched in puzzlement until she straightened up holding an unopened bottle of whiskey. Then she ducked down and groped again, found another bottle, and straightened up looking at Ackroyd.

He grinned and shook his head. All he wanted now was a bath and maybe fifteen hours of rest, then he'd go see Dr. Campbell.

XII

Dr. Campbell was not alone when Jim Ackroyd walked into his little anteroom. The man who was in the office with him was angry-voiced and profane. Evidently their discussion was ending because someone pulled open the office door and offered a few parting words.

"After three days something *is* wrong! If you don't want to join a posse, that's all right with the rest of us, but to me your damned attitude . . . oh, go to hell!"

Ackroyd turned from the front-wall window. John Donovan came through the doorway, saw the sheriff, and stopped stone still, eyes wide. "You! Where the hell have you been?"

Ackroyd answered calmly. "Up in the mountains above the hills on Dagger's northwesterly range, why?"

"Why? Because the whole darned town is on its ear. You and your horse've been missing for three days. Not a word. . . ."

Dr. Campbell came soundlessly to the doorway behind the saloon owner. He rarely showed much expression. All he did now was consider the visible chest bandage through the sheriff's shirt, then reach up to rub his jaw.

Donovan's pale eyes shone. "What happened? You look like the wrath of God."

Ackroyd smiled and moved forward, easing around the upset saloon man, heading for Dr. Campbell's examination room table. "It's a long story, John. Doctor, I've got some busted ribs."

Leaving Donovan to turn and stare, Campbell made a perfunctory gesture. "Sit on the table and shed your shirt. Here. I'll help you."

John Donovan faced completely around, then leaned in the doorway, saying nothing as he watched the ragged, filthy shirt come off. Then he stared at the improvised bandage, still without speaking.

Dr. Campbell considered the bandage. As he began to remove it, he said: "Who did this?"

Ackroyd answered quietly: "A woman. Andy Morrell's sister-in-law."

"She knew what she was doing. Now sit up straight. What the hell happened to you, Sheriff? You've got bruises as bad as any I've ever seen."

Ackroyd began speaking. He told them everything that had happened since he had left town to ride up the stage road and talk to Hudd Sawyer.

Dr. Campbell made a fresh bandage, after also making a thorough examination of the lawman. Then he lit a cigar, which lost its fire because he forgot to draw on it, and, when John Donovan finally spoke, the medical practitioner stepped back to relight his stogie and gaze at Sheriff Ackroyd.

Donovan said: "Where is Hudd? Where are the other ones?"

"The one called Marv is locked inside one of my cells," replied Ackroyd. "The two called Chet and Ryan are out back in the alley behind Doc's house . . . to be embalmed, and Mister

Morrell is going to fetch in my horse and outfit in the morning. Hudd's out back, too."

Campbell removed the stogie. "Three more? I've got the other three from up the road in pine boxes. My embalming shed is going to be full."

Ackroyd ignored that to gaze at the saloon man. "What posse were you talking about, John?"

"Six of us from here in town decided not to wait any longer, but to go sashayin' out over the countryside, looking for you. There's a lawman from up north. He was going to ride with us."

Ackroyd's interest sharpened. "What lawman?"

"Deputy sheriff from up near Denver. He didn't tell us much. Just that he was on the trail of some bank robbers."

Dr. Campbell spoke up: "He came over to talk to me, Sheriff. I showed him the three dead fellows from up the roadway. He named each one of them. Charley Walton, Mike Torrey, and Clancy Torrey. They're the men he was searching for. He wanted to know where you put the stuff taken from them. I told him, as far as I knew, it was in your office safe. He wanted to see the stuff. I told him, as far as I knew, you were the only one who knew how to open that safe, so he'd have to wait until you got back."

John Donovan was nodding his head as he listened. When the doctor finished, Donovan said: "He told me pretty much the same thing, and, when you didn't come back, an' I told him some of us here in town was worried, he agreed to ride with us. His name's Claude Perrin. He's probably down at the livery barn right now, where the others are waitin' for me."

Ackroyd was silent until he retrieved his ragged shirt and, with Dr. Campbell's assistance, got it on, then, as he eased down off the table, he said: "Disband the posse, John. I'm going up to the rooming house to clean up, change my clothes, and sleep for a few hours. Tell the deputy I'll see him in the morning."

Donovan stepped aside for Jim Ackroyd to pass through into the little anteroom. "He'll want to talk to you right now, Sheriff. He's pretty hot after those fellers."

Ackroyd lifted his hat, scratched, then dropped the hat down. From over by the door he smiled at Donovan. "They're dead, John. They're not goin' anywhere. And there are three more he'll be interested in. They're not going anywhere, either, and I'm tired all the way through. I'll see him in the morning. Thanks, Doctor Campbell."

He went out into the settling night, walked around back to lead the wagon slowly closer to Campbell's embalming shed, then he waited ten minutes, until the doctor appeared, and let down the tailgate. Dr. Campbell had no trouble with Hudd and Ryan, but he could do no better than drag bear-built Chet into his old shed. Ackroyd was unable to help. When Campbell returned to the alley and closed the shed door, panting from the exertion, Ackroyd said: "I need a favor, Doctor."

Campbell turned, looking doubtful.

Ackroyd held out a line. "Take the wagon and team down to the livery barn for me. They can care for the horses and park the outfit."

Campbell gazed at the sheriff as though he did not relish granting this favor, then he muttered something under his breath, and stalked ahead to take the line.

Ackroyd watched for a moment, then turned in the opposite direction, heading for the rooming house. There was a pleasant scent of wood smoke in the air. There were also the sounds of Cedarville around him, familiar things, and welcome. When he got up to his room, he methodically shed his soiled attire, took clean clothes with him, and went out back to the wash house.

The bath was the most relaxing thing he had experienced in

several days, and he nearly dozed off while soaking. Later, shaved and back in his room, he crawled into bed and did not move but once during the night; that was when he rolled a little in his sleep and the broken ribs let him know they were still broken.

He did not awaken until he heard the morning stage head up out of town. That would be sometime between 9:00 a.m. and 10:00 a.m. He had not slept so long in years, and, when he eased up to arise, the bruised parts of his lower body were little more than uncomfortable small reminders that Chet had put the boots to him.

His upper body felt better, but after one cautious deep breath, he knew at least those injuries were not going to go away soon, and got dressed with some awkwardness and care. It was easier to shed clothing than it was to put it on.

The sun was moving. There were birds fighting—or doing something—over along the west side of the old rooming house where an overpoweringly fragrant bush of some kind grew, and, when Ackroyd stepped out onto the rickety verandah, a broad, bull-necked man with a tanned face and a stiff-brimmed dark hat tipped far back, who was sitting, relaxed, in an old cane-bottomed chair, looked up, studied Jim Ackroyd, then arose, and said: "Good morning, Sheriff. My name is Claude Perrin. Deputy sheriff from Denver County."

Ackroyd turned, made his appraisal, and, after he had introduced himself and they had shaken hands, he invited the north country deputy to have breakfast with him. As they were moving off the verandah, Claude Perrin said he had seen the additional two corpses in Dr. Campbell's shed, and was satisfied they, too, had been with Charley Walton when the Denver banks were robbed. Then he asked about Ackroyd's prisoner, which was an indication that he had talked to either John Donovan or Dr. Campbell, since they were the only people in town

Ackroyd had mentioned his prisoner to.

Ackroyd said the man from up north could talk to Marv after breakfast, and held the door for Claude Perrin to precede him into the café.

It was late in the morning. They were the only two customers, and the café man brought their coffee as he eyed Sheriff Ackroyd. "You had the town worried," he said. "They was goin' to make up a posse and go lookin' for you."

Ackroyd nodded, smiled, and gave his order. After the café man had departed, the powerfully-built man at his side blew on the coffee before tasting it, then said: "There's a lot of money involved in this, Sheriff."

Ackroyd answered easily. "Forty-eight thousand dollars. I took money belts off the two dead men, and the one I brought in alive. I didn't count the money, just locked it up in my office safe." He was thinking of Eloise Henrichson, but said no more about the money.

Perrin leaned back as the café man slid their food in front of them, and, after he had gone away again, Perrin said: "I doubt that it'll all be in those belts, Sheriff."

Ackroyd started eating. He was one of those individuals who did not think much of his stomach; therefore, while he could go a long while without a decent meal, once he sat down to one, the repressed hunger came up all at once. He ate and had nothing to say for a long while. Evidently Claude Perrin had not missed any meals lately; he was talkative at the same time he ate.

"I did some spade work up north before taking up the trail. Walton has a wife up in Wyoming. I didn't want to waste time going up there to look for her."

Ackroyd continued to eat without speaking.

"I got a feeling, Sheriff, that she might know something. Maybe, if Walton hid part of the loot, she'd know about that.

What I can't figure out is why those men you tangled with brought Walton and those other two down here, and laid them out beside the road. But I'm damned glad you brought one of them back all in one piece."

Ackroyd reached for the cup of coffee. If this lawman talked to Marv, he was going to discover that Charley Walton's wife was not still up in Wyoming. He was also going to find out she had half the Denver loot, and had brought it down here with her. None of this troubled Ackroyd very much. What *did* bother him was the fact that this north-country lawman was also going to find out that she had made no attempt to hand that money over to the law, not up in Wyoming or down in Colorado. There were a lot of judges who would require nothing more than that to find her guilty of being an accessory.

Ackroyd finished his meal, pushed the plate aside, and drew the coffee cup to him. Then he leaned on the counter top as he spoke. "I don't know how much of that money is left, but I guess just about all of it. Maybe the outlaws spent a little getting away from Denver, but they've been moving a lot lately. Likely they didn't have time to spend much of it."

Claude Perrin was willing to agree with that. He did not seem worried about a small shortage. "There is a big reward in this," he told Jim Ackroyd. "Not just for the outlaws, but also for recovery of the money. The banks up north expect there'll be some money gone. What I'm worried about, Sheriff, is where they might have cached some of it. Maybe most of it."

Ackroyd automatically reached into a shirt pocket for his makings, and only decided not to smoke when he had the paper troughed to receive the tobacco. He crumpled the paper, discarded it, and pocketed the tobacco sack again. "Those banks up north," he said thoughtfully, "I guess they want that money bad."

Perrin looked around, surprised. "Of course they do."

Ackroyd turned, faintly smiling. "I'll get it. Whatever is left of it, which ought to be just about all of it."

They sat looking steadily at one another until Claude Perrin began to get color in his cheeks. He said: "What's on your mind, Sheriff Ackroyd?"

"The money. I'll get it."

Ackroyd did not elaborate. He continued to smile enigmatically until they had paid up and left the café, then he halted out in the sun-bright roadway and, while gazing at the jailhouse, said: "Your interest is the money, Mister Perrin?"

The lawman gazed steadily at Ackroyd for a long time before replying. "That's right. The money . . . and the people who have it. That's the third time I've told you that."

Ackroyd leaned on an upright out front of the café, facing his companion. "I've got a problem, Mister Perrin. I know where half that money is . . . not in those money belts in my jailhouse safe."

"Oh? Where is it, Sheriff?"

"That's my problem, Mister Perrin. I'll need a written agreement from the Denver banks saying they absolve the person who has the money from any responsibility in the robberies."

Perrin's color slowly mounted again. He did not seem to be a man who would compromise or make trades. The longer he stood there, returning Jim Ackroyd's gaze, the more temper showed in his face. Finally he said: "Sheriff, the law is only written one way. Anyone in possession of that money has to have been involved. I have a feeling what you're leading up to is some kind of swap . . . you'll hand over the money, if the banks in Denver will agree not to prosecute someone. Sheriff, the law don't work that way. Whether the banks will agree not to prosecute, the law sure as hell will prosecute. Now, if you're trying to make a trade with me . . ."

"Yes, Mister Perrin?"

The lawman lapsed into a rough silence. He did not seem willing to resolve it quickly. Instead, he said: "Let's go talk to your prisoner."

Ackroyd slowly shook his head. "Not today, Mister Perrin."

XIII

Ackroyd went down to the livery barn to look at the team horses. They had been corralled out back, were standing side-by-side at a manger, contentedly eating, and the light rig was parked nearby. The sun was warm; there was the customary smell of a livery barn around him, which he did not object to in the least, and, when the day man sauntered out also to lean looking in at the horses, Ackroyd said: "Harness them up for me, Will."

The day man was perfectly agreeable. "To the light wagon?"

"No. To one of your top buggies."

The day man returned to the barn for lead shanks, and Sheriff Ackroyd strolled up to the barn's front entrance and gazed northward.

The deputy from Denver County was over in front of the harness works, standing in shade, gazing southward in the direction of the livery barn. Ackroyd sighed and went back down the runway.

When he climbed into the top buggy out back, he did not drive northward up the back alley, but turned southward heading toward the lower end of town. He eventually turned westward, but not until he had all the false fronts of Cedarville's west side between himself and the roadway.

He drove at a loose trot for two miles, then halted to look back. If Perrin had discovered that Ackroyd had left town, he had not yet got a horse to ride after him; there was no one in sight.

Ackroyd eventually angled northward on a westerly course

and kept the horse at a loose trot. It was a bumpy ride; walking the horse would have made it smoother, but Ackroyd sat very erect so the occasionally jolts would not cause much pain.

It was a magnificent day, the sky was as clear as blue glass, and, as far as Ackroyd could see, there was nothing moving either ahead of him or behind.

He went around the plateau above a wide arroyo with a piddling little warm-water creek at the bottom, where trees and brush grew, saw cattle down there trying to hide from flies, and turned almost due west. He had not covered more than another mile and a half before he saw a band of riders coming toward him. There was a stand of cottonwoods between Ackroyd and the riders. He drove over into them, halted, climbed down gingerly, dropped a tether weight, slipped the bridle so the horse could crop grass, then went over to lean against one of the trees, while he waited.

The foremost rider was Andy Morrell, and he loped ahead until he recognized the sheriff, then raised a gloved hand in high salute, hauled down to a slogging walk for the last dozen or so yards, and finally halted in cottonwood shade, leaned, and looked down.

"You look fit, Sheriff."

Ackroyd had already identified the others. Morrell's wife and four of his range men were approaching. Riding beside Morrell's wife was Eloise Henrichson. Ackroyd raised his eyes. "Is she bringing the money, Andy?"

Morrell nodded. "Yeah. You were worried about it?"

Ackroyd dryly smiled. "I wasn't, but there's a Denver lawman in town who *is* worried about it." He told them about Claude Perrin, and, when he had finished, Morrell's square-jawed countenance hardened.

"Does he figure to arrest her, Sheriff?"

"He doesn't know about her, Andy. That's why I was out

here on my way to the ranch. I'll take the money back. I don't want him to know about her."

Morrell thought a moment. "What about that bastard you got locked in your cells? He knows about her. He'll sure as hell tell that Denver lawman."

Ackroyd inclined his head slightly. "Yeah. But the Denver deputy isn't going to talk to Marv . . . until I've handed over the money . . . and until I get a written statement from those bankers up in Denver they won't try to make her an accessory."

Morrell studied Ackroyd a long time, his expression relaxing. "Can you do that?"

Ackroyd laughed. "I'm sure going to try. I'll tell you one thing, Andy. In this kind of a game it's who has the money that's going to be listened to."

Morrell was doubtful. "You'll end up with your hide nailed to someone's door, Jim."

There was no time for further talk; the other riders were within earshot. Ackroyd turned to gaze at the beautiful widow. She nodded and faintly smiled at him. He smiled back, then went over to talk to her.

Morrell and his wife sat their horses in the trees. The range men swung off to take advantage of the halt to spring their knees. They looked out where Ackroyd and the beautiful woman were quietly talking, and looked at one another, but their faces were absolutely expressionless. Too expressionless. They had been up at the wagon camp, had seen Ackroyd and the beautiful woman together, and they were neither blind nor fools.

When he finished explaining to her, she wanted to ride into Cedarville and confront the Denver lawman. Ackroyd waited until she had made her indignation obvious, then he said: "If you will do this my way, I don't think there'll be trouble. If you don't . . . do you think the only reason I was up there in the hills was because I wanted those outlaws? I had an idea there was a connection between them and you. I wanted you in the clear. I want that now, too, more than ever, and all I need right now is just a little help from you. Just a little . . ."

She stood a moment, looking steadily at him, then turned without a word, unbuckled one saddlebag behind the cantle of her saddle, lifted out a bundle that was wrapped in heavy paper, and handed it to him. Then she said: "I'm going to owe you a lot, Sheriff."

He held the bundle and smiled. "The weather is beautiful this time of year. There are wildflowers out and . . . you can repay me right easy. After I get rid of this feller from Denver, if you were of a mind to, we could maybe take a couple of sandwiches and go for a day-long ride up through the foothills."

She continued to look at him as she said: "We could do that anyway. As soon as your ribs are up to it." Then she turned, rose up across the saddle, and finally smiled at him. "But I'd rather take some sandwiches and ride down and see that old ranch of yours."

He went back to the wagon, nodded to Catherine, winked at her husband, slipped the bridle back on the harness horse, put the tether weight inside on the floorboards, climbed up, and turned to drive back the way he had come.

There was not another word spoken by any of them until Ackroyd was a half mile distant, then Andy Morrell evened-up his reins in quiet thought, and glanced at his wife. "I think maybe I'd ought to sort of ride in and get the mail, Catherine."

She returned his look with a twinkle. "And take the men with you, Andy. Eloise and I'll go back . . . Andy? Just so it won't be a wasted trip, fetch back some coffee."

Ackroyd looked back only once, and saw the party of horsemen still in cottonwood shade. Then he sat forward and concentrated on reaching town. He did not see the riders miles behind him split up, the greater number of them start out toward Cedarville, too.

By the time he got back to town, the sun was past its meridian. He left the rig and hitch with the liveryman and went up to the jailhouse, let himself in by the rear door, put the bundle of money in the safe, and heard Marv swearing down in the cell room. He guessed what the outlaw was upset about, and left the jailhouse by the front door, heading for the café.

He did not see the lawman from up north. The café man made up a pail of stew, filled a bottle with black coffee, and watched the sheriff head back across in the direction of his jailhouse.

A few minutes later, when the stranger wearing the stiff-brimmed, low-crowned drover's hat entered, the café man remembered him from breakfast time, and said: "Ackroyd's prisoner ought to be mad as a bear with a sore behind by now. He didn't get no breakfast."

The bull-necked stranger turned to look out the window toward the jailhouse. He seemed prepared to go over there, then, instead, he sank down at the counter to eat, and the café man went after his food.

Across the road, Ackroyd barred his office door from the inside, then went down into the cell room where an indignant outlaw cursed and growled until Ackroyd motioned him back, and unlocked the door to put the pail and bottle on the floor. Marv said: "You figure to starve me? I already told you all I know. If I go up before a judge, I'm goin' to tell him you wouldn't feed me."

Ackroyd relocked the door and stood briefly watching Marv pick up the pail and bottle. He said: "There's a Denver deputy in town. I don't know whether he has extradition papers or not, but if he does, he's going to be out of luck. They may want you for bank robbery up there, but we want you for murder down here, and that's going to take precedent. Marv, how much of that bank loot did you fellers get rid of on the way down here?"

The outlaw spoke around a mouthful of stew. "Ryan bought the team an' wagon. Otherwise, we bought some grub." Marv swallowed and reached for the coffee bottle. "Sheriff, I've been thinking. Suppose I tell everythin' I know about those fellers. What the hell, it won't make no difference to them . . . they're dead. Maybe if I tell about all the other hold-ups they done, the judge'll figure I'm bein' helpful."

Ackroyd regarded the wiry, leathery man almost stoically. "In this country, I don't think, if you wrote it all down in a big book, it'd help much. But you can try."

Ackroyd returned to the office, closed and locked the cell-room door, and was draping his key ring from a wall peg near the gun rack when someone pounded on the door out front. He had no illusions about who that would be. He had not seen Perrin when he'd crossed over to the café, and had returned, but he had no doubt but that Perrin had seen him. He lifted the bar, hauled back the door, and met the Denver County deputy's hostile, smoldering gaze.

Perrin walked in saying: "I could have overtaken you, Sheriff."

Ackroyd did not dispute this as he kicked the door closed and went to his desk to ease down. "Maybe. But it's just as well you didn't try." Then, before Claude Perrin could speak again, he said: "You can help me count the money."

Perrin did not move from over by the front wall. "Where was it hid?"

Ackroyd turned his back and knelt to work the tumblers on the jailhouse safe. "It wasn't hidden."

When he stood up and dumped the money belts atop the desk, then placed the paper-bound bundle beside them, he said: "They bought their team and wagon with some of the money. You can impound 'em down here and force a sheriff's sale, and I'll send you whatever they bring. Otherwise, they only spent a little on grub."

Perrin approached the desk, gazing at the belts and the bundle. Ackroyd handed him a belt and took one himself. Inside each belt were three compartments with flaps that snapped. Each belt was thick, and, when the pair of lawmen drew out the folded notes and began to count, Deputy Perrin's lips moved.

It required fifteen minutes to total the money from the belts, and, after Ackroyd had written it down and reached for the bundle, Perrin's mood appeared to have mellowed slightly. He said: "Who are you tryin' to protect?"

Ackroyd did not respond; he concentrated on peeling off the paper. When the packets of banknotes were exposed, each one with a string around it, Perrin pursed his lips. "That's a hell of a lot of money," he murmured.

Ackroyd nodded and handed two bundles to the Denver County deputy. It took nearly as long for them to total the money from the bundle, and, when they added it up and Ackroyd raised his head, the Denver County deputy had already made a rough estimate.

"Forty thousand, Sheriff?"

"Forty-six thousand, Mister Perrin. They must have paid twice what the rig and team were worth. Or else they ate better than I've ever eaten."

Perrin relaxed in a chair, shoved out thick legs, and, while gazing at the money scattered over Ackroyd's desk top, heaved a big sigh before speaking. "All right. I'll give you a receipt for it and be out of your town on the night stage."

Ackroyd leaned back. "You can leave on the night stage if you want to, Deputy, but the money stays here until I get the agreements from the bankers up north that they will not prosecute anyone but the feller I've got for a prisoner in my cells. And you can't have him, without an extradition paper signed by the governor of Colorado . . . and then I think you're going to run into trouble again. I'm holding him for murder. That'll rate one up on your charge of bank robbery."

Deputy Perrin's heavy features began to redden. His hard, steady eyes went to Ackroyd and remained there.

Ackroyd waited for the angry response but it did not come. For a long time the deputy simply slouched in his chair, then abruptly arose on his way to the door. When the latch was in his hand, he said: "Where is the telegraph office?"

"We don't have one," replied the sheriff, also arising. He saw the big hand whiten where it was holding the latch. Otherwise, Claude Perrin showed nothing.

"Where is the nearest one, Sheriff?"

"Twelve miles south, down at Barneyville, or forty miles north across the mountains up at Rossburg."

The hard eyes were unrelenting. "You know what you're doing, Sheriff? Being an accessory, interferin' with a lawman durin' the performance of his duty, and . . ."

"I'm not interfering with you, Mister Perrin. I'm being helpful. I just told you where the nearest telegraph office is, didn't I? As for being an accessory, how do you figure that? Here is the bank loot. You counted it yourself, and you can have it as soon as I've got my letters from up north. Deputy, what I'm doing is trying to protect someone who didn't know enough about the law to know they can't go around carrying stolen money. That's all."

Perrin's broad, low forehead creased into two, uneven lines. "Well, hell, Sheriff, if that's all . . ."

Ackroyd began gathering up the money to return it to his safe as he said: "Get me the letters, Deputy. That's all."

Perrin stood a moment longer, watching Ackroyd replace the money and belts in the safe, then he walked out, and slammed the door after himself.

XIV

Andy Morrell entered the jailhouse office, wearing a faint frown. He jerked a thumb and said: "That feller who just walked out of here . . . Claude Perrin . . . is he the deputy from Denver County?"

Ackroyd nodded. "Do you know him?"

"I knew him twenty years ago when he was trailing cattle into the high country from over around Dodge City. In fact, I bought cattle from him. I hadn't thought of Perrin in fifteen years until I saw him crossing the road up by the stage office. I had no idea he was a lawman now."

Ackroyd felt slightly hopeful. "Were you good friends?"

Morrell nodded slightly. "But twenty years can make a difference. Especially with him behind a badge."

"He doesn't know it was Eloise, but he guessed I was tryin' to protect someone. Maybe, if you just kept away from him, things will work out anyway."

Morrell thought that over, then said: "Well, I'll stand him a drink at Donovan's place, for old time's sake."

After the cowman had departed, Ackroyd went back down into his cell room. Often, on warm afternoons, he napped on one of the cots down there. This time, as soon as he appeared, Marv hailed him, still willing to hope that if he held nothing back, and in fact embroidered what he knew a little, he might escape the scaffold.

Ackroyd listened, decided he was not going to get a nap after all, returned to the office, locked the street-side door from outside, and went over to the café for a meal.

Paul Beaman who owned the Cedarville passenger, light freight, and mail franchise, and whose six stagecoaches were ordinarily busy seven days a week, looked around as Ackroyd eased down nearby, and said: "The Denver deputy just bought passage south to Barneyville. He was in an evil mood."

Ackroyd nodded. When Perrin had left the jailhouse, he had been in an evil mood.

Then Beaman said: "Mister Morrell and some of his riders are in town."

Ackroyd nodded again, gave the café man his order, and finally turned. "You know that twelve hundred acres I bought north of your horse pasture?"

"Yeah. The old Mullins place. I had no idea the old man was thinking of selling out or I'd have been down to talk to him."

"Could a man raise a herd of horses down there, Paul?"

"Sure. That's darned good grazing country, otherwise I wouldn't own that land southward. You want to sell it?"

"No."

"You're thinkin' of goin' into the horse business?"

"Well, I was thinking that I might fix up the buildings and move down there to live . . . and maybe start a little band of quality mares, and run a papered stud horse with them."

Beaman drank coffee, shoved the cup away, and leaned upon the counter, watching the café man bring the sheriff's food. "I get some good mares now and then. Of course, I don't sell them until they develop a fault of some kind."

"Then you sell them cheap?"

Beaman laughed. "All right. But first you got about ten miles of fence to ride around and repair in some places." Beaman arose. "I'll let you know when I got a mare that'll be good for raising colts."

After Beaman had departed, the café man came sauntering from his cooking area. "You want a pail for your prisoner, Sheriff?"

Ackroyd nodded. Later, when he was heading back to the jailhouse with his prisoner's supper, he saw Claude Perrin and Andy Morrell standing in tree shade over in front of the harness works, talking and smiling.

111

Marv looked at the pail Ackroyd brought and said: "Stew again?"

The sheriff put the pail inside, locked the door, and smiled at his prisoner. "There's another way to look at things, as long as you've got stew to eat, you're still alive."

He started up out of the cell room but Marv called him back. "I can tell you where there is a cache. I think Ryan had about three thousand dollars in it."

Ackroyd waited.

Marv smiled a little. "Just drop the key outside my door."

Ackroyd returned to the office, locked the cell-room door, and went up to Dr. Campbell's place to have his ribs examined. Dr. Campbell was sitting in a tipped-back chair outside on the front porch and waited until the sheriff reached the porch before bringing his chair down onto all four of its legs.

"How do you feel?" he asked, and, before Ackroyd could respond, Campbell led the way inside to his examination room.

The pain was noticeable only when Ackroyd twisted his body, or when he bent over. Otherwise, he had become accustomed to taking shallow breaths, and there was no constant pain, just intermittent hints of it.

Campbell made his examination, then re-wound the chest bandage. As he worked, he had a question for the sheriff. "How long am I supposed to hold those fellers out in the shed? This time of year, it's a good idea to get folks into the ground without a lot of delay."

Ackroyd was putting on his shirt when he replied. "I'll go over to the saloon and see if I can raise a couple of gravediggers. If I can, and, if they'll work at it, we can plant those men in the morning."

"And . . . my pay?"

Ackroyd shoved in his shirt tails. "How much?"

"Six dollars." At the look on the sheriff's face, Dr. Campbell plunged headlong into an explanation. "Embalming fluid's gone up two bits a bottle, and there was six of them, remember. That takes time."

Ackroyd put on his hat and started out of the little room with its smell of strong disinfectant. "I'll tell the council at its next meeting. But you didn't have to embalm them, Doctor. They were going into the ground within a few days."

After Ackroyd left, heading for the rooming house, the only place he would be able to get a nap, he thought of Hudd Sawyer. Just dropping Hudd into a dark hole and shoveling dirt over him did not seem a very decent way to treat a man who had died trying to help the law. He decided that he would also request two more dollars from the town council at its next sitting, for a nice headboard for Hudd, and, if they wouldn't ante up, he'd have one made and pay for it himself.

His room was hot. That front-wall window caught all the morning sunlight. In winter it was a blessing, but summer was over the land now. He kicked out of his boots, shed his gun belt and hat, and eased down gently to lie on his back.

Sleep came soon. Ackroyd never dreamed, probably because as a rule by the time he got to bed he was tired, and this time, despite all that rest the night before, his body still required rest.

It was a pleasant afternoon. Except for a freighter wheeling up out of town with an empty bed after off-loading at the dock out behind the general store, his hollow big wagon rattling and bumping along, and later, the late-day stage coming into town from the north, making more noise, there was nothing to disturb Ackroyd's slumber.

Later, he went out to the wash house, soaked again in hot water, shaved, and strolled down to the café. The place was about half full. It was a little early for suppertime, but Cedarville had its share of hungry men who ate early.

The Denver deputy was there, wedged between two huge,

bearded, unsmiling freighters in checkered flannel shirts. Claude Perrin was a good-sized, thickly set-up man, but those two freighters made him look undersized. He saw Ackroyd and nodded.

Ackroyd nodded back, surprised because going down to Barneyville shot half a day and coming back should have shot the rest of the day, and here Perrin was in the early evening when he should not have been able to get back to town until tomorrow.

Ackroyd ate slowly. The last of his cumulative hunger pains had departed after his midday meal. He was almost back to normal again—almost, but there were still the busted ribs.

Outside, with dusk settling, Deputy Perrin was waiting in overhang shade, smoking a long, lean Mexican cigar, and looking complacent. When the sheriff emerged from the café, Perrin said: "The man's a pretty fair cook. I've eaten in a lot of greasy-spoon cafés in my line of work, and he's one of the best."

Ackroyd ignored that. "I thought you went down to Barneyville?"

"Well, I bought passage, for a fact, then I met an old friend from years back. Andy Morrell. He sent one of his riders down on the stage with copies of the telegrams I wanted sent." Perrin drew on his stogie and trickled smoke while gazing dispassionately at Sheriff Ackroyd. "Morrell and I shared a lot of campfires, back then, when we were both scratchin' hard to make a dollar. He spoke highly of you."

Ackroyd began to have a feeling of misgiving. "I'm right gratified to know that, Deputy."

Claude Perrin removed the cigar to flick ash, then plugged it back between his teeth. "Back in those days Andy Morrell was a damned good friend, and a bad man to have for an enemy. I don't think he's changed much."

Ackroyd was rummaging his mind for a way to bring this

conversation around to some position where he would be able to find out what else Morrell might have told Claude Perrin.

The Denver County deputy sheriff made it easy for him by saying: "I guess the main difference between a mean Andy Morrell back when all he had was a saddle and a horse was that, now he's got wealth, some hard-looking range riders, and can still be mean, but this time he could be *real* mean."

Ackroyd offered an admission. "He's got a reputation throughout the Pawnee Valley countryside, Deputy."

Perrin slowly inclined his head. "You could have told me about the woman, Sheriff."

Ackroyd reddened but it was not discernible in the settling night. Damn Morrell anyway.

Perrin straightened up a little. "You don't like that, do you? Well, Andy and I know each other real well. I guess better'n you and I'll ever know each other. I'll tell you something about Morrell. He'll listen . . . then he'll tell you exactly what he figures to do, and you can bet your last drop of blood that he'll do it."

Ackroyd knew Morrell this well; he did not have to have the deputy explain it to him. He said: "What did he tell you?"

"That his wife's sister was Charley Walton's wife . . . now his widow . . . and that's where the big bundle of bank loot came from. He even told me about meeting you out yonder and her handing over the money that you fetched back to town, for me to help you count."

Ackroyd's color deepened as his anger increased. That damned Andy Morrell had made a clean breast of everything. Ackroyd had to look like a fool to the north-country lawman.

"And . . . he told me something else, Sheriff. He told me that, if I so much as went out to talk to Walton's widow, he would kill me. And if those bankers in Denver don't send back the right kind of answers to my telegrams, him and his men will take that money out of your jailhouse safe, and burn it in the middle of the road."

Ackroyd wagged his head. He had reproached Morrell up at the outlaws' wagon camp, and Morrell had acted cowed; at least he had acted sufficiently impressed to leave Ackroyd with the impression he would no longer rely on his gun and his hang ropes.

"I agreed not to go near Walton's widow, to take the damned money back to Denver with me, and to close the books on this affair. I agreed not to let the prosecutor up in Denver get enough evidence to take your prisoner out of Pawnee Valley. Sheriff, I'm not all that scairt of Andy Morrell, but he was a good friend twenty years back, and for all I know he'll be a good friend again, someday. But most of all, after arguing with you, and thinking it over, I had already decided to let you keep your prisoner . . . and your secret . . . and just take back the damned bank loot." Perrin leaned to drop his stogie over the edge of the plank walk into the roadway, then straightened up as he smiled. "The money is what I came for. I'll be right glad to settle for that, and, you take my word for it, so will the bankers up in Denver. That's all they care about. That's all their kind ever cares about." Perrin yawned. "It's been a long day, Sheriff. Good night."

Ackroyd watched the bull-necked man with his stiff-brimmed drover's hat amble off in the direction of the rooming house. Ackroyd stood out there for a full ten minutes, before turning to pace his way slowly up to Donovan's saloon. He was resentful, relieved, annoyed, pleased, and that kind of a combination required a drink, maybe two drinks.

XV

Ackroyd's 1,200 acres had deep soil and it had never been opened up. The old man who had bought it thirty or forty years back had been a buffalo hunter and a trapper. His kind never owned a plow and seldom were around where people used them. After he sold out to Sheriff Ackroyd, he went to some little town up in Wyoming to live with his daughter. But he had the true range man's love of his land, and had taken Jim Ackroyd over every foot of it, which made it easier for Ackroyd to show Eloise Henrichson where the springs were, and where there was an ancient Indian burial ground, as well as to show her where two ragged old big apple trees grew. Even the old man Jim Ackroyd had bought his land from had had no idea how those two trees had got out there. But over the years he had worked out two theories, either one of which had to be the explanation. Either some emigrant traveling through, perhaps with apple-tree shoots in the bed of his wagon, had for some whimsical reason decided to plant the trees out in the middle of nowhere, or, more likely, someone from back in those days had been eating an apple as he drove along, and had tossed the core away, from which the trees had grown.

Regardless of however the trees had got there, they were huge and unkempt and broad-spreading, and Eloise told Ackroyd they needed to be pruned back. She volunteered to do it, but not until late autumn or early winter had arrived, and, as they rode southward from the trees, she also offered to help Ackroyd repair the house. The barn, she told him, intimidated her—he could do that by himself.

It was a large barn with a steep pitch to the roof. The walls were of massive fir logs. There were no openings so even at midday it was gloomy inside.

They rode southward and found some of Paul Beaman's horses through a post-and-rider fence that had fallen from age and neglect. They could have herded the horses back to Beaman's range; instead, they went over along a willow-lined creek, hobbled their horses, and ate, and afterward, with flower fragrance in the hot-day air, they relaxed in the shade and watched trout minnows feeding on May flies that hovered above the creek.

Eloise smiled and said: "It is beautiful. I think this part of southern Colorado is the most beautiful place I've ever seen. You're lucky."

He grinned. "Not always."

She understood and said: "That is over. The ribs will heal. Andy told us at supper night before last that, if you hadn't been as tough as an old horseshoe, you would not have survived up there after they beat you."

The mention of Morrell's name prompted Jim Ackroyd's smile to fade. He had thought quite often of how Morrell had revealed the secret of his sister-in-law's implication with the stolen bank wealth, and, although he knew Morrell to be a very direct, forcefully plain-spoken man, and understood how Morrell had justified what he had done to himself, for Ackroyd it still rankled.

He plucked a grass stalk and chewed on it, watched the hobbled horses eating strong late spring grass, and said: "I think your brother-in-law and I are miles apart in most ways."

She surprised him. "I noticed that weeks ago, and I am happy about it. I like Andy, and I think I understand him. But he is not my ideal man." She caught his rising glance and said more. "But that isn't going to be a problem for me. My sister doesn't believe there is another man like him. She and I have always been different in some ways." The smile returned. "How many mares can you run out here?"

He was perfectly willing to have the conversation move away from Andy Morrell. "I'd guess probably fifty or seventy-five. It would depend on how much rain we get each year and other things. And I've never ranched for myself, so I'll have to sort of feel my way along."

"More like a hundred mares and two stallions," she said matter-of-factly. "You'll have to cross-fence, though, and cut hay."

He spat out the grass stalk. He had been a range man, had worked the cow countries of several states, but he had never cut hay in his life. Settling back with his shoulders against a gently yielding willow, he said: "Did your pa put up hay?"

Her beautiful violet eyes narrowed in wry amusement. "In Montana, they either store hay or lose herds. Yes, he put up hay, but he did not like to talk about doing it. He was a rider, a scout, and a hunter, always on top of a horse, never on the ground working for them. But he got to like it. He would take me on the seat with him and we'd rake windrows all day long."

He watched willow shadows shade her beautiful face, took down a big breath, and said: "He didn't do it for himself, though, did he?"

She looked past, where the fish were jumping for May flies. "No. He did it for my mother, my sister, and me."

"I'd guess a man would need something that important to make him do it."

She continued to look past him. "Why are you single?"

His jaw dropped. He knew she was forthright. He had made that discovery up at the outlaw camp, but this caught him completely off guard. "I . . . the idea of marriage just never came up."

The violet eyes drifted slowly back to his face. "You'll marry someday."

He was still floundering, but he had always been a man who recovered quickly. "I hope to." He had more to say, but hung back.

She had the initiative and kept it. "It isn't any good unless the two of you share common interests . . . and a sense of humor."

She was gazing past him again. He knew she was talking about her own experience. "I'd guess that's about right," he told her. "I'd add one other thing. Money."

She swung to face him again. "No. My sister told me once that it is easier to be happy with it, than without it, but that's not quite true. I've always had enough money to live comfortably. I never asked where it came from. I assumed it came from Charley's cattle trades. But with just the money, and the loneliness, the money is no good at all."

"What I meant was, enough money to buy a few things when you want them, to put a new roof on the house or maybe buy another couple of brood mares. I didn't mean a lot of money."

She agreed. "That much . . . yes." Then she laughed at him. "You are a nice man. I can imagine you as a little boy. Your mother would have loved you very much. But you gave her a lot of bother."

He was grinning when he said: "What makes you sure of that?"

She sprang up and dusted off the grass before replying. "Because you have curly hair."

He stared up at her.

She laughed again. "All men who have curly hair were inquisitive, troublesome little boys. Didn't you know that?"

He got up, reset his hat, and walked with her out to the horses. "I don't know much about little boys, and a lot less about little girls." He watched her kneel to remove the hobbles, then arise to lash them behind the cantle. Her back was to him. She was a small-waisted, long-legged woman, perfectly rounded, but not overly so. He thought she had probably been a tomboy. Then she turned and caught him studying her, and leaned on the saddle, regarding him from a calm, expressionless face. He took down another big breath. "Eloise, I'll never forget this day."

She nodded with a gentling up around the eyes. "Nor will I."

"Well, maybe we could do it again."

"I want to do it again, Jim."

He floundered again, knelt to remove the hobbles, and, when he arose, glanced over. She was still leaning like that, watching him. He bridled his horse, then stepped over to do the same to her horse, and, when they had only the width of the horse between them, he said: "Was your pa's place up in Montana anything like this place?"

"I suppose it was once, when I was a small child. By the time I was old enough to understand things, he had fixed the house so that my mother loved it, and he had done a lot of work. Jim, I wouldn't mind the house just the way it is."

He pushed both palms down his trouser legs and turned with an effort. "Wood rats and all?"

She wrinkled her nose. "No. Not with wood rats."

"I'll get rid of them."

He raised a hand to the horse's mane and looked steadily at her. She neither moved nor looked away. "I'll wait," she eventually said, then she moved, and he went over to his own horse.

On the ride back toward the distant stage road neither of them said much, but with Cedarville's rooftops in sight she said: "You'll have all summer . . . on your days off. Tell me when, and I'll meet you down there. By autumn it ought to be livable."

He was silent for a half mile. His first glimpse of her had intimidated him. Later, up at the outlaw camp, she had been easier to be with; now he was no longer self-conscious around her at all. "By autumn, Eloise, we'll have time enough, I reckon."

She nodded and turned to smile at him.

★ ★ ★ ★ ★

Patterson

★ ★ ★ ★

I

Glenn Patterson was a laconic, sometimes dry, sometimes almost brilliant observer of the life scene, of Nature and animals and people. When he wanted to, Glenn Patterson could philosophize out of the cumulative experiences of a colorful, often violent lifetime, and yet Patterson was less than thirty years old. He was simply and solely one of those people to whom things had been happening since early childhood. He knew of no particular reason why this should be so, why he, of thousands of other men, should be so singled out by some mysterious providence to be always in the right place at the right time—or the wrong place at the wrong time, depending upon one's outlook.

Still, Patterson had come to manhood oak-like, narrow-hipped, and wide-shouldered, scarred and wise in the ways of surviving, like an old lobo wolf whose steely eyes lay half hidden behind the quiet droop of lids while he assessed life from a fair distance ready for whatever it threw his way. Capable, thorough, strong as rawhide, bronzed from many summer suns, a man other men instinctively respected, a man women looked back at. A good man with a horse, as someone had once said of Patterson, or a good man with a gun. It was the gun now that was uppermost.

Springtime was on the land again. Little cold winds came unexpectedly to stiffen new grass and worry tree buds, but by and large winter was now past; the days were getting progressively longer; horses and cattle were shedding; men were still riding the land in sheepskin coats but occasionally now there were rich and balmy days when this did not have to be so. As a matter of fact on the sheer barranca where Patterson sat now, his sheepskin open to the golden sunlight, it was downright hot. There was, therefore, perhaps no reason for him to wear the thing. No outward reason.

At the barranca's abrupt, brushy base was a ranch. From Patterson's eminence up there on that cliff top, it looked like a fair ranch at that. The buildings were made of chinked logs hand-adzed and fairly well-squared. The roofs were tin. There were good pole corrals down there, a windmill squeakily spinning, and out back was a scurrying little creek that tumbled out of the forested uplands farther back, up near where Patterson sat.

He had an excellent view of everything. Southward the land flowed nearly to the horizon before it met more big, black-thrusting mountains. It was good land with good forage grass, occasional shade trees, and that little creek bisecting it. A man could go a long way and never find so secluded or so fitting a place to put down his roots when his roving days were done.

The house particularly interested Patterson. It wasn't more than perhaps two years old, possibly much less. The chinking still showed dark and the siding logs had beads of sap that reflected sunlight in an amber way. There was a porch all around, after the Southwestern cow country custom; it was upon those porches folks lived out the breathless summers. Even slept out there, in case a welcome breeze should come. It looked to be maybe a four-room house. The stovepipe jumped out of a lean-to roof in the back. That would be the kitchen. For closer details, though, from up where Patterson sat his saddle, a man would need a spyglass. That was why Patterson wore the coat.

He stepped down from the saddle, reached under, brought forth a leather tube, opened it, and carefully held forth a short, heavy, expertly crafted telescopic rifle sight. Cattlemen never carried such things. Not one in 100 had ever seen one, and those who owned them were even more rare. A man had to have a very special need, to own such an expensive gadget; furthermore, if other men saw a stranger carrying such a piece of equipment, they would invariably wonder. That was why, in spite of the golden sunshine, Glenn Patterson was wearing his sheepskin this day.

He stood beside his patient horse with the telescopic sight lifted. It brought that ranch house down there right up atop the barranca to him. He even saw the door open and a lanky cowboy walk out to assess this golden new day with its dazzling dawn light and its spotless, enamel sky of softest blue. Patterson lowered the scope. That distant man jumped away from him to become small again. It was a long distance; there wasn't a saddle gun in creation that could reach that far.

Patterson turned, drew forth the rifle from his saddle boot, impassively affixed the telescopic sight to its topside hangers, screwed it into place with rough, powerful fingers, checked the gun's load, and raised it. The only thing about that handmade rifle that resembled a Winchester .25–35 ordinary carbine was the butt that ordinarily protruded above the boot when Patterson was astride. Otherwise, this weapon had a delicately tapered barrel, a flattened bolt for charging the chamber, and a range three times as far as a range rider's mass-produced carbine could hope to have.

Patterson raised the gun to his shoulder and snugged it back. That cowboy down there upon his porch was twisting to move, to walk down off his porch and head over for the barn where there'd be the morning chores to care for. As Patterson swung his scope sight to track the man, a stiff, very white fluttery movement arrested his attention. It was a curtain swaying through an open window. Patterson lowered the gun, looked with his naked eye, raised the rifle, and looked once more to make sure. It definitely was a curtain.

Sometimes, because range men came in an endless variety, one encountered a rare person who hung curtains in his womanless shack. Patterson had seen that done. But what arrested him now was that these were *clean* curtains. Only women kept curtains clean.

He raised the gun, sought out the man, and tracked him to his barn where he disappeared inside. The nicker of a hungry horse floated up the barranca's top where Patterson stood with two mangy old ageless oaks screening him.

Time passed. Patterson went ahead to the edge of his cliff, knelt, plugged one bullet into his rifle, and waited. He had lots of time. The sunlight was good across his shoulders. The air was clean and fragrant. For as far as Patterson could look in all directions there was no one else in sight. The day was ideal for what Patterson was up there to do. He was rock-steady and endlessly patient. Like the land that had been his world nearly thirty years, Patterson could wait indefinitely.

The man emerged from his barn, paused to lift his hat, resettle it atop his head, look out and around before starting on for the house where a pencil-like strand of cook stove breakfast smoke was rising straight up. Patterson raised the blue barrel, rocked the stock into his curving shoulder, picked up the man as he began to move, and brought him sharply into focus through his glass sight. The man suddenly halted; he was speaking; his lips moved. Patterson raised his thumb off the cocking hammer, raised his head, and looked ahead where a woman was crossing from the house. Something about the woman even at that distance looked ungainly, looked awkward. Patterson dropped down for a better study through the glass.

She was pregnant. Patterson watched her join the man. She was tall and blonde-headed with golden skin and she was laughing. Patterson lowered the weapon as those two came together down there, joined hands, and paced along toward the house.

"Be damned," Patterson muttered, put the rifle butt down, and leaned upon it, watching those two. "Who the hell is she and how come . . . ?" The man and woman disappeared inside. Patterson continued to hunker there on one knee for almost five minutes afterward before rising up, unloading his rifle, and stepping back beside the drowsing horse to say: "It can't be. He couldn't have a woman . . . a wife, even if he did have one, she wouldn't laugh. She wouldn't even smile."

The beautiful day remained. Everything was exactly as it had been previously—the perfumed air, the enameled overhead sky, the wonderful warmth upon loosening muscles, the benign distances. But down there where a dead man should right now be lying in barnyard dust, there was nothing, and all this depthless silence that should be echoing the peculiar, high, sharply violent snarl of that especially made rifle was as unruffled as it had been since Patterson had first ridden to this spot just ahead of daybreak.

How many times do a man's best laid plans fail him, how often does some inscrutable fate decree that a man shall not be otherwise than he has previously been, even though he strains every sinew and every resource to become different? Anyway, who is to say what constitutes murder and what does not? A musty law book written by someone long dead in whose lifetime pure logic was never touched by the turgid tides of the remembering blood? No, the law—the *frontier* law—abides by older, simpler rules. There have always been certain crimes for which blood atonement is the only salvation, both for the executioner and for the executed. There are some things for which a bullet through the head—even from a long way off and from behind—are just payment, and that bullet, not fired in anger at all, cannot make of the man who fires it a murderer.

Patterson heaved the rifle back into its boot, went to the opposite side of the horse, toed in, and raised up to settle gently across leather. He could wait; undoubtedly that man down there would return to the yard, would saddle up, and make a sashay out over his range to inspect water holes or search out heifers with calves, or hunt for loose saddle stock. He could wait, but he didn't. He turned northward and faded out back across the high plateau, then turned easterly, and rode down off the mesa where junipers, oaks, and a few scraggly bull pines concealed him to the very edge of a gray-dusted stage road. There, he paralleled one wagon rut, riding southward toward the tin roofs and weathered sides of the yonder town.

It was one thing to execute a man. It was another thing to execute an expectant father, and if, to some men, there might not appear to be a whole lot of relevancy, there was to Glenn Patterson because, executioner though he was, or at least as he'd set out to be this morning, making a widow and an orphan with one gunshot was nothing he cherished in the least. He needed more information, needed more discussion with those who had sent him out to kill that man before he'd go back again.

The morning coach, south bound out of the rearward mountains, bouncing and swaying and scuffling up an enormous gray cloud of choking dust came *rattling* down. Patterson reined well clear to avoid the dust, watched the coach whip past, threw a high-handed wave when the whip threw him one, then idly watched the vehicle lurch and swing as it sped on toward Willows. There had to be a better way to travel; if a person had never seen an ocean in their lives, didn't even know what seasickness was, they got the landlubber's initiation to both after one stagecoach ride, especially through mountainous country.

The town lay well clear of the mountains. It had a meandering broad creek behind it to the east, lined with the usual fragile, green creek willows every watercourse enjoyed—from which the town had unimaginatively taken its name. It also had that warped, weathered, patched look of most substantial cow towns. Functional, unpretty, severely utilitarian in all aspects, Willows was a place where cattlemen, freighters, range men of all kinds came and went because it was the solitary hub of gregarious mankind for forty miles in one direction—southward—and a lot more than forty miles in the other directions before another town was located.

The town's thoroughfare—called Lincoln Road for an assassinated President—ran north and south. Otherwise, there had obviously been no planning; Willows had just grown; houses were put facing in whatever direction appealed to the owner's taste. The same applied to the meandering roads leading to those houses. Still and all, Willows, because it was confined to an area of perhaps thirty acres, actually did resemble a town, and therefore it indisputably was one.

Where Glenn Patterson rode into the livery barn to put up his horse, two of those roadways converged, one to the north, one to the south of the livery barn. Bonneted womenfolk with market baskets were now moving along. There were other manifestations of domestic activity, too, indicating that the town he'd ridden out of several hours before and which had then, in the gray gloom of pre-dawn, been asleep, was now its bustling daytime self again.

He unbuckled his saddle boot, took it down, and tossed the reins to a teenaged boy. "Hay and a quart of grain," he said, turning to walk away with the rifle scabbard hooked over his bent left arm.

The boy speculated on why a range rider would take his booted saddle gun with him over to the hotel and leave his bedroll with his personal effects still tied aft of the cantle. But he didn't speculate for long. From deep down inside the barn a gruff voice bawled at him to quit gawking at every stranger who rode in and get to work at stalling Patterson's horse.

Two cowmen, dressed in fresh clothing, idly standing out front of a harness shop, silently and impassively watched Patterson cross over into the hotel. They were older men, craggy-jawed, hard-eyed, confident-appearing men. Only one of them was wearing a six-gun belted to his middle and held down with a thong. This one made a quiet low grunt and said: "Well, that takes care of that. Now we give him his other five hundred and close the book. Let's go on over and get this over with."

They strolled on across the road and entered the hotel.

II

At fifty years of age Morgan Dunstan was gray and brusque and comfortably well off. He'd spent thirty-five years putting together a cow empire second only perhaps to the empire of Bryan Holt in the Willows country; when either Dunstan or Holt told folks to yell, they didn't ask why, they just asked how loud. Morgan Dunstan was slightly less than six feet tall and he weighed a grisly, rock-hard 170 pounds. His hair and lined face showed his age but otherwise Morgan Dunstan was physically the match of any man half his age. Hard work had made him like that, and, although he no longer had to work hard, he couldn't break the habit, so he remained as durably tough and unrelenting as he'd been years earlier.

The same applied equally to his neighbor, Bryan Holt, except that Holt was six feet tall, the same height as Glenn Patterson, and also nearly the same heft, about 175 pounds. When Holt and Dunstan marched into Patterson's upstairs hotel room without bothering to knock first, their faces were closed down to keep any emotion at all from showing. No one, not even as hard-bitten a pair as these two, liked being a part of death. There were circumstances that made such an execution as Patterson was supposed to have committed undeniably necessary. Still, no one enjoyed being part of it, even though, in their hearts, they knew they were right.

Patterson was standing near the window, gazing down into the bustling road when Holt and Dunstan entered. He was hatless, his booted rifle was standing in a shadowy corner, the little sun-puckers at the outer corner of his wintry eyes showed shrewdness. He twisted, saying nothing, and watched Bryan Holt dip into a pocket, bring forth some crumpled bills tied with a string and toss them onto the bed. So far none of them had spoken. There was $500 in that little pad of money. Another $500, rolled and tied the same way was in Patterson's sheepskin, which he now shrugged out of and draped upon a rickety old chair as Bryan Holt spoke, his voice very dry and quiet.

"Five hundred in advance, five hundred afterward. That right, Patterson?"

Glenn didn't answer. After one brief look he didn't glance at the money again, either. Morgan Dunstan cleared his throat, shot a look at the closed door, and back again. "How did it go?" he asked.

"Tell me something," spoke Patterson, ignoring the question. "Did you boys know he had a pregnant wife out there?"

Dunstan blinked. Bryan Holt intently considered the fly-specked wallpaper. "You weren't sent for the woman," Holt said a trifle stiffly.

Patterson considered those two, stepped across, and picked up the money off the bed, went to his sheepskin, and rummaged for the other $500. He pushed that money at Holt, who was nearest him. "Take it," he said.

Bryan Holt's faded, pale blue eyes looked surprised. "You mean . . . ," he whispered, "you mean . . . you *didn't?*"

Patterson pushed the money right under Holt's nose and repeated his words. "Take it!"

Bryan took the money, but it was Morgan Dunstan who acidly said: "Scruples, Patterson? Since when won't a thousand dollars salve over a feller's scruples?"

Glenn gazed dispassionately down at the shorter, burlier of his two visitors. "The trouble with our kind of law, Dunstan, is that it gets blurry when fellers like you want a man tipped over. A bullet is the only cure for inveterate rustlers, sure, just like it's the only cure for wanton murderers, but where things get out of focus is when hate's behind the hiring of a gun. Like now. You understand me?"

"No, I don't understand you," growled tough Morgan Dunstan, his eyes deeply smoldering. "You were to get a thousand dollars cash for sockin' away Joe Hickman. Joe's been acquitted four times on rustling charges. Now, what are Bryan an' I supposed to do . . . go right on lettin' him steal us blind? Patterson, you know as well as I do that when the damned lousy law won't do what's right, then fellers like you come into the picture. Oh, the Cattlemen's Association calls 'em range detectives, an' they're legal-like . . . you got the badge in your pocket, sure . . . but between the three of us we know what you're supposed to do. We paid you to do it."

Patterson went back by the window. In the main, what Morgan Dunstan had just angrily stated was the bald truth. Range detectives were notorious for being exterminators; they were known throughout the West for this one specialty. Still, they were not—at least most of them were not—out-and-out cold-blooded murderers, and that's what was sticking in Patterson's craw right now. He had no scruples at all about killing a man as low and underhanded as this Joe Hickman because the crooked

134

frontier law courts slyly winked and turned successful rustlers loose every day—as long as a few hundred dollars crossed the right palm. But there was something else, too—an exterminator was not an impersonal hired gun, a cold-blooded killer for hire. At least Glenn Patterson was not, so he said: "Dunstan, I shouldn't have taken your word about this Hickman. I should have gone over the court transcripts first, should have asked more questions." Patterson turned back to face his visitors. "I think I came damned close to making a mistake this morning. I don't want ever to make that mistake. You know why? I'll tell you . . . because I've seen a lot of good men shoot first, then discover they socked away a feller someone else had a grudge against and dreamed up a lot of false charges against. After you do that once, Dunstan . . . you might just as well hand in your badge and start killing for hire. You see how blurry the difference can be?"

Dunstan stood stiffly, angrily silent, glaring at Patterson. Bryan Holt, though, thoughtfully tipped back his hat, puckered up his brow, and gazed out the window as he spoke in that same cornhusk dry voice.

"What more do you need, Patterson?" he asked. Then he shrugged, and said in a softer tone: "Sure, we knew about the woman . . . her condition an' all . . . but lice get nits. You see how we stand? Maybe she's got folks she can go back to. But, really, Patterson, that's not our concern. Hickman's had four crooked trials at the county seat where every sodbuster on the jury is dead against big cattlemen. He's bought his way clear each time, come back, and stolen more of our cattle. It's not all grudge. Not by a damned sight. Tell you what you do . . . ride over to the county seat, read the trial records, talk to folks over there includin' the sheriff, then come back." Holt paused, swung his tough old eyes to the range detective, and sadly wagged his head. "We got reason to hate him. He swaggers in the saloons an' laughs at Morg an' me. But that's not it. We got to get rid of him or he's not only goin' to steal us blind, he's goin' to encourage other ex-range riders to do the same by his example."

Bryan Holt was making sense. Patterson ignored Morgan Dunstan to say: "I aim to do that, Holt. I'm going to look Hickman up. But even if it pans out like you say . . . what about the pregnant girl out there?"

Dunstan snorted. "Know what I think?" he said to Patterson. "I think the Association sent the wrong man for this job. Why don't you just ride on back to Denver an' forget this? We'll hire another feller."

"The kind you'd hire next, Dunstan," stated Patterson, "would be the same kind I'm paid to watch for . . . gunmen renegades. And just for your information, if you think after you've hired a professional killer and he's socked Hickman away, that all your troubles will be over, let me tell you how wrong you are. Those boys never give up. They bleed men like you and Holt for as much and as long as they can, because they know damned well, if they write a letter to any local sheriff about your part in a murder, you're finished."

Bryan Holt chewed that over and began for the first time to show anxiety. "Leave it be," he growled at Morgan Dunstan. "I think we've got the right man in Patterson. Anyway, what can another week hurt? Let him ride to the county seat an' make his investigation. Morg, I don't like the idea of hirin' some night rider."

Dunstan's anger didn't lessen but his common sense told him there was nothing to be gained from pursuing this any further, so he said: "Go ahead, Patterson, make your investigation. But if it takes too long, believe me, I aim to act, not talk."

Dunstan jerked his head at Bryan Holt. The pair of them left Patterson's room. Downstairs in the small lobby two other cattlemen were idly standing in front of a window, gazing out into the roadway. At sight of Dunstan and Holt descending the stairs, those two turned without a word, walked outside, and waited. As Dunstan strode forth first, those two nailed him.

"Well?" one man gruffly asked, and raised his eyebrows to complete the question.

Dunstan uttered a raw curse and said: "He didn't do it. Hickman's confounded pregnant woman came out. Patterson saw her and lost his guts."

"Wait a minute," put in Holt, a trifle pained. "That's not exactly the way it was, Morg."

One of those other men raised his eyebrows at Bryan Holt. "Did he shoot him or didn't he?" this man demanded.

"No, he didn't," growled Morgan Dunstan. "He wants a week or so to make a thorough investigation."

That inquiring cowman let off a strong oath full of dark feeling. The other man, though, scratched his jaw and squinted up his eyes and gazed around where passers-by were strolling past. "We've lived with it four years, or thereabouts. How can one more week hurt?"

"Hurt?" snorted Dunstan. "You boys are sixty miles out. Hickman doesn't hit *your* herds. As local executives of the Association, you're interested, sure, but not like Bryan and I are interested. One week can cost us two, three thousand dollars."

Dunstan whirled. "All I know," he said in an intense, suppressed statement of angry fact, "is that he's raided my herds for nearly four years, that he's went and taken up land, and built himself a damned ranch right at the base of the uplands trails within the last eighteen months, and I don't . . . by God . . . mean to stand for it one more day!"

"Give Patterson his week," stated one of the other men stiffly, looking down into Dunstan's flushed face sternly. "You agreed to do this our way, Morgan, when you come to the Association for help. Our way was moved and seconded in secret meeting of the governing board. You go runnin' off half-cocked and get us all in hot water by some tomfool notion, and I promise you the Association'll be all over you like a rash. There's a right way an' a wrong way. You remember that, now."

Dunstan's sputtering subsided. The Cattlemen's Association was powerful; it had a long arm and a longer memory. It did not sanction the hiring of professional killers and never had, and woe to the member who dragged its name through the muddy waters of legal action by using renegade murderers who invariably talked sooner or later. Each state or territory had its local chapter of the Western Beef Growers Association—called simply the Stockmen's or Cattlemen's Association—and every local town had its individual chapter of the parent organization. The Association's headquarters was over in Denver, Colorado. It was from Denver that the quiet, deadly men like Glenn Patterson rode forth on their assignments.

"One week," mumbled Dunstan, balefully looking at his companions. "Then, if Patterson doesn't move . . ." He didn't finish it; he didn't have to; his meaning was graphically clear.

Bryan Holt broke it up by saying: "Come on, I'll stand the first couple of rounds up at the saloon." He sounded glum and looked glum as he led off, walking northward.

From overhead, at his hotel room window, Glenn Patterson saw the four of them bleakly strolling through the plank walk pedestrian traffic. He recognized only Holt and Dunstan, but no great imagination was required to guess the identity of the other two. All four of those hard older men were dressed in the expensive attire of wealthy cowmen, and only in a very general way did this kind of attire resemble the rougher garb of everyday range riders. It wasn't hard for Patterson to guess where those four were now heading, or, after they bellied up to the bar, what their muted conversation would be about. Patterson blew out a big breath, scooped up his hat, dropped it upon the back of his head, and started for the door. It was a full day's ride to the county seat. If he left Willows right now, he just might make it a little ahead of dawn the ensuing morning. What a lousy way to spend a night, and all because of the way a blonde girl big as a bloated toad had smiled at a man whose face Patterson hadn't clearly seen.

III

Devon was the county seat. It was here the county supervisors met and ruled on local law. It was also here the sheriff of Buffalo County met Glenn Patterson at the Cattlemen's Saloon, looking dusty, tired, and thirsty, about 11:00 in the morning, and, although Sheriff Will Conrad did not know Glenn Patterson, it was his custom to engage strangers in conversation. Sometimes this custom offered unexpected dividends, sometimes it didn't. But invariably it gave Will Conrad food for thought, and at fifty years of age he still found people endlessly varied and interesting.

After introducing himself and standing the first beer, Will Conrad began to fish for information. He had a time-tested method for this, but it didn't always work because strangers oftentimes had just as time-tested methods of evading queries. Glenn Patterson was better than the millrun of men, although he knew not only how not to give out information, but also how to turn the thing back upon the other man. Within fifteen minutes of their meeting Patterson had Conrad talking about the Willows country, its people, its countryside, and its problems.

"Lived over there for eleven years before I ran for sheriff," Conrad reminisced over his third beer. "Used to be town marshal of Willows."

"Seems like a good country," mused Patterson.

"It is," agreed the sheriff, a brown-haired, brown-eyed, blocky, solid-set man. "It's good cow country. The trouble is, all the best land's already taken up. Fellers like Bryan Holt and Morgan Dunstan own more range than a feller can ride over in four, five days."

"I don't know about that," said Patterson smoothly. "I saw a brand new ranch at the base of a big barranca west of Willows about seven miles. I reckon there's still some good land around if a feller looks for it." He was watching Will Conrad's face as he spoke and saw the soft shadow fall, then pass away at the mention of Hickman's place. "That feller looked right prosperous, Sheriff. Good log barn, new house, stout corrals."

"Joe Hickman," muttered the lawman, flagging for another brace of beers. "Yeah. I know him. In fact, I expect most folks around Willows know Joe Hickman, especially those two cattlemen I just mentioned, Dunstan and Holt."

"Good hand, Sheriff . . . this Joe Hickman?"

The beer came, Will Conrad looked down his nose at it, his expression showing strong annoyance. "He's a good hand, all right, Mister Patterson. He's *too* good a hand. Joe's been arrested and tried four times for rustling."

Patterson raised his eyebrows, feigning surprise and interest. Sheriff Conrad looked around, nodded, and resumed his study of the foamy beer glass again.

"Acquitted four times. I figure that's some kind of a record in Buffalo County."

"Well," murmured Patterson, lifting his glass and then holding it away from his lips. "Seems to me when a feller's arrested that many times for the same crime, there's got to be something to it. How's he manage to get off each time?"

Will Conrad also drank, ran the back of a mottled, scarred hand across his thin lips, and quietly belched. "Can't say exactly, Mister Patterson, but it's sure got a bad smell to me." Conrad's face brightened. "But I've got a theory about Joe Hickman. Y'see, I've been a peace officer one place and another for twenty-seven years. That's just long enough to appreciate that there's such a thing as the law of retribution. My theory is that, one of these days, Joe's going to wind up with a bullet hole through him . . . from back to front."

Patterson emptied his glass, leaned along the noisy bar, and turned the glass in its little sticky puddle. "You figure that's how it'll end," he murmured. "Well, if he's what you say, then you're probably right. Only . . . how does the duly elected law of Buffalo County look on things like that, Sheriff?"

Conrad pushed his glass aside and half twisted to gaze along the bar where perhaps fifteen or twenty other late-morning idlers were loafing, talking, and steadily drinking. "The law'll have to look for the killer, of course. That's what I'm paid for. That's what's expected of me. I got deputies, all good men. We'd get him, Mister Patterson. But that's all. A feller does what he's sworn to do. He doesn't necessarily always believe what he's doing is plumb right, y'understand, but that's life. You know how it is."

"Sure do, Sheriff," agreed Patterson, moving the empty glass back and forth in its puddle. "Sure do. Does this Hickman have a family?"

"He got married to a girl from down south somewhere about a year or so ago. The last time he was tried . . . and acquitted . . . she was right here in Devon with him. Pretty girl, big blonde, sturdy as oak. The kind a feller sees and somehow always remembers. I sat for two days in that courtroom wonderin' to myself how he ever got her. Wonderin' what would happen to her someday, when Joe makes his final mistake."

"Maybe he won't make it," said Patterson straightening up off the bar, looking left, looking right, then moving as though to depart. "Maybe he'll change his ways, Sheriff, or make enough off his stolen cattle to turn honest cowman."

Will Conrad grimly shook his head. "In my business you get

141

to know a few unchangeable facts about men, Mister Patterson. A thief remains a thief. A killer goes on killing until he gets himself killed. Men as old as Joe Hickman don't change. Maybe they *can't* change, but one thing I'm plumb certain of . . . they *don't* change."

"Sheriff, it's been real nice visiting with you. Maybe, if I'm over this way again, we can split a few more beers."

Will Conrad's shrewd, narrowed eyes turned soft and pleasant. "I'll be lookin' forward to it, Mister Patterson," he said, and followed Patterson's wide-shouldered form all the way across the saloon until it dropped from sight beyond the distant batwing saloon doors. Then Will Conrad took his glass, strolled down the bar to where a pair of rough, slouching men were awaiting him, both young, both wearing tied-down six-guns. "Ab," the sheriff said to one of those men, "follow him. I figure he'll head back for Willows. Trail him there, if he goes that far, and put up at the hotel. Keep me posted."

The lanky, square-jawed deputy called Ab silently nodded and walked away. The other deputy waited for Will Conrad, Buffalo County's shrewd, seasoned lawman, to speak again.

"Charley, go on over to the courthouse and ask around. If I'm figurin' Mister Patterson right, he's on Joe Hickman's trail."

Charley didn't look surprised. He simply said: "Range detective, Will?"

"I think so. Too clean-lookin' and -actin' to be a hired professional. That only leaves an exterminator. Go see just how right or wrong I am. I'll be back at the jailhouse when you get finished."

Charley would find all he had to know. Patterson had spent an hour and a half going over the records in the county clerk's office that adjoined the courtroom, where all trial-bearing transcripts were kept. Patterson had walked out of the courthouse feeling satisfied. Not elated, not even especially justified, but satisfied that everything Dunstan and Holt had told him was true. He even remembered the name of the arresting deputy sheriff each time Joe Hickman was brought in—Abner Folsom. He remembered Ab's name because he wondered what the deputy had thought each time he'd made the long ride to Willows and back again with his prisoner. After the first acquittal Folsom had to feel a little bitter; it was hard enough being a peace officer under normal circumstances but seeing dishonest law at work could be extremely disillusioning—providing the deputy himself was not part of it. Usually deputy sheriffs weren't. No one had to buy off an arresting officer. Accomplished outlaws like Joe Hickman could even laugh in their faces, because they paid out their cash money to higher authorities, so that deputies just did the sweating and the hard work, like riding seventy miles in one day.

At the livery barn where Patterson went to get his horse to ride on the trail back, he encountered a lanky, square-jawed man. They exchanged a head-on look as strangers often do. The square-jawed man was passing the time of day in idle talk with a fat hostler. Patterson rigged out the horse himself, flipped the liveryman a silver dollar, and swung up. He had no intention of knocking himself out on the ride back like he'd done on the ride over. It was another of those brilliantly balmy spring days with light and shadow alternating across an endless flow of waving green grass. There was dust on the stage road but otherwise the air was diamond-clear and full of the constantly changing scents of flowers and budding trees.

For three miles the land was flat and soft underfoot. After that Patterson's horse began a gentle climb to breast some velvety low hills. He recalled a wayside spring and calculated to make his night camp there. He had his bedroll behind the cantle; there was ample feed for his horse, anyway; there was no need to hurry. After he returned to Willows, he'd still have five days to finish his investigation. Not, he thought, that he needed any more time. Hickman's guilt had fairly leaped at him out of the transcripts. But it was no longer Joe Hickman who troubled his thoughts. It was that pregnant blonde girl out at Hickman's ranch. Perhaps, as Holt and Dunstan had made plain to him, this was not why he'd been brought to Dakota Territory from Denver, but that did not change anything to his way of thinking. Maybe Dunstan had been right, too, when he'd growled something about Glenn Patterson being the wrong man for this particular job. He shrugged that reflection away; he was here; he'd accepted the responsibility for *why* he was here, so, one way or another, he'd do the job.

Along toward noon the weather changed a little. This was the one time of year when Nature was most like a woman, sometimes warmly soft and rewarding, sometimes imperious, gusty, unpredictable. The sky remained clear but out of the snow-tipped north a ground swell wind began steadily to blow. It was cold enough to make Patterson button his collar and appraise the sky for storm sign. There was none. Then, too, about 3:00 in the afternoon, as he was progressing deeper into the broken country, which eventually ended almost within sight of Willows, the wind stopped as suddenly as it had begun, heat began piling up in the troughs Patterson rode through, the promise of a hot summer to come returned, and he unbuttoned his collar.

It was near 5:00 p.m., not more than three miles from that cottonwood-fringed spring he'd planned to camp beside, that Patterson began to get an odd little feeling up between his shoulder blades. It was an unaccountable thing, yet it persisted, and like most men of his breed Patterson heeded the hunches that sometimes strongly came and went. Finally, with the sun turning red off in the west, he halted to sniff the atmosphere, to take the pulse of this endless, empty world he was passing through, then, because of the soft earth underfoot that took and kept every shod-horse imprint, instead of changing course he abruptly turned back upon his own trail, rode to a low hill with trees atop it, got down up there, and blended quietly into the strengthening shadows.

He saw the rider almost at once, where he passed around the eastern shoulder of a side hill. The man was too distant for him to determine much more than the fellow was riding straight down Patterson's tracks, but that was all he had to know anyway.

Patterson got back astride, rode down off his hill, and stopped in a little low pass to consider. It had to be either the sheriff back at Devon or one of his men. Patterson had only spoken to two other men in Devon. One had been the county clerk, a fat, elderly man who'd have no reason to be the least bit interested in Patterson, or the bartender at the saloon where he and Will Conrad had talked. That barman wouldn't have any reason to be interested in Patterson, either. That left Will Conrad.

Patterson's lips pulled downward a little in a wry smile. Conrad—twenty-seven years a peace officer by his own admission—was no fool.

He rode on, reflecting upon that man back there. Conrad had been suspicious, which wasn't a good thing in view of what Patterson had to do. He'd also made the remark—perhaps as a veiled threat—that although, while he might personally feel no remorse at all over Joe Hickman's passing, he was still obliged by his duty to bring in his assassin. *We'd get him, Mister Patterson* had been Will Conrad's exact words. Thinking back now, Patterson had the feeling that Conrad would keep his word on that score, too. Well, things usually got complicated if a person became sufficiently involved, but there were lots of ways to skin a cat.

Patterson came to the campsite he'd remembered just as the setting sun teetered upon a raw-edged distant peak. A fiery last burst of red sunshine exploded down across the land, laying its flame atop the roundabout low hilltops but neglecting to reach farther down.

Patterson hobbled his horse, and turned him loose. He kept his saddle, his bedroll, and his booted rifle beside him while he slowly digested a meal of oily sardines and jerky. Because the jerky was salt-cured, he also drank deeply from the spring. Also, from time to time, he glanced around. If he wasn't already under surveillance, he soon would be. By his best estimates that deputy out there had never come closer than a mile.

Patterson grinned. The deputy would have jerky with him, no doubt, but as long as Patterson was at the spring, Will Conrad's man would have to suck pebbles as a substitute for drinking water. He thought, after nightfall, he'd slip back and scout that man. But he didn't do this, in the end. He, instead, rolled into his blankets and decided to let the deputy think Patterson hadn't detected him. All Patterson wanted anyway was one good look so he'd be able afterward to identify his shadow. The best place to do that would be down at Willows as the pair of them rode in.

IV

Habit is a powerful taskmaster. Glenn Patterson hadn't slept past sunup since early childhood; he was up, had his meager breakfast, and was saddling his animal before the sun's initial pale banners came whipping in from the far-off east. By full daylight he was downcountry four miles and breaking clear of the hills. He didn't look back but that telltale feeling between the shoulder blades persisted, so he knew his shadow was still back there.

Where the land opened up and flattened out, he struck the stage road again and held to it. Once, when the morning stage came *rattling* down through its eastward pass, he reined off a quarter mile as he'd done once before and in this way avoided gray alkali dust.

He was almost within sight of Willows when he twisted for a rearward look, sighted a lone horseman, small in the distance, straightened forward, and rode on until he had Willows in sight. He'd cut off nearer town, get in among some outlying sheds, and stroll back for a close scrutiny of Will Conrad's deputy.

Four horsemen came loping inward from the west. They appeared to be range riders heading for town. Since there was nothing else worth watching, Patterson kept his gaze upon those four.

They were young men, rode lightly in their saddles, came hastening along with good sunlight burnishing their sweated horses. Patterson, walking his horse, was a scant half mile away when they struck the roadway, whirled southward upon the trace, and without minimizing their gait swept along. One of them had briefly turned to glance over his shoulder. That one was familiar to Patterson. He'd watched him walk from his house to his barn two days earlier. Joe Hickman. Patterson's whole attention closed down upon Hickman, his horse, his manner of sitting a saddle, even the way his shoulders rhythmically rose and fell.

The other three were nondescript. They could have been riders for Holt or Dunstan, or for that matter riders for any cattleman in the countryside. Also, Patterson thought, they could have been cronies of Hickman's in his rustling enterprises. It was precisely this part of Hickman's life Patterson meant now especially to investigate. It didn't do much good to eliminate an outlaw unless you made reasonably certain that you also eliminated his rustling operation; otherwise, since no solitary man ever rustled on a large scale, his shadowy friends stepped in and took over, the rustling went on uninterrupted, and sooner or later you had to return and do the whole thing over again.

The riders were rapidly widening the distance. Patterson booted his horse into a long lope and rocketed along in the wake of Joe Hickman and his companions. Just short of town he got close enough to make out that the other men were roughly Hickman's age, that they were typically leaned-down, rawhide types, no different from other riders throughout the cow country West. One of them wore a wrinkled old vest that had once been tan but that was now a neutral shade of tan-gray. Another wore a left-handed hip holster, while the third man's hat was one of those stiff-brimmed, high-crowned things usually found in the Southwest where Spanish early-day influence still lingered.

At the edge of Willows, Patterson twisted, looked far back, then reined off to the right, letting Hickman and his friends dash the last 100 yards by themselves.

There were a number of sag-roofed little sheds at the upper end of town. Patterson rode in among them, dismounted where a willow thicket grew, tied his horse in dark shade, and walked back to the juncture of the northward stage road and Willows' main roadway. There, leaning against one side of a recessed doorway, he waited.

Willows was bustling about its daily chores. People came and went. The stores were doing a thriving business. Wagons, buggies, even horsemen passed up and down in the broad roadway. Across the way and southward where a big saloon stood, Hickman and his friends had left their lathered horses. Patterson wished for a smoke, but since he only used cigars and was rarely where these could be procured, his wish remained just exactly that. It was difficult to carry stogies when a man was traveling light; they invariably got rolled upon, sat upon, or broken some other way. Moreover, Patterson was not a habitual smoker. Mainly he liked to smoke when he had time to kill or a lot of nagging thoughts to wrestle with.

That solitary rider was walking his horse. He seemed in no

hurry at all, but, when he finally approached town with midday sunlight striking across his face, Patterson had his close look. The deputy's eyes, shadowed by his hat brim, were roving the yonder roadway as though in search of something special, and neglected to glance over where Patterson was slouching in that gloomy doorway. Ab didn't see Patterson at all, but Patterson saw him, recognized him as the lanky individual he'd formerly seen killing time at the livery barn back in Devon, and smiled to himself that it hadn't been a chance meeting back there after all. When he and Ab had exchanged that look back in Devon, it had been because Ab wished to get a straight, head-on glance at Patterson, so he would remember him.

Patterson watched Ab walk his critter right on down to a livery barn and turn in. He made his assessment of Abner Folsom without knowing that was his name, then returned to his animal, took it through back alleys to another barn, and turned it over to the hostler. After that, he took his booted rifle over to the hotel, washed up, and went out to eat.

At 2:00 in the afternoon he strolled along to the same saloon he'd seen Joe Hickman enter, noticed that Hickman's horse was still patiently standing outside at the tie rack, and went on inside to have a cold beer. He thought he'd also spot the Devon deputy in there, but he was wrong. He attributed this to the probable fact that Will Conrad's man had gone to hunt up the town marshal and perhaps ask the marshal if he knew anything about Glenn Patterson. There wasn't anything the marshal could tell about Patterson because, although his first two hours in town Glenn had made a point of singling out the town clown, taking his measure, he'd sedulously avoided any other contact, which invariably was his way.

Hickman, with his friends, was heatedly engaged in a heckling conversation with a barman over some recent horse race. The barman, badly outnumbered, was stubbornly sticking to his guns, but Joe and the others were rattling him badly with their remarks, their loose laughter, and their bantering scorn. The barman was glad to have a legitimate excuse for breaking it off. He got Patterson's order for a beer and filled it. Afterward, he wagged his head and said to Patterson: "Why don't you danged cowboys stay out on the range?" He said this in an almost plaintive manner that made Patterson smile.

Joe Hickman was flat-bellied and narrow-hipped. He was right at six feet and honed down to a wiry toughness. His face was lean and sun-darkened. The eyes were pale and bold and challenging. He was, Patterson thought—not entirely without envy—the kind of a dashing, confident, and forceful man who could sweep a handsome girl off her feet. Hickman had an air of arrogance that usually accompanied a man successful at his calling whether that calling was inside the law or outside it. It, also, was usually encountered in men who were making money faster than they can spend it. Altogether, in Patterson's view, Joe Hickman was a typically prospering outlaw who knew all the ropes. He belonged to that brotherhood of night riders who had learned how to survive in spite of the law. There were not many like him. When a person came across them, they were ordinarily condescending, deceptively wily, and as deadly as men weaned on gun barrels could become. If they were not accomplished gunfighting killers themselves, they always had accomplices who they were enriching who would do their killing for them.

For that reason Patterson also covertly studied the three with Hickman. He was still studying them when the deputy sheriff from Devon strolled in, shot one piercing glance over at Patterson, then sauntered up to the bar, and bought a drink. Immediately Patterson sensed the change in the atmosphere. It was as though an electric shock had abruptly run up and down the bar. Joe Hickman glanced at the lawman. His loose, arrogant smile faded the smallest bit, he turned and looked, then he said: "Hello, Ab. Long piece from home, aren't you?"

The deputy got his beer, picked it up in a heavy-knuckled hand, turned, and looked along the bar at Hickman. Totally ignoring Hickman's friends he said: "Not so far the smell of you didn't reach me, Joe. Care for a beer?"

Hickman threw back his head. When he was through laughing, he said: "Why don't you get over it, Ab? I told you before . . . bein' my friend's a heap better'n bein' my enemy."

Ab drank, cleared his throat, and let off a long sigh. "We're friends, Joe. About twice a year I pay you a call." He finished his drink, pushed the glass away, and shook his head at the barman who was lingering close by. "One of these days it'll stick. Either that . . . or you'll step on the wrong toes once too often and I won't have to come down here any more."

Patterson, listening and watching, recalled the name of the deputy sheriff who had brought Hickman in each time the rustler had been tried. Ab, as Hickman had called him, would be Deputy Sheriff Abner Folsom. Patterson also noticed something else. Although Hickman was bantering at the lawman, none of his three companions ever smiled at Ab. They stonily regarded him as stray dogs eye one another. There probably wouldn't be any trouble. Still, it could come. It depended on just how far this oblique conversation went and whether Hickman or Folsom drew a little blood with their veiled sarcasm. Patterson watched and waited and, meanwhile, made his assessments of these tough, resourceful, deadly men.

Hickman said: "Ab, forget it. You're goin' to be chasing your tail a long time and you still won't get within a country mile of my dust. You're the ploddin' kind. When I was range riding, I knew a hundred just like you."

Folsom might have been the plodding kind, as Hickman had said, but he wasn't slow-witted. He came right back at the rustler. "Those fellers you knew, Joe, they'll still be plodding long after you've walked your last mile. You think you're smart as a whip, but you're not. You're just clever . . . not smart."

One of Hickman's companions growled something under his breath. Hickman looked down. He straightened up off the bar. "Gotta go," he threw at the deputy. "Have another beer, Ab . . . on me." Hickman dropped some silver atop the bar. "On your kind of pay a man can go a long time between drinks. When you get some sense, Ab, come see me. Maybe I can find a slot for you."

Patterson saw Ab's cheeks get rusty. "Save your money, Joe. Headstones are expensive. Anyway, I'm partial to the kind of cash that pays for my beer."

That remark stung one of Joe's friends. He was the swarthy, black-eyed cowboy with the high-crowned hat. Stepping back one foot from the bar, this man said: "Deputy, you got a real nasty way of talkin'."

Patterson saw Ab's long-legged frame faintly stiffen, saw Ab's eyes slide away from Hickman and alight upon the swarthy man, rake him up and down to take his measure. "Well, now, mister," Ab said quietly, his tone lacking all inflection, "if you don't like the way I talk, there's a wide roadway out yonder."

The conversation had taken that downhill dip Patterson hadn't been able to say it might, or might not take. He twisted casually from the waist so as to be prepared if swift movement away from the line of fire became imminent. But the man upon High-Crown Hat's left nudged him and growled a low warning. In front of High-Crown Hat, Joe Hickman adopted a prudent attitude, also. He squared up between those two bristling adversaries and dropped another of his smiling innuendoes.

"Drink your beer, Ab," he said smoothly, "and wash the trail dust out of your throat. There's nothin' here in Willows for you. See you around." He turned, looked pointedly at High-Crown

Hat, and started away from the bar. The others followed him. High-Crown Hat did, too, but he stepped along a little stiff-leggedly, putting Patterson in mind of a fighting rooster. When the four of them disappeared out through the doorway, Patterson continued to stand, twisted half around so he could view Ab Folsom head-on. He considered there really wasn't much point in continuing this game. He knew Ab; Ab knew him.

"Deputy," he said quietly, "how'd you enjoy your supper last night . . . kept away from the spring water?"

Ab's smoky gaze, still smoldering from his near brush with Hickman's dark friend, ran up and down Patterson, stopped upon his face, and lingered. "Well, I'll tell you, Mister Patterson, I got damned dry, to tell you the truth."

Patterson grinned. The deputy grinned back. Still, there wasn't any warmth in either of those little smiles. Instead, there was the hard, uncompromising recognition of candid enemies, which was, at least in Glenn Patterson's view, a lot better than the kind of deceptive venomousness that had previously existed between High-Crown Hat and the Devon deputy.

"So you saw me an' figured things out," murmured the lawman with a small shrug of his shoulders. "Maybe it's better you did."

"You think so, Deputy?"

"Yeah. Ridin' this far's bad enough. Ridin' back with a corpse tied over a saddle horse is a sight worse."

"You figure you'll take me back that way, Deputy?" asked Patterson.

Ab shrugged again and signaled for another beer. "Who knows, Mister Patterson? Only thing I'm sure about is that I sure don't want to."

"I don't think you'll get the chance."

That brought Ab's wintry glance up again. He studied Patterson a moment before replying. "You givin' up on Joe?"

It was Patterson's turn to shrug. "Hang around and see, Deputy. I'll tell you one thing. I don't back-shoot."

That registered with Ab; he furrowed his brow and stared a long time into his beer before he said: "Mister Patterson, let me give you a word of advice . . . maybe you don't back-shoot, but don't go bankin' on it that Joe won't."

Glenn digested this. He hadn't pegged Hickman as a killer. Now he wondered. "Thanks," he said, and strolled out of the saloon.

V

Seven miles out—seven miles back. He got an early start after a good night's rest in his hotel room. In fact, when he left Willows, there were scarcely other folks abroad. The sun didn't lift until he was almost atop that old tan barranca, but when it finally did lift, it showed full promise of hosting another beautiful springtime day. He wanted to do all the looking in the vicinity of Hickman's ranch he had to do, then get back to town ahead of evening. He had in mind looking up Bryan Holt or Morgan Dunstan for a little palaver.

Atop the barranca a brightening world lay emerald green and breathlessly still for as far as he could see. Once, a dainty-stepping doe with twin fawns showed herself southward of the Hickman place in among the creek willows. She was undoubtedly having a breakfast of tender new willow growth. Hickman's place was still and peaceful. Patterson thought of the man down there, of his grinning ways and his bold, flashing stare. He also thought of the beautiful girl.

He rode west along the barranca's cliff edge, but back through the screening trees, until, where the cliff began to melt westerly back down upon the open country again, he found a dozen fresh cattle trails. From here, by gazing off to the north, he could orient himself. The land tipped up, ran along through a series of smooth hillocks that steadily increased in height until they became full-fledged mountains farther off, complete with dark and gloomy big stands of pine timber. He did not imagine rustlers would push fat cattle through those hills and kept on riding until he was eased gently back down upon the plain again.

Here, he found his first cattle. They were dark red and greasy fat. They were also alarmed at the sight of a horseman, ran off a little distance, swung, and lifted their heads to watch him intently. They were branded along the left ribs with a big JH. He sat a moment considering those animals. Obviously they were Hickman's legitimate critters. He made no count but estimated their numbers to be in the neighborhood of a 100, perhaps 150 head. These wouldn't be all Hickman's cattle, though. What kind of a damned fool risked his life stealing cattle when he already had enough of his own to make a decent living without stealing?

He rode southward for a while, encountered more fat red-backs, came across several respectable little springs that hadn't been cleaned out yet this year, appraised Hickman's graze, and shook his head. There was everything here a man needed to live well, not opulently, but well. Ample land, good graze, water, sheltered places to winter feed. Even a snug home and a good tight barn. The more he explored, the less he thought of Joe Hickman. Many men exactly like Glenn Patterson spent lifetimes working just to achieve the variety of independent existence Joe Hickman had, yet Hickman had also to strut and swagger and sneer, had to rustle other folks' cattle to show the world what a clever, wily man he was. Sometimes there were mitigating circumstances, sometimes when hard times overtook a man he stole to keep his family fed, or to try and get back on his financial feet again. With Joe Hickman, these things did not apply.

The sun climbed steadily. Eventually Hickman's JH critters

began to be mixed in with some B-Bar-H cattle. Those B-Bar-H animals would undoubtedly belong to Bryan Holt, which meant down where Patterson now was, Hickman and Holt bordered. He swung eastward now, the lay of the range firmly fixed in his mind.

It was while he was riding in this new direction that he spotted two other horsemen abroad on the land. He became both cautious and curious about those two. He probably would have avoided them altogether had this been possible, but this was all open land with occasionally a solitary old oak tree for shade. There was no place to hide, so he watched those two spot him, gradually turn their animals, and head in his direction. He thought the pair of riders would be Holt riders, but when they were closer, he saw his mistake. One was that left-handed friend of Joe Hickman's; the other was that hard-faced man with the faded vest. As he rode along watching, he wondered at those two being down here on Bryan Holt's land. It was still early; wherever High-Crown Hat was, those three undoubtedly had their camp.

When they were close enough, the pair of horsemen spoke briefly back and forth. Obviously they were discussing him with the same quick interest and long curiosity with which he was studying them. One of them raised his hand in a careless salute. Patterson responded in the same manner, drew rein, and waited for the other men to cross the last 100 yards to him.

Neither of Hickman's friends had shaved; neither looked pleased about this unexpected meeting. The left-handed man solemnly nodded, saying: "Howdy, mister. You a rider for one of the outfits hereabouts?"

Patterson studied those small, close-set pale eyes ahead of answering. Left-Hand was mean, not just dangerous but also vicious. The stamp of dissipation, too, lay across his hatchet face.

"Just traveling through," Patterson cautiously replied. "Got up kind of early and figured to hit a town ahead of suppertime." He was banking on neither of those two having noticed him in the saloon the day before. His reason for doing this was elementary. If those two thought he was simply another grubline rider, they might grow expansive. Otherwise, they would not.

"You'll hit it long before suppertime," said Tan-Vest, loosening in his saddle and throwing a look out around, then back to Patterson again. "About five, six miles the way you're ridin'. It's called Willows."

"Good," murmured Patterson. "You fellers work hereabouts?"

Tan-Vest's slightly bloated-appearing face faintly, sardonically smiled. "You could say that, stranger. We work hereabouts. It's a pretty good country."

"Any outfits needin' riders?" Patterson asked.

Left-Hand shook his head. He was watching Patterson closely. His expression wasn't exactly suspicious, but it seemed to reflect some inner doubts the man was having. "I think I've seen you before," he said. "Don't know where, but I've got that feelin'."

"Maybe," conceded Patterson, putting his attention back upon the other man. "I can't say you look familiar, friend, but then I've worked in a lot of camps between here and the Little Laramie. It's a mighty big country."

"Don't happen to have a bottle in your saddlebags, do you?" Tan-Vest asked, and Patterson knew then what it was about the faintly flushed, bloated face before him that had earlier struck a chord. Tan-Vest was a drinker, a habitually hard drinker.

"Sure don't, but it's not a bad idea." Patterson softly grinned at Tan-Vest. "I'll be in that town come evening. If you boys show up, I'll buy the first round."

Tan-Vest inclined his head. "We'll be there, stranger. My name's Gard. Simon Gard. Folks call me Sim. This here pardner of mine is Bill Blevins."

Patterson nodded at them. "My handle's Glenn Patterson." He squinted at the sun, lifted his rein hand. "See you in town this evening. S'long."

He rode on, slouching as a bored traveler might ride, did not once look back, let his animal pick its own route and its own gait, and speculated a little about the whereabouts of the other one, the man with the Mexican coloring to him who wore the stiff-brimmed, high-crowned Southwestern hat. Something else that intrigued Patterson was the reason those two were so far south so early in the morning. They'd have to have had a camp somewhere close by, otherwise they'd have had to get up long before sunup to be that far south of the Hickman place. He wondered whether or not they were staying at Hickman's ranch. He also wondered if, since they'd been scouting down across Bryan Holt's land, they might not have been out that early so none of Holt's riders would see them. If that were so, then it was only reasonable to assume they were studying the drift of Holt's cattle, which meant, since they were clearly cronies of rustler Joe Hickman, that someone might very well be planning a raid on B-Bar-H.

By the time he was within sight of town again, Patterson was beginning to believe he'd inadvertently put his toe into muddy water. He'd had several miles to make calmly all his judgments and decisions. If those two hadn't been scouting up B-Bar-H for a strike, it wouldn't matter if some of the Association men lay a day or two in fruitless ambush. If they were planning a raid, he smiled to himself, patted his horse's neck, and rode on into town. Sometimes things fell into place; some days were good for a man; some days weren't.

He put up his animal, went along to a little hole-in-the-wall café, ate a big midday meal, returned afterward to the sidewalk, and lit a stogie he'd bought from the café counterman. The taste was strong, the bite sharp, the aroma good. A man's pleasures in this life came from the little things, the small, physical things.

Willows was alive with people as it always seemed to be about high noon. Across the way he saw the town marshal and another older man sitting relaxed upon a wall bench shaded by an overhang, desultorily talking. The marshal was a big old man. Twenty, thirty years before he'd been one of those men who could walk into a saloon full of brawling cowboys, lay aside his .45, and wade in with both fists like a fellow thinning out wildcats. Then the other man raised his hat-shaded face and Patterson recognized Morgan Dunstan. He waited a long time for Dunstan's careless gaze to drift across to him, then turned, and strolled on along to the hotel where he turned in and went upstairs to his room.

From the roadside window he could still see the wall bench. Now, though, the town marshal was sitting there alone. Patterson turned and waited for the knock he knew was coming. It came. He called for Dunstan to enter, flicked gray ash out the window, and motioned Dunstan to a chair while he tossed aside his hat and dropped down upon the edge of his bed.

Dunstan wasn't as fired-up as he'd been two days earlier. Now he impassively watched Patterson from his chair and quietly said: "Heard you got back yesterday. Also heard you brought back Ab Folsom right behind you."

Patterson nodded. "You've got real good ears. Ab trailed me. I met him in the saloon afterward. There wasn't much point in the pair of us playing hide-and-seek. He told me Hickman's a back-shooter."

Dunstan lifted his shoulders and dropped them. "I don't know about that," he said. "As far as I know, Hickman's never gotten into any trouble around Willows."

"No, he wouldn't do that, Mister Dunstan. Only a damned dumb owl fouls his own nest. By the way, do you know three men Hickman runs with, one's left-handed, another is dark looking and wears a high crowned hat, the third one . . ."

"Wears an old scruffy tan vest," interrupted Dunstan. "Yeah, I know them. When Hickman holds his roundups, those three work for him. They hang around town once in a while. You think they're part of his crew?"

Patterson puffed. "Well, what do you think? If Hickman makes big strikes, he doesn't do it alone."

"I think maybe they're part of his crew. But I can't back it up with anything."

"Tell me something, Mister Dunstan. Just how does Hickman get away with it when he rustles? I rode all over that country this morning, and except for the northward mountains it's all open country. If you and Mister Holt didn't actually see him driving off your cattle, you could not help but see the dust, unless of course he cuts up into the mountains, but by golly I didn't see any wide trails up there, and anyway those hills would slow a herd down to a crawl."

"You're overlooking something, Patterson," stated the cattleman. "We don't see any dust an' we don't sight any big drives. Never have, an' both Bryan an' I have put men to watching."

"How does he do it, then?"

"Night time. We've picked up his trail several times, but since we never know when he's going to strike, he's usually a day or two ahead of us." Dunstan leaned back, crossed one leg over the other, and eyed Patterson dispassionately. "What did you turn up over at the county seat?"

"Enough to convince me you and Holt were right. Does that satisfy you?"

Dunstan gave his head a very stiff, very slight nod. "I reckon. So now you'll take care of him. Right?"

"Right. But not like you're thinking, because that won't take care of his three friends, and, if I sock Hickman away, what's to prevent those others from keeping right on with it?"

After a thoughtful moment of silence Dunstan said: "I see. You're right, Patterson. I underestimated you. I apologize."

"Forget it, Mister Dunstan. Just round up Bryan Holt and meet me here tonight after dark. We're going to plan a little surprise for Hickman."

VI

It was well after supper before Dunstan returned to Patterson's hotel room with Bryan Holt, and evidently those two had discussed a number of things including Patterson because Holt said, shortly after entering the room and making sure the door behind them was securely closed: "Patterson, if you're satisfied those three cronies of Hickman's are in this, too, I figure we'd ought to make a strike at Joe's ranch with all our riders."

Patterson let that suggestion go past and, instead of commenting on it, told the cattlemen about his meeting with Sim Gard and Bill Blevins, down on Holt's range that same morning. Holt's initial reaction was surprise. Moments later the astonishment passed and Holt became apprehensive.

"Gettin' the lay of my cattle," he said. "What else would they be doin' down there so early in the morning?" When neither Dunstan nor Patterson answered, Holt looked at them both with increasing anxiety. "Listen, we've got to get right on top of this, boys. If that bunch hits me once more, I'm goin' to be hurt plenty."

Patterson said smoothly: "I reckon it's time we baited a little trap. I suggest you fellers post some of your riders atop the barranca overlooking Hickman's place. I may be wrong, but I figure Hickman's pardners have to be stayin' at his place. If so, your men will see them move out one of these nights. They can trail 'em."

"Hit 'em," growled Morgan Dunstan. "Hit 'em with everything we've got. Kill the lot of them. Wipe them out once and for all."

Patterson regarded the yeasty older man a moment. Dunstan was one of those brave men who acted first and reflected later. There were a lot of graves in Dakota Territory, and everywhere else for that matter, filled mistakenly by such wrathful zealots. Patterson was not a hot-tempered man; he didn't like being with men who were hot-tempered.

"Not until we're all together, Dunstan. You remember that. A premature strike can scatter those boys like a covey of quail. I didn't ride a thousand miles just for the fresh air. Holt, you have your men up near the juncture of your range and Hickman's land. Somewhere out there's a good-sized herd of your B-Bar-H cattle. It'll be that bunch the cow thieves'll have their eyes on. Now tell me something, you two. When the cattle are rustled, what direction are they driven?"

"West, then southward down through the badlands which lie about thirty miles south of here," stated Holt.

"And you've trailed them the same way every time?"

Holt nodded.

"How many shod horses were along?"

Holt frowned. "We never could really tell, Patterson. You see, the cattle tracks blotched things over pretty well except back in the drag. Back there usually we found two separate sets of tracks. But we've done a little speculatin' and it looks like maybe as far as those badlands there aren't more'n maybe four, five men pushing the cattle."

Patterson lifted his eyebrows. "Four or five, you sure about that many?"

Morgan Dunstan said: "Something else you've got to know, Patterson. Down in those badlands . . . you can see the black slopes from here in town . . . live a lot of renegades. We think Hickman's in with a band of them, because as soon as we've got close to that country, the tracks have showed where men have come out of the draws and cañons."

"To help drive the critters?" Patterson asked.

Dunstan nodded. "It's always looked that way. But the hell of it is that's thirty miles off. We've never been able to get down there without being seen long in advance. On top of that, those fellers in the badlands are almighty shy around strangers, especially when we come with fifteen or twenty armed riders. There's something else, too. Once you hit the lava-rock flats down there, which is what most of those black mountains are made up of, you lose all tracks."

Patterson felt around for a cigar he'd bought after supper, lit up, and blew out a cloud of strong smoke as he regarded Morgan Dunstan. "You ever try riding down there alone, and at night, Mister Dunstan?"

Dunstan didn't answer. Patterson saw in his face, though, that the question embarrassed the cattleman, probably, Patterson thought, because Dunstan had never thought of going into the badlands like that. He sucked on his cigar, waited for one of the men to speak, and, when Holt finally did, Patterson listened with his head lowered while he considered the white ash of his stogie.

"Wouldn't do any good, Patterson," Holt stated. "Those men down there would recognize either or both of us. You see, they come to Willows for their grub and what not. They come and go. We don't know them but they'd know us. Especially if they're mixed up with Joe Hickman."

"Which," Patterson said dryly, "they undoubtedly are, and that solves a puzzle for me. I couldn't figure out how Hickman did it so smoothly."

"He's no fool," growled Dunstan.

Patterson arose, crossed to the window, and silently gazed down into the speckle-lighted roadway. Range men came and went down there, some boisterous from drinking, some less noisy but equally as effervescent. It seemed to Patterson, in view of what he'd just learned, that to stake out Hickman's ranch now would be putting the buggy in front of the horse. If a running fight with the rustlers ensued, and if they had friends among the badlands renegades, some good men might very easily get themselves killed. He faced back around, still chewing his stogie. "We'll postpone that ambush at the Hickman place for a day or two, until I can ride into the badlands, have a look around, and ride back again."

Bryan Holt immediately protested: "Hell, Patterson, suppose he's set to raid me tomorrow night or the night after? I can't afford to take no such chance as that. The shoe's beginnin' to pinch with me, from losin' cattle."

Dunstan supported his friend. "This'll be the first decent chance we'll have to catch Hickman red-handed, Patterson. As far as the outlaws holed up down south are concerned, they'll be thirty miles off. We can cut Hickman to pieces before he even gets close to . . ."

Patterson interrupted sharply: "You said yourself, Dunstan, you've picked up horse tracks well this side of those badlands where Hickman's friends meet him out on the range to take the herd farther along. Suppose there happens to be a big strike planned, suppose they meant to raid Holt of two, three hundred head? That'd mean they'd have possibly twenty riders meet them. With Joe and his sidekicks, Gard and Blevins and that dark one, you'd maybe win out, but with that many guns throwing lead at you, someone would get badly cut up. No, we'll postpone the stake-out until I've had a chance to scout that southward country. I'm in this to see that it's cut off and finished once and for all. That means Hickman's friends as well as Hickman."

"Well, suppose like Bryan says," exclaimed Dunstan, "they

raid him tomorrow night?"

"They won't do that," stated Patterson, and Dunstan turned sarcastic.

"No? You got a crystal ball or an Injun medicine bundle that lets you see into the future?"

"Mister Holt, you have your riders out all night starting tomorrow. Keep them out until I get back. Have them patrol your range up near where it borders with Hickman. Have them build fires and make noise so Hickman'll see them before he tries anything. How many riders have you got?"

"Twelve," muttered Holt, then in a stronger tone he said: "Patterson, all we wanted you to do was take care of Hickman. That's all."

Unexpectedly now, Morgan Dunstan supported Patterson's earlier contention. "Bryan, the man's plumb right. We can't just sock Hickman away. We've got to break the back of the whole damned ring."

Holt turned on Dunstan. "Sure. But dammit, Morg, those are *my* cattle that're going to get taken off, not yours."

Dunstan colored, but fought down his annoyance. "I'll bring over some men and patrol with you fellers. The more I think about it the better Patterson's way sounds to me. Listen, we agreed to give him a week . . . he's still got a couple of days to go."

Holt turned a little sulky toward his friend and neighbor. "You're the one, the other night, who was all for goin' out there and doin' away with Hickman when the rest of us talked about holdin' fire. You're sure switchin' around, Morg."

But it was evident that, despite his subsiding protests, Bryan Holt was also coming around to Patterson's way of thinking. When Dunstan fell silent and Patterson strolled back to drop down upon the edge of the bed again, Holt glumly bobbed his head up and down.

"All right, Patterson, we'll hold off until you make your southward scout. But if those damned thieves come skulkin' down on my range in the night, and I catch 'em at it, you won't earn your thousand dollars. I'll take care of Hickman my own way."

"Just keep the fires burning, keep your men patrolling, and there won't be any rustling," stated Patterson. "But you better remember this . . . both of you . . . if Joe Hickman gets killed while I'm gone, all we'll have accomplished is to drive his friends underground for a week or two, maybe longer, then they'll bounce right back under some other leader and raid you all over again."

Dunstan stood up. Everything that they'd met to discuss had now been talked over. "Patterson I'll tell you something," he said. "One slip down in those dark cañons while you're nosing around, and none of us will ever see you again. You won't be the first man to go into the badlands for a look-see who never came back."

After the two cattlemen had departed, Patterson sat a while smoking and thinking. He came to a conclusion, too. Except for that big smiling girl of Joe Hickman's he never would have stumbled onto the whole matter of Hickman's organization. He'd have shot the rustler and gone on back to Denver.

He got up, stood beside his window gazing down into the lively night-time roadway until his cigar was finished. He then decided to go have a drink of his own and left the room for the outside soft coolness.

It was a balmy night with an endless array of blue-white stars overhead in the dark vault of the heavens. As he stood just beyond the hotel doorway deeply breathing, he decided he didn't want that nightcap after all, turned, and slowly paced his way southward along the plank walk.

There weren't many people abroad down there in the

southerly end of Willows for the simple reason that the gaming rooms and saloons were at the opposite end of town. However, he did encounter a number of shadowy young couples walking along, hand-in-hand, as well as an occasional older couple out to enjoy the pleasant night. Not until a man spoke his name from a gloomy doorway and stepped out where pale light struck across his features did Patterson's attention turn back again to the dangerous present.

"Hello, Folsom," he greeted the shadowy man in front of that gloomy doorway. "You lost? The saloons are up the other way."

Ab Folsom's teeth shone in a white, stark way against the rugged darkness of his smooth, bronzed skin. "Thought I'd say the same thing to you. Fine night, isn't it?"

"Real fine," murmured Patterson, wondering. "Were you expecting me down here?"

"No, not exactly. I was just watching some men who rode in a few minutes ago. You walked right past and didn't look their way. Joe Hickman and his runnin' mates. They went on up to the saloon."

Patterson, eyeing the Devon deputy carefully, said: "Is that so?"

Folsom made a little deprecatory gesture with one hand. "What's the point in us playin' games, Patterson? I know what you're up to."

"Why don't you stop me, then, Folsom?"

"You haven't done anythin' yet. You got to make your move before the law can step in."

"Then it just might be too late, Folsom," said Patterson, and was suddenly struck with an idea. "How long are you supposed to spy on me?"

Folsom shrugged, stared, and said nothing. He was, in Glenn Patterson's sight, a tough, capable, and resourceful antagonist.

"All right, Folsom, I'll make you a proposition."

"Not interested."

"Hear me out."

Folsom shrugged. "Go ahead then, but you'll be wastin' your breath."

"Maybe. Maybe not. I'm leaving town tonight." As he made this statement, Patterson saw Ab Folsom's eyes suddenly mirror hard interest and surprise. "Got a little riding to do. I'll be gone maybe a couple of days. Now, if your orders are to keep me in sight, I'll make this proposition. You go fetch your horse and ride along with me."

Folsom stood there stonily staring and considering this. He was suspicious. He seemed also full of an aroused curiosity. He wouldn't ask the obvious questions; he clearly wasn't that kind of man. Still, he had those same questions in the depths of his thoughtful eyes. Finally he said, dragging out the words: "You got a pardner, Patterson? Is that why you want to take me galli-vantin' around the hills tonight . . . so's he can pot Hickman without any danger of being spotted?"

"You don't believe that, Folsom. You know a loner when you see one."

Patterson waited. He smiled a little down around the mouth. He had gotten Folsom into a pocket; the deputy was bursting with questions he'd never ask. Ab was in a dilemma. He didn't know anything about Glenn Patterson. He had his orders from the sheriff; if Patterson rode out, he'd have to follow him anyway. Finally he said: "Where d'you keep your horse?"

"In a different barn from yours."

"Go get him, Patterson. I'll meet you here in twenty minutes."

They grinned at each other. It was a nearly hostile, challeng-ing grin. Like stray wolves they were circling and circling, wait-ing to spring.

VII

Patterson didn't use his own horse. He hired a fresher beast at the livery barn, a jugheaded, gimlet-eyed, ewe-necked buckskin gelding of fourteen hands that was built to endure and that had been put together by an unkind destiny both to carry a man and punish him mercilessly at the same time. But he was tough, which was what Patterson wanted. He and Ab Folsom had some thirty miles to cover before sunup.

Folsom was waiting when Patterson rode up. Ab was smoking a brown-paper cigarette and somberly gazing up where the saloons were sending forth their noise and their tawdry lights. He studied Patterson's mount, gauged the animal correctly as any lifelong horseman would have done, flung away his smoke, and gave his head a short, hard wag.

"If that one doesn't jar your kidneys loose, then he'll crack you between the eyes when you dismount."

Patterson had his own saddle, bridle, and booted rifle. He said nothing until the pair of them was riding southward out of town and Folsom asked how far they'd ride. "Thirty miles," Patterson replied. "But that's about all I can say with any degree of knowledge."

Ab puckered up his forehead and squinted through the soft-lighted gloom. "The badlands," he said, making a solid statement of it. "You got friends down there?"

"Would we be riding at night if I didn't care about being seen?" countered Patterson.

Ab didn't answer. They rode for a solid hour without another word passing between them. They loped a while after that, pushing the miles steadily behind them.

Eventually Ab, rocketing along with both reins looped while he twisted up another brown-paper cigarette, said: "You ever been in the badlands before, Patterson?"

"No. Have you?"

"Yup. Several times. Never went there voluntarily, though."

"Well, you're doing it now."

Ab lighted his smoke, inhaled, exhaled, looked balefully over, and said: "Like hell I am. If you weren't going there, I wouldn't be, either."

"That bad, eh?" murmured Patterson. "Tell me about it."

"Not much to tell. Every renegade between Dakota Territory and the Kansas plains tries to get down into those black damned mountains before the law overtakes him. There's a settlement in there. It's got no name I ever heard, but it's called the Roost. If you're lookin' for someone in particular, I'd suggest you go to the Roost and sit around. Sooner or later they come slippin' out of their mountain hide-outs for a few drinks. That's all there is to the Roost, one saloon, a big public corral, a card room, and a greasy-spoon café."

"Do they know you in there?" asked Patterson, and watched Ab shake his head.

"They don't know me. But if my badge happened to fall out of a pocket, any of them would salt me down before I could bend over to pick it up."

"How come Sheriff Conrad doesn't clean the place out?"

"You'll see, come sunup, why he doesn't. In the first place those lava-rock mountains stretch east and west nearly a hundred miles. In the second place, no one sneaks up on those fellers. In the third place, it'd take an army to round up all the outlaws in those hills." Folsom smoked for a while, then fell to studying Patterson. Finally he said: "You from Denver?"

"I've been there," Patterson replied.

Folsom dryly said: "I'll bet you have. How much do you Association exterminators get for a hide like Joe Hickman wears?"

"You interested in a job?" countered Patterson quietly.

Ab went on silently smoking for another few miles. He'd probed Patterson, had been turned off with each probe, which he'd expected anyway, and now fell to considering the round-about balmy night. When he ultimately spoke again, though, the words showed that his thoughts hadn't strayed any.

"Maybe you're smarter than I figured, Patterson. Maybe you've already set me up with the boys at the Roost. That'd be one sure way to get me off your trail, wouldn't it?"

Patterson reached up to resettle his hat, to swing his head around to see what could be seen of the changing land this far south. Then he said: "You're smarter than that, Ab. If I'd wanted you out of the way, I wouldn't have had to go to all this trouble."

Again Folsom fell silent.

They had been riding for a number of hours now. Glenn's ugly buckskin was just as fresh as when they'd left Willows. There was as yet no way to separate those southward, dark mountain tops from the purple sky, but by the gritty footing under hoof Patterson knew they were getting close.

A band of tough little night-grazing mustangs heard them coming and broke away in a swirl of drumming sound. Folsom listened, then said: "Lots of wild horses down in this part of the country. When I was a kid, we used to snare 'em. Trouble was, they were all too small for men an' too mean for kids. We got a half dollar a head for them from buyers up around Willows."

"You know this country, then," stated Patterson.

"Well enough," answered the deputy from Devon. "Well enough to know where to hide if I have to."

"Tell me something," said Patterson, relaxing as he slowed the buckskin to a loose and long-legged walk. "Who, down in those hills, would buy bunches of stolen cattle?"

Ab made a wry face. "That'd be no problem. Behind the hills southward are more towns. The farther south you go, the bigger and richer those towns are. There'd be plenty of men willing to pay low dollar to rustlers, take the critters on through the mountains, into Wyoming or Idaho, and sell them at a five hundred percent mark up."

"Would they have any trouble getting them through?"

Folsom emphatically shook his head. "None at all. If you mean, would the renegades in the hills bother 'em, the answer is no. If they stole them, they couldn't resell 'em. Anyway, if the hills got a bad name for something like that, the buyers'd quit coming in there. If you meant, would the critters scatter, the answer is the same. No. The slopes are slippery lava rock. There's damned little feed until you get up near the high meadows, and the passes are so steep only a few men could drive a thousand head through without danger of losing a single head."

Patterson murmured: "Ideal cow-thief country, Ab."

"It is that, Mister Patterson, and in more ways than one." Folsom cleared his throat, spat earthward, and said thought-fully: "And if you're going to all this trouble to locate Hickman's friends up in here, you're more likely to wind up dead than I thought you were."

"He's got friends in here?"

"Of course. This is the only place he can get rid of stolen cattle."

Patterson blew out a big breath. "I'll be damned if I understand why your sheriff hasn't busted up this ring by now, Ab. You know who the ringleader is. You know where he takes the cattle. You even know how he sells them."

"Mister Patterson," said the deputy in a pained tone of voice, "you already know we've had Joe Hickman arraigned four times. I've been the man who's brought him in each time. After he's been acquitted for lack of sufficient evidence each time, I've also been the man who handed back his wallet, his gun, and his spurs. We've tried until we're blue in the face. The law courts don't just take my word or Will Conrad's word about Hickman. They demand solid proof. Just how do you produce that unless you catch Hickman in the act . . . which no one has ever done . . . or unless some pardner of Joe's will talk . . . which none of them ever will?"

Patterson had no answers so he kept silent.

Two hours later they were able to make out the saw-toothed, rough spires of those hulking dark mountains on ahead. Patterson tried to estimate the time. He thought it had to be at least 3:00 in the morning. He also thought they could afford a half hour's rest to favor their animals, and to this Ab Folsom heartily agreed, saying only that it wasn't so much his horse that needed a respite, as much as it was he himself.

They kept going until they came upon some haphazard boulder fields. In one of these, safe from accidental discovery by men or animals, they got down, loosened their saddles, hobbled their animals to permit a little grazing, and stamped the circulation back into their backs and legs.

"Sure a hard way to serve the Lord," commented Folsom. "Pays a mite better'n punching cows, but sometimes I'm not sure all the extra guff a feller has to take is worth it. Like now . . . ridin' down here with you."

Patterson smiled. "You don't like my company?"

"Not if it's going to get me killed, I don't."

"You didn't have to come," Patterson said.

Ab Folsom made a grimace about that. "You know a danged sight better'n that, Patterson. But kickin' this around doesn't change anythin'. What we've done is done. What comes next . . . I sure don't know . . . but I got two eyes and a good right hand just like everyone else, so I'll just wait my turn and take my chances. If you baited me into a bushwhack, all I got to say is that you'd better be almighty fast with your six-gun because I don't figure to let you out of my sight."

Patterson turned a little where he slouched upon a big rock and gazed down at those darkly standing, crumpled mountains.

How did a stranger in those hills find exactly the men he was looking for, without them first finding him? He asked Folsom and the deputy, making a cigarette with his head lowered, simply said: "They tell me, Mister Range Detective, that there's a sort of moccasin telegraph system in there, that newcomers, even ones who'll appear among 'em like we dropped out of the sky, get dang' well scrutinized by some sort of committee. If the judgment is favorable, we're welcome at the Roost. If it's *not* favorable . . ." Ab popped the cigarette into his mouth, lit it, snapped the match, and made a wolfish grin. "You know how the song goes . . . 'He'll not see his mother when the work's all done this fall?' "

"All right!" Patterson exclaimed. "What are we? We can't go in there as snoopy lawmen, obviously, so do we go in as renegades on the run or maybe as cow buyers, or as a couple of riders looking for some fast work and easy money?"

Folsom flicked ash off his quirley. "It isn't goin' to make much difference. They're goin' to snort us up no matter what we say. Maybe we'd better just say nothin' at all. Let 'em wonder and puzzle over us a bit."

Patterson ran this suggestion through his mind, found it acceptable for a number of reasons, and said so. He then told Folsom that, if the lawman had a badge in his pocket, he'd better put it in his boot, or maybe hide it under one of the rocks where they were resting.

Ab shook his head, his eyes sardonically bright. "You got one too, Mister Exterminator. My guess is that it's an Association badge out of Denver. You know something, Patterson? You got any idea why I'm not more scairt of you gettin' me killed in the badlands than I am? I'll tell you. Outlaws hate peace officers, but they particularly despise Association range detectives. As long as you've got an Association badge in your pocket, no matter what you *tell* those fellers at the Roost, all I've got to do is ask them to look in your pocket. Patterson, those men would kill you by inches."

There was no arguing with Ab's logic in this matter. But Glenn Patterson had long since taken this into consideration. He'd even thought of leaving the badge back at the hotel. The reason he'd decided not to was elementary. If he found himself in a situation that required credentials, the badge would suffice. Now he stood up, surveyed the rocks and peaks ahead, and said: "Forget it, Ab. Keep your badge. I'm keeping mine. As for the rest of it . . ."—Patterson slowly brought his head back around—"you can trust me or not as you please. All I ask is that you stay close, keep the tie down off your gun, and watch what you say."

"You got my word on all three counts, Patterson. You're a feller I'd like to trust. I figure you'd be a hard man to beat in a fight. But I got my gizzard to watch out for, too."

They smiled at one another.

Patterson stretched and yawned. He swung to listen for their horses, swung back, and watched Ab kill his smoke. There was a slight chill to the air that hadn't been there a half hour before, and, although the distant east was still darkly obscure, dawn did not seem to be far off.

Suddenly Folsom said: "Patterson, tell me one thing. Do you always go about your little chores so thoroughly? I mean like goin' over all the evidence against a rustler? Even ridin' into a place like the Roost to be sure you're on the trail of the right man?"

"Always, Ab. Did you ever shoot the wrong man?"

"No. But then I'm not an exterminator, either. I don't shoot for pay."

"The hell you don't. The difference is pretty vague, Ab. You do it with one kind of a badge. I do it with another kind. But the men we go after are just as dead."

"Maybe. But I get the feeling there's more to this than just gettin' Joe Hickman."

"Do you?"

"Yeah. But that's all right. Keep it to yourself. It's none of my business anyway."

"In that case let's get the horses and ride on."

They walked out to their animals, bridled up, knelt to off-hobble, and, afterward, as they were tightening cinches and latigos, Patterson said over his shoulder: "You're a pretty good man to have along, Ab. It's the girl."

Folsom finished with his horse and swung up. He squinted over at Patterson. "The girl? You mean Joe's wife?"

Patterson didn't move for a moment. He gradually turned to face the deputy. "Yeah," he murmured, "Joe's wife. I saw her out at the ranch big as a spring heifer."

Ab carefully evened up the reins he was holding. He faintly scowled but he said nothing. After Patterson was also mounted, Ab swung southward and pushed his horse straight toward the nearing foothills. He seemed to be grappling with some unpleasant thoughts of his own.

An hour later they got into the first breaks. After that the mountains opened up for them, allowed them to pass up into a belt of shaggy bull pines, and later, when daylight finally came, the land over which they'd traveled in the night was as empty as though they'd never been back there at all.

VIII

Ab knew his way around up here. He demonstrated this knowledge by first making for a pleasant small glade with a cold-water creek running through it. All around them were sharp upthrusts of shiny black stone. Occasionally trees grew out of silted-up crevices or where the eons had encouraged dust to settle in endless layers. But the general appearance of these badlands was of gloom and solemnity. Only rarely did they sight a bird or other wild creature, which moved Patterson to say the badlands were aptly named.

Their breakfast consisted of a deep drink of cold water, filling enough but not very lasting. Ab struck a traveled trail and pointed along to where it followed around a stony slope and dipped down, eventually, into a shadowy cañon where tree tops were distantly visible.

"The Roost's down in there. So is the main trail through the hills." Ab paused to swing his head up and around. "There's a sentry around there somewhere, on a peak or a high place. He'll be spottin' us about now. We'll be another hour or two reachin' the Roost. By then they'll know we're comin'."

A little more than an hour later Patterson saw just how true Ab's observation had been. They came swinging along on their downward path and saw the Roost while still a half mile out. It wasn't much. As Ab had said, it consisted of three or four rough log buildings, a big corral in a grassy clearing, and an undefined trail that passed directly between the buildings, meandering from north to south. There was smoke rising straight up into the bright, still morning from the larger of those several log shacks down there, and where a tie rack stood out front of that same building four saddled horses were patiently standing.

"A little early for folks to be abroad, isn't it?" Patterson asked wryly, eyeing those four saddled animals.

Ab's reply was pointed. "I told you there'd be a spy atop some damned hill who'd see us coming and pass the word. That'll be the welcoming committee down there."

They slid through 100 feet of shale and came finally to the pine-needled level ground where the aroma of that breakfast fire reached them. After that it was simply a matter of weaving their way in and out of the trees until the road was reached. By then they were well within the boundaries of this hidden small outlaw village called the Roost.

There wasn't a soul in sight. Each building looked as gloomily deserted as though the Roost was a ghost town. Ab led on up to the tie rack, stepped stiffly down, loosened his *cincha*, tied up, and stamped his feet as though fresh out of the saddle after a long ride. Patterson did the same, but, as he cared for his animal, he also shot a quick, hard look around. He had that odd little sensation up between his shoulder blades again.

They stamped over the porch of the close by building, walked on inside, and were met by a tantalizingly inviting scent of frying side meat. Two men were sipping coffee at the counter. Two other men were sitting silently upon tilted-back chairs over where an iron heating stove merrily *crackled.* The two by the stove looked straight at the newcomers but the two at the counter didn't even let on that they'd heard the door open. There was an air of hushed tension in the room. A fat man in a dirty candy-striped pink shirt came padding out of the back room, wiping large hands upon a soiled flour-sack apron. He was shock-headed, unshaven, loose-lipped, and skeptical-looking. His fast once over of Ab and Patterson seemed an automatic reflex. He nodded with no show of friendliness and said: "Fried spuds an' side meat's all we got if you boys want breakfast. Dollar a plate with coffee two bits extra."

Patterson, stepping across the counter bench, nodded at the man. The prices were high, especially for coffee, but he wasn't much inclined to protest. The fat man dourly grunted and padded back out of sight again. Ab dropped down, hooked his elbows upon the counter, and rubbed balled fists into his eyes. Except for the sounds of frying meat there wasn't a sound in that dingy log room. The pair of men sipping their black java ten feet farther along never once turned to look at the newcomers. Back behind them where the other two sat on their tilted-back chairs, someone opened a knife and started whittling.

There was menace in the atmosphere; the depthless silence heightened it almost to the breaking point.

Just before their food came, the whittler back there *clicked* his knife closed with sharp finality, heaved up out of his chair, and strolled across to the far end of the counter where he leaned down and gazed straight up at Patterson and Ab Folsom. He was a black-eyed, pockmarked man with thick shoulders and a bull neck to match. His eyes were sunken and his mouth was a bloodless, cruel slash across his lower face. When he spoke, his eyes showed more cruelty; their expression was the same look a mountain lion might show while it played with a dying doe.

"You fellers are a long piece from home, ain't you?" this man asked, making a little velvety smile up the counter. "Don't recollect ever seein' you hereabouts before." The man hitched at his gun belt and settled into a more comfortable position at the end of the counter.

Patterson's food came. He dug out some silver and dropped it on the counter. He lifted his coffee cup left handed and turned toward the black-eyed man, saying quietly: "Care for a cup of java, mister?"

The black-eyed man's little smile winked out. He and Patterson exchanged a long glance. "Got some reason for not answerin' my question?" the black-eyed man asked.

"Maybe," replied Patterson in the same soft tone. "When I was a kid, my pappy told me once it was kind of rude to go around askin' personal questions."

Over by the stove that other tilted-back chair came down off the rear wall, its occupant dropping his elaborate affectation of total indifference. On Ab Folsom's right one of those men down the counter slowly turned and looked Patterson and Folsom up and down. For a moment there was nothing more said. Patterson sipped coffee and Ab cut into his side meat using his left hand with obvious awkwardness. His right hand, like Patterson's right hand, was resting with deceptive innocence in his lap, only several inches from his holstered .45.

"Did your pappy ever tell you it could get a man killed . . . *not* answerin' personal questions, when they was asked of you?" said the black-eyed man.

Patterson put down his coffee cup, placed his left hand upon the counter top, pushed himself upright, stepped over the bench, and walked back ten feet. He then turned back, facing forward, and said, with everyone in that room well in view: "Blackie, I never killed a man on an empty stomach before, but they say there's a first time for everything. You've got a gun on . . . straighten up over there and use it. Or else sit down and we'll have a cup of java, and forget the personal questions."

Both those men farther down the counter turned fully around on their bench but neither of them stood up. Ab Folsom, watching those two and thoughtfully masticating, was content neither of those men had a hand anywhere close to the guns they were wearing. Both of them were studying Glenn Patterson with grave interest. Even the other man, over near the iron stove, seemed disinclined to make a wrong move. That left the black-eyed man to make his appraisal and his decision alone. Patterson expected at least some bluster, some face-saving snarl of some kind, but all Blackie did was knock on the counter top twice with his left fist, all the time bent over the counter there, staring straight at Patterson.

Another man might have been fooled, Patterson wasn't. "Try again," he said to Blackie. "Maybe he didn't hear you knock."

"He heard me, all right," Blackie growled as the fat café proprietor stepped forth from his kitchen with a shotgun in both hands, its sawed-off twin barrels pointed belly high at Patterson. "He hears real good, stranger. Now, then, you still want to declare war?"

Ab Folsom had stopped masticating. His right hand lay still

on his lap. He was slightly to the right of the fat man and his scatter-gun. Ab said: "Cook, you're a sight better at frying side meat than you are at using a gun. Put that thing down before I blow a hole through your fat gut."

One of the men on Ab's right said: "How do you figure to do that, mister, with me 'n' my pardner set to salivate you the first time you bat an eyelash?"

Ab answered without taking his eye off the cook. "Real easy, friend. My pardner's the fastest man in this room with a gun. The minute I go for mine an' you go for yours, he'll pop your skull like a rotten melon. That's all the time I'll need for 'possum belly an' his riot gun, because, friend, like I just said, 'possum belly's a better cook than a gunman. He forgot to cock that blunderbuss. Before he can cock it now, I can slam three slugs through this counter into his lard-bellied carcass." Ab paused, softly smiled at the gray-faced cook, and said: "Any time you want, Patterson. I'm ready."

For a moment no one moved or spoke. Blackie eventually drew back his lipless mouth in a wide smile and growled at Patterson: "Forget it, mister. I'll have the cup of java with you." Blackie straightened very carefully, turned, and jerked his head at the cook. After one stricken glance at Ab, the cook lowered his shotgun, and hastened back out of the room. Over by the stove that other man's shoulders suddenly dropped and down the counter that pair of seated men turned without a word or another look, and picked up their coffee cups again.

It had been a very bad moment. It had come, not only with unexpected suddenness, but also with an unmistakable deadliness. Patterson went back to the counter and dropped down with Blackie between him and Ab. When the gray-faced cook brought three fresh cups of coffee, he avoided all their eyes and scuttled back out of sight as fast as he could.

Blackie picked up his cup and blew on its contents. "I'll tell you," he said carelessly, "in these hills it pays for us all to be real careful."

"That's what we've heard," agreed Patterson. "In fact, that's sort of why we're in these hills."

Blackie swung his head and showed humor in his dark glance. "I figured as much. Still, you know how it is. We got reason to wonder about strangers. An' like I said . . . I never seen either of you before."

"We haven't been exactly lookin' for companionship," muttered Ab around a big mouthful of fried spuds. "Only, after a while, livin' like hermits can make a feller sort of looney in the head, so we decided to come on down here." Ab poked toward the southward ceiling with his upraised fork. "Saw your friend up atop his roost watching, too. Got an idea from that, you boys weren't exactly hoping for a big posse to ride in here."

Blackie put aside his cup, glanced at Folsom, and seemed to be on the verge of some comment. But it may have been a personal one, so in the end he didn't say it. He simply banged the counter and bawled for his breakfast. "We knew you fellers were ridin' down," he explained. "We decided to wait an' see what come of it. Anyway, I was hungry before, and now I'm twice as hungry. Hey, Ralph, dammit take a drink back there so your hands'll quit shakin', and get me m'breakfast!"

Ralph was evidently the slovenly cook, for out of that unseen rear room came the fresh *clatter* of frying pans and dishes.

The café's atmosphere lost most of its thickness, most of its wary tension of moments before. The man by the stove sat back down and remained that way, briefly, then arose and sauntered on out of the place. On a hunch, Patterson twisted and watched that man through the window. He stood a moment upon the yonder porch looking left and right, then stepped over beside the tie rack, studied the brands on Patterson's horse and also on Ab Folsom's mount, then strolled on across toward one of the other log buildings. Patterson turned back to his breakfast, thinking he and the deputy were not yet out of the woods. To allay the suspicion that still lingered, he said that he'd been a day or two down in Willows looking around, that he'd rented a livery animal down there because he'd pushed his own beast too far, too fast, getting into Dakota Territory.

Blackie took it hook, line, and sinker. "When I first come here couple years back, I done the same," he confided. "All the same, we don't court no trouble in here. You'd better take the horse back and fetch back your own critter. No sense in getting the law out there all het up over some silly horse-stealin' charge."

Patterson agreed to this. When he and Ab finished eating, they sat a moment sipping coffee. One by one the other men left the café. Even Blackie seemed anxious finally to depart. When he eventually arose, tossed down payment for his breakfast, and stepped back over the counter bench, he said: "Across the way is our saloon. It's not much, but the liquor's plentiful an' it's cheap. If you boys are figurin' on hangin' around for a spell, drop on over. That's where us fellers transact our business."

Ab looked up skeptically. "What business?" he asked, and made a gesture with his hand. "This place's as dead as a graveyard."

Blackie slowly dropped one eyelid in a wise and raffish wink. "You might be surprised," he murmured. "Every now 'n' then there's a little excitement around here."

"Like what?" Ab asked, sounding doubtful.

"Oh. Maybe like a cattle drive southward through the passes." Blackie eyed Folsom thoughtfully. " 'Course, if you boys brought plenty of loot in with you, there'd be no point in suggestin' that maybe you wouldn't want to pick up a few dollars. But if you didn't . . . well, later on drop over to the saloon."

As Blackie departed after that enigmatic remark, Patterson

and Ab exchanged a long look. So far, that look said, they'd managed to stay afloat in this murky sea of suspicion and deadliness, but things had a way of changing in places like the badlands in a twinkling. Still, it was an auspicious start. They, too, arose and walked out of the café. At the door Ab turned. Ralph was standing in his partitioned-off kitchen doorway, looking steadily back. Ab made a slow grin. "A feller learns something every day, doesn't he, Ralph? Next time, cock it first."

IX

As the morning wore along, Patterson noticed other shadowy figures come and go at the Roost. He and Ab sat on a bench outside the café after taking care of their animals by turning them out across the road in the big public corral. Once, two lean riders approached the saloon, but at sight of two armed strangers idly sitting in the shade veered off and went out and around to come to the saloon from behind.

"No one's asleep in the saddle around here," Patterson murmured, and drew from Ab a grunt with that remark.

Ralph came around from the side of his café, saw them, and swiftly looked straight ahead as he padded on across to the saloon.

"Got the hell scairt out of him this morning," suggested Ab with a lift of quiet amusement in his words. "Needs a jolt of valley tan to stiffen up his backbone again. Funny thing, but every one of these hoot owl roosts I've ever been in had at least one like Ralph. My guess is that sometime a long ways back, he stole a horse or held up a mail coach and ever since has been drinkin' to calm his nerves. No one'll even remember who he was or what he once did, but as long as he lives Ralph'll be jumpin' every time a shadow falls across his path. Some men are cut out for it . . . some aren't. Ralph's kind aren't."

A tall, thin, bronzed cowboy strolled out of the saloon across the way, stood stockstill for nearly a full sixty seconds, staring straight over at Patterson and Folsom. He lifted his right hand, crooked a finger, jerked his head, too, swung about, and reëntered the saloon.

"Looks like the committee's been goin' over us," said Ab. "Now, we walk over there and either stand the drinks, or . . ." Ab stood up. "No way out. Let's go see what the decision is."

Patterson, also, stood up. He glanced up and down the crooked wide roadway. "I had the place figured to hold more men than we've seen," he murmured. "If these hills are as full of owlhoots as you say they are . . ."

"Maybe this is the wrong day," replied Ab, eyeing that yonder log building. "Ever get butterflies in your belly, Patterson?"

"Sure. Got 'em right now."

"Me, too. Let's go."

They stepped down into roadway dust and walked on over to the saloon. Inside, the moment they stepped through out of bright sunlight, a shadowy coolness redolent of spilt liquor, tobacco smoke, and horse sweat assailed them. Blackie was at one end of the bar nursing a shot glass of amber whiskey. He looked at them impassively as they entered. From Blackie's face, though, there was nothing to be read.

There were seven men in the saloon. Four of them were seated with a bottle and glasses at a scarred old card table. These four included that bronzed cowboy they'd seen moments earlier. At the bar, ranged up and down, including Blackie, were the others. Ralph, who they'd both seen enter the place, was nowhere in sight. This gave Patterson a brief bad moment; he had Ralph pegged for a coward. Cowards, when they sensed trouble coming, had a way of disappearing. If Ralph had been standing along the bar, too, Patterson wouldn't have felt the icicles behind his belt.

Blackie, though, broke the spell. While everyone else, including a surprisingly youthful-looking bartender who came forth from a back room with dusty, unopened bottles in his arms, openly and candidly studied the pair of newcomers, Blackie said: "Who stands the first round, you fellers or me?"

Patterson felt rather than saw Ab's body loosen. Ab said in a thin, inflectionless voice. "I'll stand the first round. Only first, let's get the cat out of the bag." He looked over where those four hard-faced men were lounging at their card table, unblinkingly regarding him and Patterson. "You boys want to drink . . . or fight?"

That same long-legged bronzed man who'd beckoned them over to the saloon pushed back his glass, leaned rearward in his chair, and smokily regarded Folsom. "Kind of hard talk seein' there's only two of you and better'n three times that many of us, mister," he drawled.

Ab nodded. "True," he said frankly. "But I got a bad habit of wantin' to know which side of a fence I'm on, friend. If I've got to fight, I'd a damned sight rather do it before I drink than after."

Blackie, who Patterson was watching, showed something close to respect in his dark gaze. "There wouldn't be any after," he said. "Not with odds like these."

Patterson smiled at Blackie. "You had your chance to test that once before. We're still here. Want to test it again?"

Blackie's obsidian gaze drifted a little, settled upon Patterson, and clung to him. "Naw," he growled. "Forget it. You boys buy the first round. We'll buy the second."

Patterson was satisfied, not so much by Blackie's assurance as by his look. Blackie was not a complicated man; he wasn't intelligent enough to mask a thought or a mood, and right now he wasn't looking sly; he was looking bored with this fencing.

"Set 'em up," Ab said, stepping over to the bar.

The men at their card table got up, sauntered over, and

leaned on the bar. The bronzed man moved in between Patterson and Ab Folsom. He didn't glance at either of them as the youthful-looking outlaw behind the bar started up along his counter pouring drinks, but he said: "This ain't like Willows. In here we sort of look a feller over. We got to."

Patterson lifted his glass, reared back his head, and dropped the liquid lightning straight down. It was as green as grass and many times more potent. If that breakfast hadn't been down below, he felt like that whiskey wouldn't have stopped but would have burned a hole right on through him and the floor planking, too.

Ab also downed his rotgut, but Ab gasped and dashed at the sudden rush of tears in his eyes. "Say," he growled at the barman, "what d'you make this stuff of . . . turpentine?"

The barman's youthful face lit up with a big Irish smile. "No," he answered up. "But all the same, mister, if I was you, I wouldn't light no cigarette for a while. You could explode."

Several of the outlaws laughed. Blackie fished out some coins and flung them down. "Fill 'em up again," he commanded.

The bronzed man, Patterson noticed, put his palm over his glass, declining another drink as the bartender passed up the line again. He turned and regarded Patterson impassively, then he jerked his head and walked back to the card table, kicked out a chair for Patterson, and dropped down in the opposite chair. As Patterson sat, the bronzed rider said: "Mister, how long you been hidin' in the hills?"

Patterson's answer, like his glance, was cool. "What's the difference? You ask that kind of a question, friend, you get that kind of an answer. Is that all you wanted?"

"No. Sit still. You got a name?"

"Sure. I'm partial to Smith . . . but my real name is Patterson. You got a name?"

The bronzed man's blue eyes hardened slightly toward Patterson. "You'll learn it soon enough. Let me give you a little advice, Patterson. I run the Roost. When I ask . . . men answer. You made Blackie eat crow over in the café. Don't try it with me. Over there your sidekick said you were fast with a gun. Well, I'm faster."

"You sure of that?" Patterson inquired, the little shrewd lines around his rock-steady eyes puckering up. "Maybe we ought to step outside and find out."

The bronzed man lazily shook his head. "I don't get into shoot-outs to prove anything, Patterson. I don't have to. Y'see, when I first came into the badlands, I had my share of battles to prove who was top dog. At the south end of town we got a boothill. Walk down there and look at the names and dates. You'll recognize some of those names. They were famous men . . . on the wrong side of the law. Now, they're dead."

Patterson's appraisal of this hawk-faced, lean man with his steady eyes and long, compressed lips inclined him toward the conviction that what he was hearing wasn't any idle boast. The top dog wasn't that kind of a man. He was cold and smart and more deadly than any other man at the Roost.

Patterson said: "Let's leave it like that, then. What else is on your mind?"

"I need two good men."

"Just like that? Ab and I just showed up and so you need two good men."

"Well, it's not quite that simple, Patterson. There was a drive through here three days ago. I didn't figure there'd be another one through so soon, so I let five of the boys go out. That leaves me pretty damned short-handed."

Patterson rolled his head backward to indicate the drinking men along the bar. "You've still got a sizeable crew," he commented.

"Can't strip the place bare, Patterson. Got to leave four or five fellers here all the time. We got to have sentries atop the hills. Besides, everybody in these hills isn't on my side. We got rivalries just like they have everywhere else. So . . . I need two more riders to help push a herd through. How about it?"

"What's the pay?"

For the first time the bronzed man's face relaxed. He came near to smiling. "You'll do," he murmured. Louder, he said: "Ten dollars a day and beans. That's a third as much as you'd make cowboying in a lousy month."

"High pay," stated Patterson, "could mean stolen cattle. What's the danger?"

"Isn't any. Not once we pick up the herd and get it into the hills." The bronzed man signaled for a bottle and two glasses. He said no more until the bartender had brought these things. As he afterward poured, he said: "The name is Buck. Well, Patterson, how about it . . . ten dollars a day, beans, and no shooting?"

"One question, Buck," murmured Patterson, reaching for his glass. "Are these critters comin' in from the north? Because if they are . . . well, Ab and I got reason not to be caught out there on that damned plain by lawmen from the north country."

Buck sipped his whiskey and eyed Patterson closely. "They're coming from the north, but you 'n' Ab got nothing to sweat about. There'll be four of us riding with you. If we run into lawmen, it'll be the first time. You see, Patterson, we've got a good set-up. We've got a pardner outside who knows the lay of the land like he knows the back of his hand. If there's anything around that doesn't smell just right . . . no drive. It's been working like clockwork for three, four years now. No reason for it suddenly to go haywire."

Patterson put both elbows on the table and looked down into his shot glass with a faint frown. This affectation of uneasiness inspired Buck to pour him another drink and to say: "I told you . . . there'll be four of us with you. Even if the law showed up, they couldn't get you."

"Sounds all right," Patterson finally said, letting his frown fade. He then framed the question he'd been seeking for a way to put forth: "Anyway, I reckon, if there's riders visible, those sentries atop the peaks'll see 'em in broad daylight before they get close."

Buck walked right into Patterson's little trap by saying: "Not daylight. We move these cattle by night. That's the only way our outside man can get them down this far before the owners discover they're gone."

Patterson had his answer. He'd been sure the stolen herd was coming from Bryan Holt and perhaps Morgan Dunstan, but this clinched that suspicion for him. "Maybe that's even better," he said to Buck. "If there's bad trouble, a feller can always get off a few rounds in the dark, then run for it without much chance of being caught."

Buck nodded, downed his second drink, and set his glass down. "Tomorrow night. You an' your pardner be here at the Roost ahead of sundown so's we can get organized and head out while there's still enough light to see by. All right?"

Patterson said: "When do we get paid?"

Buck faintly smiled again. He reached into a trouser pocket, brought forth a big roll, peeled off some bills, and tossed them across the table. "Figured you two might be hurting a little. This'll hold you. And Patterson, if you boys work out, there'll be other drives. Sound all right to you?"

As Glenn picked up the crumpled bills, he said: "Sounds better all the time, Buck."

The bronzed man got up, turned, and walked out of the saloon.

Patterson leaned back and pushed his legs out fully under the table. Beyond the doors bright midday sunlight was burnishing the timber circle around the Roost to a greenly dark brightness. For some reason, that sunlight made Patterson feel good. Perhaps it wasn't just the good warmth, although he'd now had four drinks of that potent brew.

Across the way Ralph came out onto his porch with a broom and industriously swept away a big accumulation of dust. Behind him at the bar Blackie and Ab were laughing at something one of the other men had said. Somewhere, a long way off, some Association cattlemen were probably dropping wearily into their beds after a hard night of protecting their cattle. Patterson wondered how this would now end, for Holt and Dunstan weren't likely to relax their vigil until he and the deputy sheriff from Devon got back, which meant simply that Buck was in for a surprise. Hickman wouldn't dare hit Holt's herd as long as the ranchers and their riders were on guard. He almost wished there was some way to get word out to Holt and Dunstan to let Hickman attempt his raid. That way, at least, he and Ab could get the outlaws out of their back hills onto the open plain where they could be perhaps surrounded.

The men began drifting out of the saloon. The last man to leave was Ab. His face was flushed, his eyes were slightly glassy, and he paused at the table to give Patterson a hard, triumphant gaze. Patterson arose and followed Ab on out into the dazzling sunlight.

When they were close together on the saloon's porch, Ab said softly: "Anything doing?"

Patterson took Ab's arm and led him in the direction of the big corral. As they walked along, Patterson explained what he now knew, and what he also suspected. Ab listened and threw his arms across the top stringer while he gazed in at their grazing animals.

"That's nice," he said when Patterson was finished. "Now what do we do? Hickman won't get those cattle. Buck's going to wonder . . . and since we're newcomers . . . he just might get to wonderin' too close to home."

Patterson didn't think they were in any danger from that direction and said so. "He couldn't do any more than send someone out to Hickman to find out what went wrong."

"Yeah?" muttered Ab, turning to gaze at Patterson, his flushed face getting beaded with sweat from the sunshine. "Suppose Hickman comes here instead?"

"What of it?"

"I'll tell you what of it, in case you've forgotten. Joe Hickman knows me better'n he knows his own brother . . . if he's got a brother. That's what of it!"

Patterson stared blankly at the deputy. He'd forgotten that. Ab twisted to look all around. They were alone. No one else was within shouting distance. He turned back. "I told you this was a hard way to serve the Lord," he grumbled. "And another thing, if one of us turned up missing, these boys are goin' to be over the other feller like fleas on a dog's back." Patterson fell to thinking. This thing was getting to look less and less like he wished it looked.

X

The obvious solution, Patterson thought, was for both of them to saddle up and get back out of these badlands. But just as obviously, as he explained to Ab, if they did that, Buck and the others would find out that they were gone, would be alerted to something suspicious going on, and not only wouldn't go out to meet Hickman and his cronies to take delivery of the stolen cattle, but just might make a concerted dash to catch Patterson and Ab as well, before they could reach Willows.

"Any way you look at it," said Patterson, "it's trouble."

"Possibly not," mumbled Ab. "Suppose we just hang and rattle. Just let things take their normal course. Buck's not goin' to find any rustled herd out there tomorrow night . . . we know that . . . so we'll all come back to the Roost. After that, he'll make some contact with Hickman, but that needn't concern you or me, not even if Joe comes here, because now that we know he might come here, we'll just sort of find us a campsite up in the trees out of sight somewhere and lie low."

They agreed on this. Lying low and keeping discreetly out of sight wouldn't strike any of the outlaws as odd. If anything, it would seem perfectly in character and normal for supposed renegades such as Patterson and Ab were pretending to be.

They found a good spot for their camp, a half mile southward beyond the Roost where a thicket of round-leaved manzanita made a perfect screen between their camp and the Roost's log buildings. To this place they brought their saddles, guns, and bedrolls. Here, too, they brought some groceries, mostly tinned beef, peaches, sardines, and coffee. Not the best diet in the world but for the time being quite adequate.

They spent the balance of the day getting settled. There was a pool at creek side not more than 100 feet away, the ground was covered with pine needles, and with only a little effort they constructed a stone-ring for their cooking and heating fire.

That evening they drifted down to the café for supper, drifted over to the saloon for a couple of drinks, then departed early for their camp. As Patterson built a little fire, he said: "Ab, you notice anything at the saloon?"

"Sure, Blackie wasn't around. My guess about that is that Buck's sent him out to see Hickman. Or else it's Blackie's turn to stand sentry, go on top of the hill overlookin' the northward plain."

Patterson continued working with his little fire. He had another thought about Blackie's disappearance. Buck could be curious; he could've sent Blackie up to Willows to ask around about Patterson and Folsom. If that were so, Blackie just might pick up enough gossip around town to make his ears burn, also to make him scorch the prairie getting back to report to Buck that they had some spies in their camp.

Patterson didn't mention this, though. He coaxed his little fire into a brisk, *crackling* blaze, crossed his legs, and hunkered there with the red light dashing itself against his square, rugged features. One conclusion he came to, sitting there, was that the longer he and Ab remained at the Roost, anywhere in the badlands for that matter, the more dangerous their predicament became. They had what they'd ridden thirty miles to find out, had gotten their information, in fact, so easily and swiftly, it almost seemed like some act of providence. Actually then there was no longer any reason for them to hang around. Moreover, with nightfall settled over the land again, now would be the auspicious time for them to light out back the way they'd come.

Ab came over, settled low upon the ground, propped his head upon one hand, and eyed Patterson thoughtfully. After a while he quietly said: "That livery horse of yours . . . you reckon, if we set him loose, he'd head back to Willows?"

Patterson didn't reply immediately. He was struck with the relevancy of the thought in Ab's mind behind that question. When he lifted his head to say softly—"Hell, I should have thought of that myself."—Ab hauled himself up off the ground, cocked his head a moment, then threw Patterson a warning look. Someone was approaching their camp through the trees. Patterson also heard those booted footfalls stepping over the dry needles. Ab, moving fast, sprang up, threw Patterson a little warning gesture, and stepped away from the fire. Patterson sat on, gazing into the coals as though lost in private thoughts.

Buck came out of the northward night, halted, looked around, stepped up where Patterson could see him, and said: "You've got a good spot here. Until you boys lit your fire, I didn't know where you'd gone."

Patterson motioned to the vacated spot opposite him and glanced up to watch the bronzed, rangy outlaw move across to sit down. "What's on your mind?" he asked.

Buck shrugged, looking around. "Where's your pardner?"

"He was here a while ago. Maybe strolled down to the saloon. Why? You want to see him?"

Buck said: "Naw, not particularly. Just sort of walkin' around tonight. A man gets restless sometimes, in this place. It's a good enough hide-out, but it leaves a lot to be wished for. Dance-hall girls, for instance, and bright lights. You ever been to San Francisco, Patterson?"

"No."

"Every man ought to go to San Francisco at least once. The trouble is, once you've been there, returning to places like the Roost make you damned conscious of all you're leaving behind."

As the renegade spoke, firelight played across his hawkish features, turning them to a reddish copper color. He looked to Patterson like an Indian. He had the raw-boned, sinewy build to go with it. But, whereas earlier he'd been impassively cautious and watchful with Patterson, now he seemed more like he truly was, thoughtful and speculative and restless. Lonely, too, apparently, and tired of being cooped up in the badlands. He was one of those perfectly healthy, perfectly co-ordinated men who exuded energy even when sitting relaxed, as he now was by Patterson's little fire. He rarely smiled, and never really seemed to smile at all, only to grin partially, but a lot of men whose lives had been blasted from a harsh environment were like that. Patterson himself was not a man who smiled easily.

"After a few more drives I'll head back to Frisco," Buck murmured, his eyes filmy with warm memories. "It takes money to live high, out there." He paused, centered his eyes upon Patterson, and changed his tone as he said next: "How about you? Every man's got some place he'd head for if he could."

"Cheyenne," stated Patterson, picking a place he was familiar with but which actually held no great allure for him. Denver was *his* town. But Denver was also known for being the Association's headquarters and even mentioning it here and now wouldn't be prudent.

"It's a good little town," Buck agreed without much warmth. "But not like San Francisco. Cheyenne's too small. Too many fellers a man can run into accidentally in small towns. Beside, Cheyenne smells of shippin' pens and working range men."

Buck, Patterson thought, was not a born and bred Westerner. He was undoubtedly a top hand, but he hadn't been raised to it. Still, this wasn't unusual, either; the West was full of Southerners, Easterners, even Northerners, who'd come to the wide plains and big mountains for their own reasons. The West wasn't so much a place as it was a state of mind. Some men required lots of room to mature, to concoct their schemes in, to become whatever it was their fates had decreed they should live out their lives being.

"Anywhere west of the Missouri suits me fine," murmured Patterson. "Otherwise, the world's too cluttered with people and bad smells."

Buck's bold glance lingered upon Patterson's face. "You've got the right idea," he softly said, and made that very faint, vague little grin with his lips. "Maybe, when we get to know one another better, Patterson, we can work something out. A man gets damned weary of ridin' all his trails alone. I sized you up today. You're no fool."

"Neither are you, Buck, except for one thing."

"What's that?"

"Your ability with a gun."

Buck continued to study Patterson's face. "Maybe," he ultimately said, "but if you're as fast as I am . . . then I hope we never have to fight, because that's one thing I learned long ago.

Two fast gunmen kill each other and no one wins."

Patterson inclined his head. That was true enough. But Buck hadn't said all of it. Any time two gunmen suspected each other of being equally as deadly, they didn't shoot it out in any stand-up face-to-face combat. One or the other of them stepped behind a tree or a building, or even his saddle horse, and ensured his own survival by murder. It wasn't very pretty but it sure was final.

"It probably won't ever happen, though," stated the outlaw chieftain. "I pay well. No one who works with me works very hard. What else do you expect?"

"Nothing," agreed Patterson. "In fact, when we rode here today, we didn't expect even that much. Like you say, Buck, it may never happen."

"About tomorrow night . . . ? Something you said today at the saloon got me curious. If you 'n' your pardner don't want to run across any lawmen from the north country, you pulled something up there. I'm curious."

"Why should you be?"

"You're broke, Patterson. You picked up that money I gave you today like it was a life-saver. Now, you don't strike me as the kind who'd pull something that didn't pay off. What happened?"

"What always happens," replied Patterson, being very careful now with his choice of words. "The law came a-helling it, and broke things up before we got the little job done. Sometimes a man's best laid plans don't jell. You ought to know that."

"A stage, a bank . . . ?"

Patterson gave Buck a cold, hard look. "Why don't we talk about the future, not the past," he suggested quietly, conveying strong displeasure without any difficulty because now he wasn't acting at all. He'd been in this situation before, and, while he didn't genuinely believe Buck had set what could be a trap by having some of his men question Ab at the same time he was probing Patterson, with their lives at stake he didn't mean to take that chance.

Buck nodded carelessly. "Sure. The past is done with." He gazed for a moment into the fire's little bed of coals as though something cold and distant and sad had brushed over him. Then he looked up and said, his voice turning as crisp and business-like as it had been that afternoon at the saloon: "There'll probably be two hundred head in the drive tomorrow night. It's hard enough drivin' cattle through strange country in broad daylight, but in the night it'll be harder. I wish to hell I hadn't let the rest of my crew go out with another drive. We're going to have to look sharp tomorrow night."

"Well," suggested Patterson smoothly, "why not get some of the men who'll be bringin' the herd down here to go along with us?"

Buck emphatically shook his head. "Can't risk that. They can't be missing from their own stamping grounds when the law from Willows joins the ranchers in tryin' to overtake the herd."

"Oh, local boys," murmured Patterson. "I see. Well, in that case I reckon we'll just have to do our best."

"That's about the size of it," said Buck, and whipped his head and shoulders around as Ab came stepping forth out of the pine shadows.

Ab stopped at the sight of Buck as though surprised, then he walked on up, sank down, and swore with strong feeling as he said: "That damned buckskin horse you got up at Willows busted out of the corral, Patterson. Whoever built that danged thing sure was skimpy with his nails and wire."

Patterson said a violent oath. "You look for him, Ab?"

"Sure I looked for him," Ab growled, playing his part to perfection. "Only he busted out a couple hours back and by now he could be anywhere in these stinkin' hills. How d'you expect anyone to find him in the damned dark?"

Buck, listening to this irate exchange, said: "No sweat, boys. I'll have a couple of fellers track him in the morning. But even if we don't find him, we've got plenty of spare mounts around. It's nothing to get upset about."

Ab said grumpily: "No one'll find him. We got him up at Willows. Those danged old barn-sour livery horses got more homin' instinct than a pigeon. By sunup he'll be halfway back to Willows."

Buck arose. "Forget it," he said. "I'll have another horse for you in the morning." He nodded, turned, and strolled back the way he'd come.

Neither Patterson nor Ab spoke until Buck's farthest footfalls had died away. Then Ab sighed, rolled up his eyes, and muttered: "Brother, if that damned buckskin *doesn't* light out for Willows, and Buck's men track him down in the mornin', I'm a dead duck." He fished around for his tobacco sack. "I wrote a note to the town marshal at Willows instructin' him to go tell Holt and Dunstan to stop their patrollin' and let Hickman hit their herds."

Patterson sat perfectly still watching Folsom make his cigarette, bend low to light it from their fire, and rear back exhaling a big grayish cloud. Ab removed the smoke, gravely considered its ragged little red tip, and, avoiding Patterson's gaze, said: "Well, it was sink or swim and I figured we'd better swim. Sittin' around here waitin' for Hickman or someone else who'd recognize one of us to ride in wasn't any good. This way at least Holt and Dunstan'll know what's goin' on. I told them to stay well out of range and trail the rustlers with their crews of riders."

Patterson dropped his gaze back to the coals. Like it or not, it was done; nothing he could now do or say would undo it. Possibly it would work out. One thing he felt reasonably sure of, that ugly buckskin wouldn't stay in the badlands where there was no graze, so he just might leg it for home. He was the barn-sour type, all right.

"Let's bed down," he said to Ab, and stood up to head for his blanket roll.

"You sore?" Ab called after him.

"No. But I don't exactly feel like singing, either."

XI

They were up ahead of the dawn, washed at the pool, and stoked up the fire to get warm by, for although the days were benign enough, in this fold of the obsidian hills night grayly lingered with its pre-dawn chill. Ab fried some tinned beef that they ate without coffee and Patterson said it had to be a habit with Ab to eat poor food when all they had to do was walk down to the Roost, rout Ralph out, and make him fry them some spuds and fill them with hot java. Ab's reply was succinct.

"It's not my belly I'm worrying about, it's my neck. Let's go see where that damned horse went."

They got down to the log buildings, but except for the tin stovepipe above Ralph's place, there wasn't smoke rising anywhere. No one was abroad.

They crossed to the corral. Ab showed Patterson the place where he'd turned the buckskin loose. It looked sufficiently like a genuine break in the old poles to pass inspection.

From there, they had no trouble tracking the animal northward for nearly a half mile, until he crossed one of those exposed glass-rock areas and left no noticeable sign.

"Heading out of here," muttered Patterson with strong relief in his voice.

They crossed over, quartered until Ab picked up the trail again, and kept going until the foothills opened up to show the big prairie beyond. It was gray and hushed out there. They paused to stand perfectly still watching for movement. There was none; for as far as either of them could see the land lay drowsily still and silent. Patterson let off a big sigh and turned.

"He's heading home, Ab."

Folsom didn't nod. With only partially assuaged misgivings he said: "At least he's goin' in the right direction, Patterson. But if Blackie's out there somewhere for Buck, and sees him, we can still wind up lookin' like a pair of riddled turkeys."

They turned back. Before they reached Ralph's place, the sun came out on the plain. At the Roost, however, night still stained the slopes and buildings.

Ralph was up, front door was unlocked, and, when his first customers of the new day walked in, Ralph was sitting behind his own counter drinking a cup of black coffee. He looked up, recognized Folsom and Patterson, jumped off his stool, and nasally said: "Fried beans and side meat one buck a plate, and coffee . . ."

"Yeah, we know," growled Patterson. "Two bits a cup. All right, Ralph, rustle it up and make it snappy."

Patterson and Ab exchanged a wry look, stepped across the counter bench, and dropped down. Ralph brought their coffee and padded back out of sight again. Moments later the door opened, several men entered, nodded as they sat down for breakfast, and from that moment on, until they'd had their morning meal and could depart from the café, neither Patterson nor Ab Folsom spoke. There was only one thing now uppermost in their minds—the ugly buckskin horse. They certainly could not speak on that topic around others, so they were silent even after returning to the roadway.

Sunlight came quite belatedly to warm the wooded gulch where the Roost lay. But it was welcome, late though it was. Two men mounted on fidgeting mounts brought in a gather of saddle horses across the way and southward of the saloon where that large corral was. Patterson and Ab sauntered over to lean there, examining those beasts.

"Every brand under the sun," muttered Ab, whose professional lawman's instincts were working. "If the owners of those critters had any idea where they were, we'd have half the lawmen in the northwest comin' in here with warrants."

"Any local marks?" asked Patterson, eyeing the animals casually for a good one.

"Buck wouldn't be that dumb," muttered Ab. "One thing to rustle cattle, another thing to steal a rancher's best horses. Buck isn't the reckless type. He'd do his horse stealing a long way from home."

From southward down where the dusty trail began to broaden as it approached the buildings, a man's fluting call was raised. Patterson turned. So did Ab. At the saloon several men sauntered out also to gaze southward. Over at Ralph's café other men appeared. It was difficult to see that rider clearly just yet because of the backgrounding trees, where night haze still lingered, but he was riding closer all the time, coming steadily nearer the open land where strong sunlight lay.

"Good God," whispered Ab, standing up stiff and straight off the corral. "The buckskin horse, Patterson."

It was Blackie. He was leading Patterson's livery barn animal by a loose lariat with which he'd apparently roped the animal out on the plain.

Ab whipped around as though to spring inside where those loose horses had just been turned in. Patterson's hand flashed, his fingers closed hard around the deputy's arm. "Stand still," he commanded. "Act natural. We can't get away now, anyway. Not on foot."

Blackie came slouching along, his hat brim tugged forward to shield his eyes from sun smash. The same hat brim effectively concealed his expression so that Patterson, scarcely breathing now, couldn't make out anything from the pockmarked outlaw's cruel face.

Buck, over on the saloon porch, stepped down and paced out a little way. Catching sight of Folsom and Patterson in the sunshine at the corral, he called forth: "Patterson, there's your buckskin! Better go get him. This time you'd best tie him up somewhere."

"Yeah," replied Patterson, and watched Buck turn and strike out back for the saloon again. The others, standing idly here and there, also turned to go back to whatever they'd previously been doing. Patterson said shortly: "Come on, Ab. Maybe we can still salvage this thing."

They hiked on down toward the wide end of the trail where Blackie was coming on. As the outlaw saw those two approaching, he straightened in his saddle, squared up, and drew rein. Just for a moment Blackie considered the pair of approaching men. Then he lifted his head to look farther on up where the building stood. Patterson, closely, intently studying the outlaw, distracted Blackie by saying: "Where'd you find him?" Patterson didn't care where Blackie had found his horse; he simply wished to divert the man momentarily from crying out again to his friends farther along. They were by that time close to one another, close enough at last for Patterson to get a good look at the outlaw's face.

Blackie's expression showed nothing. He bent, tossed the turk's head end of his lass rope to Patterson, and cleared his throat of trail dust, spat aside, and said: "Some danged shag poke had him. The feller was ridin' up toward Willows when I recognized your critter. The feller acted sort of funny, like maybe he was tryin' to steal the horse. When I told him to hand over the shank, the feller commenced to argue. I told him I knew the feller who owned this critter, an', if he didn't hand him over, I'd take him to the law for horse stealin'." Blackie dismounted, grinning broadly. "You should've seen how quick he give me his lass rope. Didn't even ask for it back. Said he'd broke camp ahead of sunup an' found the ugly critter walkin' along toward town. Said he just sallied out and caught the brute an' was ridin' on when I came up."

Blackie continued to grin. Patterson glanced over where Ab was stroking the buckskin's ewe-neck and running his hand up toward a ball of matted hair in the beast's black mane. "Thanks," Patterson said to the outlaw. "He got loose in the night. We tracked him out to the plain this morning."

All the time he was speaking, Patterson was watching Ab's exploring fingers probe that matted ball of hair. When Ab turned so that Patterson could see his face, Ab's expression showed bafflement and purest wonder.

"Well," Blackie said, drawing on the reins to hike along with his own horse, "I'm hungry as a bear. See you boys later." He went shuffling on up the wide trail toward Ralph's café.

Ab stepped up and said in a low whisper: "It's gone, Patterson. The note I braided into his mane is gone."

They gazed at one another for a moment saying nothing. Patterson turned and started leading his horse back toward the corral where those riders who had brought in the loose stock were profanely patching up the break Ab had made the night before.

"Patterson," asked Ab suddenly, "you suppose that feller Blackie saw with your horse found that note and took it?"

"If it's not where you braided it in, Ab, that's got to be what happened. Unless the thing just fell out or got brushed out."

"No chance. Not the way I fixed it into the hair. Someone'd have to cut it out."

They were at the corral. The two men who had patched up the poles and wire sauntered over to cast looks of strong disapproval at the buckskin horse. They were the same two who had been sitting at the counter over in Ralph's place the day before when Patterson and Folsom had first entered. One of them called the buckskin an unflattering name and said: "Once they get breachy won't no danged fence hold 'em."

Patterson agreed and watched those two head on around where they'd left their saddled animals tied. Ab, also gazing after that pair of outlaws, said quietly: "Suppose Blackie found it, Patterson? Suppose he's in there right now with Buck showin' him my note?"

Patterson didn't think that likely for the elementary reason that, instead of going into the saloon straightaway where he'd seen Buck disappear, Blackie had struck out for the café. He said something about this but Ab wasn't convinced.

"That black-hearted devil'd like nothin' better than to let us sweat while he eats his breakfast . . . then goes over to see Buck. He knows blessed well we can't ride out of here in broad daylight."

"We're sweating, all right," muttered Patterson, and started for the corral gate with the buckskin horse in tow.

Ab didn't go along. He, instead, put his shoulders against the corral bars and kept darkly watching Ralph's place for sight of Blackie. He was still watching when Patterson returned and quietly said: "Come on, it's a little early for drinking, but let's go have a beer anyway . . . and be on hand when Blackie reports to Buck."

They moved along toward the saloon. Out back somewhere, someone was shoeing a horse. Between ringing sounds from a struck anvil whoever was out there vented his wrath at a reluctant horse with sizzling blasts of loud profanity. Otherwise, the Roost was quiet enough. Patterson's ewe-necked and gimlet-eyed buckskin effectively put to rout the strange horses that pranced over to snort him up, and there was nothing from that direction but a few irritable squeals.

Inside the saloon Buck was sprawling at the same table he'd held down the day before. He nodded as Patterson and Ab strolled in. At the bar five men were watching the baby-faced barman and another outlaw roll dice for drinks. The entire atmosphere here was one of languid indifference to everything but those *clinking* dice.

Patterson called for two beers, interrupting the dice game briefly. He and Ab took their glasses over by a grimy window where there was a bench. From that point they had a clear view of the outside and the inside.

But Blackie didn't come over, not for nearly another half hour, and, when he did walk in, his hat was tipped far back, his pockmarked face was sweat shiny, and he was sucking on a toothpick. Buck motioned him over; the two of them hunched across Buck's card table and spoke back and forth in short, quick sentences. At no time did Blackie bring forth a paper for Buck to see.

Ab, grimly holding his beer glass, eventually began to relax. He tilted back his head, drained off the beer in two big swallows, blew out a ragged breath, and gave Patterson a long, relieved look as he said under his breath: "That grubliner found it, sure as the devil, Patterson. That's why he was actin' funny when Blackie came up demandin' your horse back. All we got to do now is pray he reaches Willows and hands the note to the marshal."

"That's not quite all," demurred Patterson. "We've also got to hope Dunstan and Holt obey it. Let's get out of here. For some reason this place makes me feel like I'm starving for fresh air."

They left the saloon, sought shadows alongside one of the unoccupied buildings, and dropped down, feeling as though they'd just been reprieved from a certain sentence of death.

After a long while of saying nothing at all, Patterson turned to Ab with a quiet suggestion: "Next time you feel foxy, Ab, let me know in advance, will you?"

Folsom breathed a quiet "Amen," and set about making himself a cigarette which he badly needed.

XII

Blackie and Buck and two other men came sauntering around toward the corral. Patterson and Ab watched them. It was afternoon with the sun dipping a little off center. Buck hooked one booted foot over a rail and gazed in at the mounts.

"Doesn't leave much to chance," observed Patterson, watching the outlaw chieftain.

"Doesn't dare," mumbled Ab. "One slip and he'll wind up dead. But they're all good horses."

Patterson silently agreed with that; the animals, regardless of legal ownership, were mostly young and durable. Wherever the band kept them, there had to be plenty of good, nourishing graze; their hides shone with the glisten only the hair of perfectly healthy animals ever showed.

Patterson stood up, dusted himself off, and jerked his head. They walked on over to join the others outside the corral. Blackie looked around, grunted, and said to Patterson: "Don't know why I bothered bringin' him back." He was speaking of the ugly buckskin. "He looked sorry enough when there wasn't anything around to compare him with, but in the corral with them other critters . . ." Blackie shook his head from side to side.

Buck spoke briefly to the other outlaws, who turned and walked back toward the buildings. He then turned and eyed Patterson and Ab Folsom. "A little hitch," he said, "but it's still set for tonight."

Patterson said: "Hitch?"

Buck made a little careless gesture with his hands. "Nothing much. Last night the cattlemen were out with riders guardin' their ranges. Our man up near Willows who's to run off the critters told Blackie it smelled funny to him. Still, I figure it's just the cowmen are beginnin' to hurt a little from their losses. Every time a cloud passes across the moon, one of their riders probably thinks he's seen a band of raiders coming. It's nothing. All the same, we'll change our tactics a little tonight. You 'n' Ab will ride with Blackie 'n' me. The others will trail us a half hour. That way, if there really is anything out there, we won't all blunder into it. The four of us'll do the advance scouting." Buck glanced at the sun. "Better go fill up on grub now," he said, stepping away from the corral. "A feller in this business never knows when he'll eat again."

After Buck had walked back toward the saloon, Blackie said: "He's a careful one, that Buck. But I reckon that's why he's never been hauled in. Now you take Joe . . . he's a regular devil-may-care type."

"Joe?" said Patterson blankly.

"Yeah. Joe Hickman. The feller who scouts the herds up north, organizes the thing, then runs 'em down here to us. Joe's a regular fancy Dan. Buck says someday we're going to have to bury Joe and find a replacement for him in the Willows country. Well, I know I just ate, but, like Buck says, a feller never can be sure . . . come on, I'll chow down with you boys."

Patterson hung back. "Go ahead," he said to Blackie. "Ab and I'll catch up a little later. Want to be sure that damned horse doesn't get any more funny ideas."

Blackie walked off, and Ab started on around the big corral ostensibly to examine all its weak places with Patterson. When they were a long way around, Ab said: "Well, if we didn't know before, we sure know now. Joe Hickman. Y'know what I think, Patterson? I think that the fifth time I take Hickman in will be the charm. Twenty years he'll get."

Patterson listened to Folsom but said nothing back until they'd completed their walk and were heading on over toward the café. Then he murmured: "Ab, there's one hell of a good possibility that Joe Hickman will never see the inside of a jailhouse. Not if he gets caught by Holt and Dunstan. Especially Dunstan. He's hell on wheels when he's stirred up. Hickman and his men will be south of Dunstan, Holt, and their riders. If Hickman tried busting back, they'll kill him for sure."

At the café nearly all the outlaw band was assembled. Fat Ralph was scuttling like a feather in a hot skillet. The outlaws ate heartily; they were tough, hungry men at any time. Now, with Buck's advice still fresh in their ears, they were loading up.

Blackie turned, threw a look around as Patterson and Folsom walked in, turned back with a careless wave, and resumed his eating. Buck was not there, but one thing Patterson had noticed, the outlaw chieftain did not mingle freely with his men.

After eating, everyone trooped on across the road to the saloon. The youthful barman, no longer wearing his apron but wearing in its place a tied-down .45 and a light-weight fawn-leather rider's coat and hat, looked out of place serving drinks. He obviously was going to ride with Buck and the others as soon as it became decently gloomy enough for them all to leave the badlands.

Buck came in an hour later, also spurred and coated, ready to ride. He seemed absorbed by some inner thoughts. None of the others, Patterson noticed, approached him, even with offers of a drink. Buck went to his table, dropped down at it, and flagged for a bottle and glass.

There was a quiet edginess creeping into the otherwise casual atmosphere now, Patterson noticed. Although all the outlaws acted confident, including their chieftain, they were too noisy or too quiet. At Patterson's side Ab got the same way—quiet. He drank two straight shots and toyed with the third. Once Patterson caught Ab watching him through the backbar mirror. Another time he saw Ab sizing up Buck and Blackie. It wasn't hard to guess Ab's thoughts. If there was going to be bad trouble—and Ab clearly believed there was—he meant to have all his foreknowledge, all his previous decisions made and nailed down, so he'd be free for other action when the time arrived. It was, in Patterson's mind, a good way to be. A man apprehending trouble came out of it standing up eight times out of ten. In Patterson's line of work a man banked on the odds heavily.

The sun gradually fell away. Up above, where a sentry lay atop the rocks with a mirror for flashing messages or warnings, the world got dipped in red. Lower down, shadows began to firm up and creep out. Buck suddenly stood up, went across to the door, cast a look up and around, sniffed, then turned, and, saying nothing to the men, jerked his head. They were all watching. Patterson thought they all knew Buck's mannerisms very well. The moment he peremptorily jerked his head, every outlaw in the saloon put aside his glass and walked on out of the building behind their leader.

Ab caught up with Patterson just after the others had stepped down into the dust beyond the porch, bound for the corral. "Good luck," Ab said. "Either we see a big herd tonight or the note never reached the right hands and we'll sit out there for two, three hours with everyone gettin' fidgety, and see nothin' at all."

"In either case," murmured Patterson as the pair of them hiked along behind the others, "tonight's our last night at the Roost. One way or the other, when we get the chance, we head out. A man can push his luck just so far, Ab. I reckon we've pushed ours even a mite farther than that."

The men caught horses at the corral, led by Buck, and turned to bitting up and rigging out. There wasn't much talk; this was the other side of the renegade nature. At the saloon there had been more or less forced conviviality. Now, though, these men were cold and brisk and business-like. No more laughter or banter or easy smiles until the work had been done. The difference, Patterson thought, between these experienced range riders and legitimate cowboys was simply that these men, in the course of their work, could be legally shot or lynched by anyone catching them at it. They would not, therefore, be as chipper as their legal counterparts. Neither would they be as indifferent to things around them, as they rode to their rendezvous.

As for Ab and Patterson, they had still different feelings. As Ab said after he'd mounted and had reined in close beside Patterson: "They watch out for their necks an' we watch out for ours. And if that note got through, Patterson, one side or the other's goin' to get it in the neck sure as hell's hot."

Buck, one of the first among his riders to get astride, saw Ab and Patterson also across leather and reined around to join them. He looked calm enough, when he came up and halted, looked almost casual or indifferent.

"We'll take delivery about ten miles out, but it'll be possibly a little more, dependin' on how fast our friends can push their gather."

Patterson said, glancing around where the others were beginning to mount their horses: "Starting kind of early for no more'n a ten mile ride, aren't we?"

Buck nodded. "Yeah. But you 'n' Ab 'n' Blackie and I'll ride on farther. We'll make a big scout of the land in all directions. Our pardner up near Willows probably's not right, but he told Blackie there's something odd goin' on up there."

"Sounds like bad nerves," muttered Ab, and Buck shrugged.

"I reckon," he said. "Anyway, that's what we four are going to find out before we take delivery of that herd. Well, looks like everyone's aboard . . . let's go!"

Buck turned and walked his horse out the broad trail without looking back. The other men began to stir, to nudge their animals, to follow after Buck. Patterson and Ab let most of the others get ahead before they also rode out.

There were shadows darkening the cleft where the Roost stood now, but beyond the farthest slope could be seen reddish, rusty sunlight still softly mantling the yonder prairies. Still, by the time Buck led his men out of the badlands, dusk was sootily settling out upon the plain, too. Patterson idly thought that Buck had made this same foray many times before. He knew, from the location of the upcountry shadows, exactly when to leave the Roost and arrive upon the plain after daylight failed. Patterson wondered what other tricks the bandit chieftain knew.

Blackie came up from behind, squeezed in, forcing Ab and Patterson to give way for him, and offered his tobacco sack around. He got no takers. Ab had his own tobacco and Patterson preferred cigars or nothing at all. Blackie looped his reins and went to work with both hands.

"Be money in our pockets next week," he said cheerily, rhythmically swaying to the steady gait of his mount. "Buck says after this drive we split up and ride out for a while."

"Is he figurin' on trouble?" Ab asked, holding up a match for Blackie to bend into.

"Naw. We don't get any trouble as long as we stay in the badlands. But he says we've been pretty busy this spring, the cowmen'll be bringin' in range detectives pretty quick to stop their losses, and Buck's like Joe Hickman where those danged Association men are concerned."

"How's that?" asked Patterson.

"Well, like Buck says, you can smell a sheriff a mile off, but those lousy range detectives look like anybody else . . . until they start shooting. He doesn't want to run the risk of havin' them swarm down here, so we'll all ride our different ways after we cash out this drive, and meet next fall at the Roost."

"Makes sense," murmured Patterson, watching the dusk mantle the range. "Where are we going to take this drive?"

Blackie rolled his head. "Back through the Roost an' on southward sixty miles. Buck's got contacts on both sides of the badlands. Hickman supplies us, we drive 'em through and down where the goldfields are, and the emigrant towns, we see 'em to the cattle buyers. It's like clockwork."

Ab exhaled a gust of smoke. "Buck's a clever man," he said, gazing up ahead where Buck was riding at the head of his outlaw column.

"Better'n just clever," corrected Blackie. "Plumb accurate with a gun, smart as a whip, tougher'n catgut, and a good business head to boot. You boys'll see . . . wait till we get down to the settlements an' peddle the herd. You'll see just how sharp a trader he is, too."

"How about this Joe Hickman?" asked Patterson casually. "He's got to be pretty smart, too, to rustle from his neighbors and never get caught."

"Oh, hell," exclaimed Blackie, "he's been caught! They've tried him four different times, and had to turn him loose each time . . . thanks to Buck."

Ab's head swung. "Buck? What'd Buck have to do with it?"

Blackie raffishly winked at Ab. "Buck knows folks, Ab. He sent a couple of envelopes of money up to the county seat each time."

"Bribed the judges?" Ab asked.

"Yeah. Partly that. But like I said, Buck knows people. It wasn't just bribin' them, it was puttin' little notes inside them envelopes remindin' them bigwigs up at Devon about some things out of their past that would ruin 'em if they got to be generally known. Then, to top it off, he promised to send me 'n' some of the other boys up there to salt 'em down with lead, if

Joe was convicted." Blackie beamed. "Smart, eh?"

Patterson agreed that Buck was very smart, but Ab Folsom choked on some smoke and coughed, his face as red as a beet.

Patterson said: "Seems to me, though, that Hickman could become a lead weight around Buck's neck, getting arrested and all. I'd guess a real smart man would get rid of him and put someone else up there in his job."

"He can't very well do that," Blackie explained, scowling at the tip of his cigarette. "I know how you're thinkin' on that because I used to wonder the same thing myself. But he can't replace Hickman."

"No? Why not?"

"Well, you see, Hickman's married to Buck's sister."

Patterson rode along, saying nothing more. On Blackie's other side Ab Folsom, too, seemed lost in thought, seemed no longer desirous of continuing with this conversation. After perhaps a half mile of riding between those two silent men, Blackie killed his smoke, spurred on ahead, and joined Buck up in front.

Patterson and Ab exchanged a look. They were now the last riders in the column. Still, it was too risky even back at the end of the party to mention what was in their minds, so they simply rode along, thinking and saying nothing.

Behind them, the badlands were barely visible against a darkening sky. On both sides of the column the land was also darkening along toward full nightfall. The daytime warmth was fast failing.

XIII

For a long time the outlaw band poked along. They had plenty of time to cover their ten or so miles; none of them was anxious, and, even after the three-quarter moon arose improving visibility immeasurably, they did not increase their casual pace. The men talked a little, joked some, and smoked. Buck reined back to come in beside Patterson and slouch along back there. The men kept no particular semblance of riding order; they paired off, or sometimes rode in threes and fours, conversing.

"Like they're goin' on a picnic," stated Buck, looking ahead, then over toward Patterson again. "It's an interesting thing . . . they're always glad to get back to the Roost, but when it's time to ride again, they're glad to get out of the hills."

"It's a confining life, back there," suggested Patterson, watching Buck's hawkish profile. "Last night you said so yourself."

Buck inclined his head, rode some little distance without speaking, then he looped his reins, letting his mount trail along and said: "Patterson, what's your ambition?"

On this warm, gloomy night it was possible for men riding into they knew not what to become quite philosophical, confiding less difficult than it usually was. And this outlaw chieftain was not, in Patterson's eyes, the typical trigger-happy butcher of his breed.

"The same as most men," answered the range detective. "A place to settle down and live quiet. To be able to step outside at dawn and smell the new day. It's always seemed to me that was how man was meant to live. Not forever with a pistol under his pillow or on his hip."

Buck listened and remained impassive throughout. When Patterson fell silent, he said: "Where do men get off that trail, Patterson? Somewhere along the line something begins to grow in a man, to change him away from what his folks taught him to be. What is it?"

Patterson, without a proven answer to this, simply said: "It's always looked to me, Buck, like bravery isn't what fellows like you and me call guts. Bravery is something special in folks. It's the ability to *not* hate, the ability to forgive, to overlook, to tolerate . . . and never to lose sight of a man's prime goal in this life."

Buck looked over. "You've done your share of thinking," he said quietly. "I had you pegged like that day before yesterday. You're different from the others. I think you 'n' I are a lot alike. Tell me, how many men have you killed?"

Patterson shook his head from side to side. "Talking about the past doesn't change the present nor much affect a man's future. You ever stand up in the first light of day and feel like everything that's passed before was wiped out, like each day is some kind of a promise to a man that he can do better, be better, if he's got the courage to really try for that?"

"I have. But before sundown it's always the same, all over again. Patterson, a man's chained by his yesterdays."

"I don't believe that, Buck."

"Then you're stronger than most of us. Still, you're on the Owlhoot Trail like I am, Patterson, like Ab and all the rest of us. So you weren't strong enough, were you?"

Patterson looked at his horse's bobbing little ears. "But tomorrow always comes, Buck, and tomorrow is our renewed chance to change, to try and get clear of the sordid things. I think most men try very hard a lot of times, and I figure a lot more men finally make the transition than you or I know about. There are judges and lawmen and even senators who've managed to get clear of what they've been. They manage somehow to hide their pasts. They struggle almighty hard and a lot of them succeed. But we don't know about that, because we didn't know them in other times."

Buck was looking at Patterson with an odd expression. After a while he said: "I reckon a feller who'd blackmail those judges and lawmen an' senators about their pasts would sort of be like their murderer, wouldn't he?"

"I'd say he would," agreed Patterson, knowing exactly what had prompted the outlaw chieftain to make that statement. "Maybe he'd even be lower than a common killer, because he'd be trying to assassinate their souls, their spirits, all that's true and brave and good in men."

Ab fell to making a smoke. He hadn't said a word throughout this exchange, but his lowered face mirrored a strangely respectful and admiring look. On Patterson's far side Buck, too, was silent now. Clearly Patterson had just given him much to think over, and for a while yet, since they were still a long way off from their ultimate rendezvous, he would have the time for solemn reflection.

Patterson had not meant to interject that comment about blackmail; it had just come to him as a part of what he'd had to say in reply to Buck's question, so he'd said it. But as he now rode along, he thought, since Buck was so obviously much different from his outlaw band, was a man in whom there still reposed some spark of conscience, was a gunman instead of a common killer, he would be nagged by Patterson's statements. This was, in Patterson's mind, an encouraging thing, for while he made no compromise with the lawless and never had, on the other hand he'd never before met an outlaw quite like Buck, either, and in spite of himself he respected him. It was a difficult thing to put a finger upon, this respect, but there was something to Buck other outlaws lacked. He felt that, knew it to be true, and yet it eluded his definition.

Buck eventually pushed aside his private reflections, straightened in the saddle, and studied the landscape around them. "Getting close," he stated. "Pretty quick now you two will come along with me for the scout. Keep watch for my signal." This was the brisk, cold-toned, efficient outlaw chieftain speaking again, and Patterson understood. Buck had two distinct sides to him. But then, so did all other men.

As Buck loped on up to join Blackie at the head of the column, Ab blew smoke after him and softly said: "Deep, that one. Deeper than any like him I've ever run across before. He didn't come out of no sod hut on the prairie. I got to admit it, Patterson. There's something about him I trust and respect, even though I know he's an outlaw and maybe, before dawn, will try to kill us both."

The men, seeing their leader reverting to his old wary self, broke up their little cliques, got back into a sort of loose-riding formation, and became quietly alert again. It was wetly gray and soft-lighted in the dead world they were passing through. Every now and then one of them would cock his head in a listening manner, straining to hear ahead through the nightfall and perhaps pick up the bawling of driven cattle. But there was nothing like that to be heard; in fact, except for the occasional sharp snippet of abrasive sound where a shod hoof struck down across rock, there was nothing foreign to be heard at all.

"He's signaling," said Ab. "Let's go."

He and Patterson joined Blackie and Buck up ahead. The group halted. Buck twisted to look back and say: "The rest of you keep going. We'll lope on ahead and scout a little. If I fire a gunshot, turn and hightail it back for the Roost. Otherwise, keep coming at the same gait we've been riding until we join you again."

"Hey!" a shadowy rider farther back called out. "Buck, what's wrong?" This man evidently was suddenly anxious.

"Nothing," Buck blandly said, "but only damned fools go out to do what we're here for, without making doubly sure. Now do as I say." He squared up in the saddle. "Patterson, you and I'll scout northwest. Ab, you two scout off to the northeast. Remember, no shooting. No matter if you see danger . . . don't shoot." Buck speared Blackie with a hard look. "Keep that damned gun in its holster," he growled, as though he knew Blackie very well, which he undoubtedly did.

Ab looked at Blackie. They turned off and rode away in their specified direction. Buck and Patterson watched them go briefly, then they also swung away from the main party of outlaws and also loped away.

A half mile out Buck hauled down to a stiff walk and soberly eyed Patterson's buckskin. "A man'd have to want lots of power and endurance under him to pick that animal to ride," he said, and raised his eyes.

Patterson had a good answer. "What's a little discomfort? If a feller might have to rely on power, he's better off to take a little inconvenience to get it, isn't he?"

Buck made that vague, very faint little grin of his, but it was too dark for Patterson to see it. Meanwhile, Patterson, who did not know the country they were passing over, swung his head from side to side, looking and remembering. They angled northward after a while, the rockiness left them, and silt replaced it. From this alone, Patterson deduced that they were well enough along upcountry to be soon within the area where Hickman would probably be coming with his stolen herd—*if* Ab Folsom's note got to Willows, and *if*, after it got there, it had come into the proper hands.

Buck had nothing to say for a long while. Not until he eventually halted with a steady little northerly night wind blowing into their faces and Buck's horse pricked up its ears as though that breeze was the bearer of some kind of animal tidings.

"This'll do," the outlaw leader said, and swung down to stand beside his horse. "There's something up there. You and I can't smell it yet, but the horses can."

"I wasn't much counting on the scent," said Patterson, also dismounting. "I was counting on the sounds."

"They could still be a long way off. This breeze'll bring the scent a long way, maybe three, four miles. We wouldn't be able to hear anything that far off."

All this was elementary conversation, Patterson knew, and let it die with his companion having the last word. For a while

219

Buck stood there with one arm draped across his saddle, gazing northward into the pewter night. He finally said: "I think this is my last trip, Patterson. You want to inherit an organized band of pretty good cow thieves?"

Patterson was slow to answer. He wasn't as much surprised at the outlaw's statement as he was at being offered Buck's position as outlaw chieftain. He said: "No thanks. The way it is with me, Buck, isn't the same as with you. I wouldn't be efficient enough. Why are you quitting?"

"It's a feeling I've got." Buck looked over. "Premonition they call it east of the Missouri. Out here it's called a hunch. I've gone about as far as a man can go without stumbling. I need to quit anyway. I've got plenty of money. I never particularly liked the life. Never got any thrill out of having to prove myself to every half-baked brute wearing a gun who came riding along looking for another notch."

Buck turned, toed in, and rose up to settle across his horse's back. He waited until Patterson had followed his example, then he lifted his rein hand and led out northward again. He had no more to say for a while, seemed instead acutely interested in the surrounding night. But a mile later, when he again halted and keened the night, he spoke once more.

"You put something into words for me tonight I've been floundering with for a long time, Patterson. Courage isn't just a gun in a man's hand, and each new day is a new chance. I can't take that chance until I get rid of these cattle we'll get tonight, but within the next couple weeks, after we all split up, I can, and I aim to make the effort. Patterson . . . ?"

"Yeah?"

"Roll your hoop with mine. We'll go down to San Francisco, relax a few days, then hunt us up some legitimate business."

With Buck watching him Patterson was very careful about his selection of words. He very slowly said: "You don't need me,

Buck. You don't need anyone for what you're going to try. In fact, it'd be better if you didn't have anyone along to lend a hand. Besides, as I've already said . . . my leanings are in a different direction. You head to San Francisco. I'll head in another direction altogether." Patterson gazed steadily at the bronzed, lean man across from him. "Tell me one thing. What about Joe Hickman?"

Buck's eyebrows lifted slightly. "What about him?"

"He's a fool, Buck. He's going to break your sister's heart."

Buck said—"Oh?"—very softly. "You know Hickman that well. I thought you said you came through the Willows country on the run."

"That's right. Ab and I did come from there, riding fast. But men like you and me, we look and we listen. Hickman's well known. I say he's going to get shot or jailed. How about your sister, then?"

Buck's brows dropped; his steady eyes didn't waver. "I told her not to marry him. I told her he was a loud-mouthed four-flusher." Buck started to say more, but suddenly a note of bitterness crept into his expression and he said: "What's blinder than a girl in love, Patterson, do you know? Well, neither do I. Moreover, I blame myself. She met Joe through me."

"She's going to have his kid, Buck. What happens then?"

Buck shook his head. It evidently did not occur to him to be curious about Patterson's knowledge of this intimate scrap of information because of his own overwhelming thoughts. "The Lord knows," he muttered. "I don't. My sister and I were orphaned in our teens. It doesn't matter where, but I managed for both of us. Then we came here and she fell for Joe. That's another reason why I want to quit, Patterson. You're dead right about Joe. He'll get it one of these days. He's one of those smart alecks that, the more they make, the bigger their hats keep getting. He is a fool. But she loves him. What does a man do about a thing like that?"

Patterson understood Buck's torment but he had no answers for it, so all he said was: "I think we'd better scout on ahead."

They poked along for a half hour, then heard the first faint echoes, far off and faint, of lowing cattle. Buck instantly reverted to his old alert, wary, and efficient self again, which was just as well, because Patterson's feelings suddenly became mixed; it showed in his face that in a way he was relieved that Ab's note had, after all, gotten into the right hands. At the same time, too, his expression showed both resignation and anxiety. Whatever happened now, he and Ab were in very great personal peril, more so, perhaps, than any of the other men riding with Buck's outlaw band.

"It's Hickman," said Buck, "and right on time. Let's head back and round up the others."

They turned and booted their mounts into a swift lope back the way they'd just come.

XIV

Ab and Blackie had also picked up the detectable sounds of Hickman's oncoming herd. When all the outlaws were together again, Ab managed to ride off and stop beside Patterson while Buck gave short orders and hard commands to his men. None of the others seemed aware that neither Ab nor Patterson was listening.

Ab said: "All right, Patterson, now we're in it up to our necks. Hickman'll recognize me the second he rides up."

"And," responded Patterson, "his three pardners . . . the ones you nearly tangled with in that saloon up in Willows last week . . . they'll recognize me."

"Well, then," prompted Ab, beginning darkly to scowl, "what do we do now? We can't run an' we can't stay."

"We stay, Ab. We stay . . . but we ride out to the herd and

keep our faces hidden. We act like we're holding the critters. Unless I miss my guess, they'll need some holding. Those beeves will want to cut back for their home range. What I'm sweating out, though, is something altogether different."

"Yeah, I can guess," exclaimed Ab dryly. "Holt and Dunstan, and whoever else they brought along. In the dark, if they charge the outlaws, we're goin' to be out there with their stolen beef. Folks tell me, Patterson, that gettin' shot accidentally hurts just as much as gettin' shot on purpose."

Patterson smiled and Ab, fingering a chapped lip, smiled back, but there wasn't as much genuine humor in Ab's smile as there was ironic understanding of where this long trail had led the pair of them. As he took his finger away from his mouth, Ab looked over where Buck and his men were still speaking, and made a wry observation.

"The first gunshot, Patterson, puts us in double jeopardy. Buck an' Blackie and their friends are going to know damned well someone got the word to the cattlemen. You'd never convince them this is any coincidence. And who'll they think of first, among their crew . . . us. You an' me."

Patterson urged his horse ahead. "Come on, stay close and play the cards as they fall."

Ab shrugged and followed Patterson on over where the others were beginning to break up, to haul back on their reins to get out of their tight little rough circle around Buck and Blackie.

Now, the lowing was more audible. Moreover, there was a definite rumble echoing from the northward ground where a large herd was coming along. Finally the strong scent of cattle filtered down through the night. Patterson sat his saddle, wondering just how far back the cattlemen might be, and also wondering how many of them were out there.

Buck said: "Patterson, you and Ab ride to the west and come in from that direction. I'll ride straight on up and meet Joe. The rest of you . . . split off to the east and close in so the critters don't scatter or try to cut back."

As the men moved to obey, Ab rolled his eyes at Patterson. So far so good. Buck had ordered them to do exactly what they'd had in mind doing.

Blackie materialized out of the crowd, attached himself to Ab, and rode along upcountry, saying cheerily, entirely unsuspectingly: "Well, I told you fellers it'd go smooth as clockwork."

Ab looked at Blackie but didn't answer. Patterson didn't even look around as they rode on closer to the noisy herd. Someone up ahead in the night bawled a raucous curse at some critter trying to cut back. The distinct, sharp slap of rawhide over a furry face came along in the wake of that angry shout where a rider had backhanded a critter across the nose, turning him back into the herd.

Patterson saw the cattle fanned out ahead. There was a solitary point rider but he'd evidently sighted Buck coming directly forward and was looking off slightly to the east. Joe Hickman, Patterson thought, and veered away a little farther so as to minimize a dual recognition.

A horseman had spotted the three of them and reined out from the plodding herd. The cattle were nearly bawled out; for the most part their protests at being pushed hard and fast from their home grounds had turned into hoarse imitations of their usual loud lowing. Patterson turned to get on the far side of Blackie. Ab followed his example as that oncoming drover swerved in to accost them. Blackie, paying his companions no heed, saw the stranger and drew rein, leaned far forward, straining to make the man out, then reared back and boomed out a bull-base greeting.

"Hey, Sim!" Blackie rumbled. "Sim Gard, it's me! Over here, it's me, you old hop toad, you. Boy, you fellers sure took your time about gettin' down here."

Patterson saw Gard but was too far away to make out much more than his silhouette in the night as he and Ab swung around to head in toward the drag of the shuffling, dusty herd of cattle. He heard Gard call back a profane and bantering greeting to Blackie, then those two reversed their courses and went indifferently riding along, talking back and forth. Neither Patterson nor Ab Folsom could make out anything they said because of all the other sounds, the clouds of dust, and the low bawling of the cattle.

They got almost into the drag before either of them saw a rider coming upon them from the west and farther out. This man had spotted them first. They did not, in spite of their wariness, spot him until just before he called out a short greeting in Spanish.

"*¿Quién es?*" he sang forth. "Who is it?" He expected only friends, but still he didn't recognize either Patterson or Ab. The minute Patterson swung his head, though, he recognized the other man. It was that swarthy outlaw in the high-crown hat they'd seen with Joe Hickman up at Willows, the man who looked half or two-thirds Mexican.

Patterson stopped and began to turn his horse as he called back in a deep down tone of voice: "Hey, who'd you think it'd be . . . Abe Lincoln?" He kept turning, kept coming alongside the swarthy man. Ab, too, was heading back, riding hunched in his saddle and with his head tipped down so the brim of his hat effectively shielded his face. He said something, the swarthy cowboy swung his head, and Patterson reined right in, drew his gun, and viciously chopped a short overhand blow that crunched down through that high-crown hat into scalp and skull. The swarthy man crumpled without a sound and fell. Ab lunged, caught his mount by the reins, and looked quickly over at Patterson.

"Get rid of it," Patterson hissed, indicating the horse, then turned and rode into the drag of the dusty herd, hoorawing the laggards back as though chousing a drag was all he'd ever had on his mind. 100 yards farther along he twisted to look back. High-Crown was no longer to be seen back there upon the dark earth where he limply lay.

Ab came hastening back, several hundred yards farther along. He said: "Hobbled the critter with his own reins. It'll hold him a while, but sooner or later someone'll come onto him out there."

"If it's later," growled Patterson, "we won't give a damn. How'd he get behind us like that, anyway?"

Ab didn't answer. They kept in the drag, pushing footsore and sluggard critters through billows of churned-up dust and watching through slitted eyes for approaching horsemen. None drifted back for a long while, and meantime the herd continued to move along.

Up ahead men were calling back and forth. It struck Patterson that whatever undertakings were in progress up there must soon terminate. He had deduced from things he'd heard from Buck and others that Joe Hickman and Joe's outlaws from up around Willows would soon turn back. The sooner, he told himself, the better.

Ab rode in close and pointed. Three riders were coming through the dust from the head of the herd. They were riding lazily. It was difficult to discern them because of the poor light, the dust, their shadowy movement, but Patterson was certain who they would be: Hickman and his two companions, heading back northward again.

Ab growled: "Where the hell is Dunstan? Where's Holt with his lousy riders? If they ever expect to catch this gang all together, now's the time."

Almost as though Ab's bleak words were some kind of cue, Hickman and his companions, riding out a little way, suddenly lifted their heads, straining northward. Patterson and Ab Folsom noticed this and also twisted to look back. There wasn't anything to be seen, but then the night was murky. But within moments Patterson *heard* something.

"Horsemen!" he said. "And a lot of them!"

Joe Hickman, farther westward, evidently had a better vantage point because he abruptly hauled back on his reins with his left hand, pointed through the dusty night with his right hand, and called out in alarm to his companions: "Riders, a damned army of 'em. Run for it! Break up and run for it!"

Behind Patterson and Ab the oncoming men began to firm up through the dusty darkness. Ab yelled—"Look out!"—and dropped over on the off side of his mount as a gunshot tore night apart with its lancing orange dagger of fierce light.

Patterson felt the breath of that bullet and jerked violently on his reins. As he spun off eastward, Ab shot out ahead of him, riding low and with his six-gun in one hand. A burst of ragged pistol shots exploded far back. Over to the east, where those charging riders were curving inward upon the herd, Joe Hickman and his two friends were swamped in a wild mêlée.

Men's shouts rose up above the quick, frightened bawling of the herd. Cattle that had previously been dragging one leg after another became in a twinkling full of panic. Muzzle blasts and thunderous explosions put them on the verge of stampeding.

Far ahead, up where Buck and Blackie and the men from the badlands were, came sudden howls of astonishment and alarm. Someone up there threw three fast shots rearward, which was a mistake, because those converging riders from the north turned their attention away from Joe Hickman and his two surviving friends, and let go with a withering blast toward the front of the column. Because all the attackers seemed at last to be in range and firing, the resultant deafening thunder turned the confused cattle inward where they briefly bawled their terror and trampled one another, then they swung completely around, broke over into a shambling run, and went thundering back northward, the way they had come.

Patterson and Ab got clear of the farthest wing of this blind rush of large animals by hard riding and quick maneuvering, but afterward, because of the nearly impenetrable dust scuffed to life by the herd, they couldn't make out friend from enemy. In other quarters, though, men seemed not to have this problem, or else they didn't care at whom they fired, for the red flames of gunfire erupted constantly throughout this swirling, eerie battle.

The men from the badlands were trying to break off, were trying to get free enough from the press of numbers converging upon them, to make their dash for the Roost. It took Patterson a little while to discern which were the guns of Buck and his men and which were not. He still hadn't seen any of the men up close who were attacking, but was quite confident who they were.

Ab came in close and bent to bawl out something over the tumult of stampeding cattle, gunfire, and men's ardent outcries.

"We know where Buck's going to take his men, Patterson! Dunstan and Holt don't know that! It's up to us to get ahead of the outlaws and slow them! Come on!"

Patterson's horse swung in his excitement and plunged along behind Ab's animal as the deputy sheriff went racing southward. By the time Patterson had made his assessment of what Ab was desperately seeking to do, it was too late to turn back anyway, so Patterson permitted himself to be borne along.

They whipped past the last of the terrified cattle, swept up within range of two mounted men who ignored them to pepper away in the direction of the attacking cowmen, then got almost up where the main party of outlaws was stubbornly fighting. Here, someone shouted at them in a fluting call that seemed to be demanding identification. Patterson saw Ab Folsom lift his

.45, squeeze the trigger, and that yelling man let off a loud howl as Ab's slug cut the air within inches of his head.

Then they were past and hidden in the tawny dust.

Patterson hadn't sighted Buck or Blackie; for that matter, even if he'd seen them, been able to make out their silhouettes in the maëlstrom of noise, dust, and night gloom, he probably wouldn't have been able to recognize them anyway. He caught up with Ab a mile southward where the acrid dust was thinner. He leaned to call over: "That pass we came through leaving the Roost. Make for it, Ab! We can hold 'em for a while there."

Ab nodded vigorously and plunged ahead.

The battle was raging behind them now. It crossed Patterson's mind that perhaps he and Ab were running away from the one place they might be able to do the most good; it didn't sound to him as though the outlaws were going to be able to fight clear of that overwhelming force of gunfiring range riders. But, with the miles fleeing rearward under the hoofs of their horses, Patterson began to notice that the fighting back there was, in fact, beginning to sound less confined and more scattered, as though the outlaws had indeed broken clear after their initial surprise, and were now running southward.

Ab was riding twisted, his gun hand raised in case a target came along from behind them. He saw Patterson looking at him and gave his head a hard wag. "Damned fools!" he bawled. "Why didn't they split up . . . have half their men get around southward of the outlaws?"

Patterson did not reply. Tactics such as Ab was suggesting belonged to soldiers, not cowboys. Those cattlemen back there, Patterson thought, had done famously well to trail Hickman this far before being detected. Normally range riders wouldn't have evidenced even that much restraint.

The fighting became even more sporadic back there, and, as fast and far as Patterson and Ab had come, the sounds of battle seemed also to be keeping pace with them. Buck had indeed broken free and was making his desperate dash for the Roost. If Patterson and Ab couldn't stop the outlaws before they got back into the badlands, all the range riders in the county wouldn't be able to flush them out of their endless hiding places throughout those black and forbidding mountains.

XV

Their horses were stumbling badly as the first low peaks showed dead ahead. Up above, where a rash of silver stars stood above the higher peaks, it became possible to make out the highest rims of the badlands. Patterson called over for Ab to slow down, to save their animals, that they were far enough in the lead not to kill the beasts. Ab obeyed, but he kept swinging to look back.

The drum roll of hard-riding horsemen came distinctly and steadily over and above the crashes of occasional gunfire back where the outlaws were in full flight before their enemies. Patterson put their separating distance at roughly a mile, a mile and a half. He could easily make out the pass on ahead, so he reached forward, tugged out his booted rifle, and balanced it across his lap to be ready, when the moment came, to hit the ground, abandon his horse, and run for a vantage point on one side of the looming pass. Ab, also, drew out his carbine; it was a typical range rider's Winchester saddle gun, fairly accurate up to 200 yards, neither accurate nor even dependable beyond that range.

They swept into the pass, hauled back, sprang down, and let the horses run ahead up the trail. Less than a mile onward lay the log buildings and the large public corral.

Patterson waved Ab off. "Take the other side," he commanded. "And be careful . . . Dunstan and Holt are out there, too."

They split up, sprinted for cover among the boulders and bull pines on each side of the pass, got into position, and had time enough for only a moment of very brief respite before the red flashes of gunfire showed farther out.

Ab fired first. He shot off four rounds almost as fast as he could lever and squeeze off. Patterson, uncertain of their targets, held his fire. Ab's shooting threw the oncoming outlaws into confusion. So near safety, they evidently had never once considered the likelihood of enemies being in front, as well as behind them. Men cried out warnings as they squared around to meet this fresh challenge. They frantically yanked their horses off to the left and the right of the pass.

Patterson saw one burly rider duck down over his mount's mane and shoot ahead. This man was pinning everything on a forlorn hope that he could dash past and reach the safety of the yonder trees before either Ab or Patterson would check him. It was a fatal error. Patterson put aside his rifle, stepped out from his protective rocks, let the oncoming man run straight at him, and, after the outlaw glimpsed Patterson and wildly fired at him, Patterson drew and squeezed off one shot from the hip. The riderless horse gave a violent bound forward as his rider went off backward, struck the ground, bounced, rolled five feet, and lay still.

The other nearest outlaws saw the killing, and, if they'd pinned their hopes on the dead man's wild rush, they abandoned those plans at once and, firing in Patterson's general direction, sawed their reins to get clear.

Ab fired his carbine empty and drew his six-gun. But the outlaws were hurling lead with desperate violence now. Ab had to duck far down. So did Patterson. He threw himself back behind his boulders and remained flat. But they had both accomplished their purpose for the renegades broke up, some fleeing westward, some eastward, along the more rugged foothills of the badlands where there were no convenient passes. Behind them, hooting and howling, now that their foemen had been checked, went the cattlemen. Patterson thought it would only be a matter of time before this unequal battle came to its grisly end. He also thought it would be better for Buck and Blackie and their riders if they died fighting, because, otherwise, with an abundance of bull pines around, the survivors would surely be hanged with their own lariats.

"Hey!" Ab called over. "You all right?"

"I'm not hit if that's what you mean," answered Patterson dryly. "How about you?"

"Someone shattered the stock of my carbine, dammit all."

"Stay down, Ab. We turned 'em off. Lie low a while longer and our end of it'll be over with."

The sounds of strife gradually diminished, but an occasional distant yell of triumph floated back to the waiting men, coming from either the east or the west where the cattlemen were running their enemies to earth.

Patterson eventually arose, dusted himself off, picked up his carbine, and stepped out through the rocks and trees where he could see the northward plain. Dust lingered out there, dimming the moon and stars. The smell of animal sweat mixed with burned gunpowder was strong, but otherwise that vast sweep of northward land was empty.

Across from him, also standing up, Ab said: "Those cattle will be back on their home range come sunup. Dunstan and Holt ought to be glad about that."

Patterson tilted his head. The sounds of gunfire were diminishing now, and they were distant, sounding more like small twigs popping underfoot than weapons of death. He hooked the rifle over one crooked arm and strolled over to Ab Folsom.

"A hard night's work," he quietly said. Ab nodded, looked out over the plain, then backward, on up the cañon.

"If any got away, they'll probably try to get back to the Roost sooner or later. You expect we ought to walk on up and wait?"

"I reckon," muttered Patterson, and turned to start up through the trees to that wider, broader place in the trail where the log buildings were. Just before he and Ab stepped through the final belt of pines, Patterson said, squinting ahead: "Maybe, just to be on the safe side, we'd better ease around behind the café. Ralph's got his scatter-gun, you know."

They did this, stepping lightly around the eastward side of the Roost and coming in toward the café without making a sound. Ralph's café was dark and hushed.

"Maybe all that gunfire scairt him into runnin'," opined Ab, studying the dark rear windows. "He's had plenty of time to saddle himself a horse and hit the southward trail out of here."

Patterson said—"Maybe."—without sounding either hopeful about this or entirely skeptical, either. "Let's go find out."

They moved stealthily down to the last fringe of trees and paused there. The café was utterly without life, but then, as Patterson mumbled, it would be that way, for fat Ralph was not the type to grab a gun and rush out to fight. They stepped out into plain view and walked ahead, each with a gun cocked and ready. Nothing happened. They reached the rear door. Ab gave it a push. The door swung inward; all the greasy odors of Ralph's unkempt kitchen came thickly out to them. Patterson stepped through first, then Ab. The floor *squeaked*. They parted, each man stepping to one side of the opened door.

Patterson said: "Ralph? Hey, Ralph, where are you?"

Unexpectedly a raspy voice bleated out of the deeper darkness of the next room. "Who's that? What's happened? What was all that shootin' about?"

Patterson looked across where Ab's face was a blurry pale blob. They both started for the opening that led from Ralph's kitchen out into the other room. Patterson kept talking as they did this.

"Bunch of damned cattlemen were following Hickman with the herd, Ralph. They jumped us about six, eight miles out when we were taking delivery of the herd from Joe."

Patterson eased through into the front room. Ab came through right behind him. They could dimly discern Ralph, sitting cowed and terrified over near his iron stove. An ominous sheen from some weapon in his lap indicated that frightened Ralph was armed. Patterson didn't give him a chance to speak, to ask questions. He kept talking as he slowly advanced across the unlit room toward the stove.

"There was a cussed army of them. They ran us back here and split off at the mouth of the pass when the boys raced off, every man for himself."

Patterson halted, standing in front of the cook. He bent, took hold of Ralph's shotgun, and lifted it away. Ab, holding out a free hand, took the weapon, broke it in the middle, and ejected both cartridges. As he snapped the empty weapon closed again, he said: "You might not believe it, Ralph, but the gang's done for, finished, busted up. Any minute now those cattlemen'll come ridin' up here with any of the boys they happened to take alive."

Ralph cringed. "You're those two new fellers," he whispered. "How'd you two get clear if the others couldn't?"

"Well, now," Ab said quietly, "you see, Ralph, it was Patterson and me who got into the pass first and turned back Buck and the others so's the cattlemen could overhaul them before they'd get into the mountains."

Ralph's eyes got round. "You . . . done that?" he whispered, his voice fading noticeably. "You two . . . done that to Buck . . . ?"

Patterson nodded. "We had to, Ralph. You see, Ab here is a deputy sheriff and I'm an Association man."

Ralph made a faint bleating sound in his throat and shrank

back. Patterson strolled over to the doorway, looked out, listened, heard nothing, saw nothing, and walked back. To Ab he said: "Let's go over to the saloon and wait. I need a drink, you need one, and I can tell you for a fact that Ralph never needed a drink so badly before in his life."

They had to nudge the fat cook to get him up out of his chair, and once the three of them were outside, Ralph seemed more fearful than ever. He shied at the shadows and the utter stillness. Inside the empty saloon, glasses still stood at random upon the bar top where the rustlers had left them when they'd ridden away hours before. Ralph put out both hands to steady himself.

"Don't faint," said Ab, going around behind the bar to get two bottles, one of which he set down in front of the demoralized outlaw. "Relax, Ralph. Whatever else you're wanted for, at least it's not for rustling cattle tonight."

Ralph said: "It's dark in here."

"And it's going to stay that way," Patterson replied, joining Ab at the card table Buck always used. "Sometimes things don't work out exactly right, Ralph. Sitting in lamplight can get men killed. Take a drink. You'll feel better."

Ralph splashed whiskey in a glass and drank. Ab and Patterson also had a drink, but only one each. Not so Ralph, he had two more fast shots before he turned, placed his back to the bar, and said: "I never trusted you fellers. Not from the first time you rode in."

Ab shrugged. "The others did. Buck did. That's what counted."

Ralph's face was getting red; his eyes were brightening steadily with Dutch courage. Those three straight shots had put some iron into his backbone. "They'll get you two for this!" he exclaimed. "Your friends can't get 'em all, and the ones that escape'll hunt you down for what you done tonight!"

"That," returned Ab Folsom, "is the oldest song in the world, Ralph. Have another drink and don't worry. If every man who'd set out to salivate me ever got the job done, I'd look like a piece of that foreign cheese with all the holes in it."

Patterson suddenly stood up, listening. At once both Ralph and Ab Folsom became alert and stiff. For a few moments there wasn't a sound, then each of them picked it up—the slow approach up the pass of many shod horses coming on at a slow but persevering walk.

Ralph said: "Buck! Buck's coming! Now you two'll sweat!"

But Patterson and Ab knew better; there were entirely too many riders moving up toward the Roost for it to be the outlaws. There were more horses out there coming up the trail than Buck had originally had, even before the fight out on the plain. No, it wouldn't be Buck and the outlaws; it would be the cattlemen approaching.

Patterson picked up his rifle and went with it over to the door. He stepped out upon the dark porch and gazed southward. Ab remained inside.

The riders were coming along in a bunched-up party, their naked guns resting across their laps. Moonlight glowed against them, making each of those riders appear bleak and lethal and unrelenting in appearance.

Patterson waited until the foremost men were close enough, then called out to them: "Holt? Dunstan?"

The horsemen halted. One man got stiffly down and tossed his reins to another man. He walked on over toward the saloon. Patterson recognized him when he stopped at the foot of the porch steps.

"Hello, Dunstan. What happened after we turned them back from getting up into the pass?"

Dunstan didn't speak right away. He stalked on up onto the porch and peered inside the saloon over the batwing doors, then he sighed, and turned back. "Killed four, winged another one, and three got clean away. So it was you that turned 'em at the pass. Good work, Patterson. Who was with you, that deputy from Devon?"

"Yeah. Ab Folsom. He's inside with another one."

"I see," muttered Dunstan quietly, gazing out where his riders were silently sitting. "One got through, eh?"

"No. This one didn't go out on the raid. He's their cook. Where's Bryan Holt?"

"Had to send Bryan back," said Dunstan in the same quietly rumbling tone of voice. "He got hit pretty bad in the side. We made up a travois and sent him back with the one we winged. The town marshal from Willows and five of our crew went back with Bryan. Those five were hit, none of 'em too bad, but bad enough to need medical attention."

Dunstan looked back into the saloon again. Ab was lighting a lamp in there. Patterson said: "Dismount your men. There's whiskey inside. Across the road's their café. We can rest the stock until sunup, then head back."

Dunstan nodded, stepped ahead to the porch edge, and gave the necessary orders. As his range riders began to swing out and down, there was a little rustle of talk among them. Evidently they hadn't expected their fighting to be over when they'd ridden up to the Roost. As they led their animals away, the men looked with interest and strong curiosity at the Roost, its log buildings, its big corral, its dark and forbidding natural setting.

"I need a drink," muttered Morgan Dunstan, and pushed on into the saloon with Glenn Patterson right behind him.

XVI

Patterson left Dunstan and his crowding-up riders at the bar right after the cattleman told him the dead outlaws were tied across their horses outside. Ab joined Patterson outside in the cooling night. Behind them, orange lamp glow made a pleasant brightness in the otherwise darkened outlaw village. As they strolled down to look at the dead men, three more cowboys came slouching up, leading two more corpse-laden horses.

"Who've you got?" Patterson called casually, and the grumbled answers stopped Patterson in mid-stride.

"The one with the Mex hat. The cattle run over him on their way back home. And Joe Hickman."

Ab said: "Hickman? Is he dead?"

"Dead as a gut-shot bird," bleakly replied one of the riders, pushing on past. "Where's everybody?"

"Up where those lights are burning," stated Ab, his sober gaze upon Patterson. "It's a saloon. Go on over and help yourselves."

Patterson started walking again. Ab didn't mention Hickman and neither did Patterson. They went down where the tired animals were standing and examined the cooling bodies. Simon Gard was there. So was Bill Blevins, Hickman's other outlaw companion. The other corpses were recognizable as Buck's men from the Roost. Ab stepped back to roll a smoke.

"That finishes it," he softly said, and lit up. "A good night's work, Patterson. Not pleasant at all, and for a while out there I wasn't too damned sure we wouldn't wind up belly down over our saddles like these fellers, but, still, it came out pretty well."

Patterson returned to Ab's side, shaking his head. "We need a couple of fresh horses, Ab," he said. "Buck's not here and neither is Blackie."

Ab looked up with a dogged scowl. "You crazy? We'll track them down come sunup. Couldn't find them in the dark anyway."

Patterson was adamant. "Only half the job's been done and you know it, Ab. If Buck and Blackie are left free, they'll come back, and we'll have it all to do over again."

Patterson turned to head across to the big corral where several unused horses were idly picking grass. Ab watched him go for a moment, then hurled down his smoke, stamped viciously upon it, and spoke a hair-raising oath as he, also, hiked on over to catch a fresh horse and drag an outfit over and put it on. All the time Ab was doing this, he was growling protests and powerful oaths. All the time Patterson was rigging out he was stonily silent. As the pair of them led their horses out, closed the gate, and swung up, a burly, stiff-walking older man came up and stopped to put a puzzled look forward. It was Morgan Dunstan. He said: "Hey, is that you, Patterson? Folsom?"

"It's us," growled Ab, reining clear of the gate. "Who'd you think it might be, the Angel Gabriel?"

"Well, where the devil do you think you're going this time o' night?"

"Ask him," growled Ab, jerking an irate thumb in Patterson's direction.

"The outlaw chieftain's not here," said Patterson, shortening his reins. "We're going after him."

Dunstan looked troubled. "But where?" he asked. "Where'll you find him in the dark in these damned mountains?"

Patterson didn't answer; he simply reined past the cattleman and struck out for the northward trail that led out of the Roost.

"Wait!" Dunstan called. "Wait until I can mount up the boys. We'll come with you."

Patterson kept on riding. Ab looked back, looked forward to Patterson's wide-shouldered silhouette, shrugged, and also kept on riding.

The night was well advanced; there was a little swirl of cool air coming out of the cañons; the scent of sage and pine sap and dust hung in the air. Out beyond the pass where soft silver moonlight drenched the empty world, Patterson swung unerringly westward. He didn't know where Buck and Blackie might have gone, west or east, but since he had to start his search somewhere, he turned west. At least, in a very general way, this was the direction of San Francisco. He rode along, thinking of the things he and Buck had said to one another. None of it made him anxious to overtake Buck, yet on the other hand he knew Buck's breed of man. Buck would never permit himself to be vanquished like this. Even though he'd meant for this to be his last cattle raid, he could not now allow that judgment to stand. Men like Buck had more than intelligence and spirit— they also had pride. Buck's pride alone would make him return to the Roost, reorganize his outlaw crew, and make at least one more slashing raid against the cattlemen of Willows country. That was why Patterson was on his trail now. Because he knew full well that Buck had to be personally stopped, and tonight; otherwise, as he'd said to Ab back at the Roost, they'd have it all to do over again.

"Hey," mumbled Folsom, coming up to ride stirrup with Patterson. "Why west? How d'you know they didn't go east?"

"I don't know they went west. I don't even know they're together. But I *do* know one thing, Ab. If we don't find them, we won't have accomplished a damned thing permanent tonight." Patterson looked around. "You don't have to trail along. You've done all anyone could have expected you to do. Why don't you go on back?"

Ab sniffed. "You're forgettin' something. Sheriff Conrad ordered me to keep *you* in sight . . . no one else. Besides, I kind of like ridin' in the night."

"Sure you do," muttered Patterson, and smiled. Ab grinned back. These two understood one another. They had not originally gotten involved in this as friends, but it's hard for men who have fought desperately hard side-by-side not eventually to become friends.

Patterson said: "You can forget Hickman. Conrad had in mind that I might sock him away. Well, he's socked away and Sheriff Conrad's going to be disappointed he can't nail me to the wall for it."

"Not Will Conrad," said Ab stoutly. "No one on this earth wanted him put away one way or another worse than he did." Ab was thoughtfully silent for a while, then he said: "But this Buck feller . . . whatever his name is . . . Will Conrad never heard of him. Neither did I. You know, Patterson, we *could* go back to Willows and get out some flyers on him. They'd pick him up sooner or later. All of them get caught someday."

Patterson had no comment to make. He rode along with the Black Hills on his left, probing the onward land which was strange to him. He had a fifty-fifty chance of being right in his choice of directions. A man couldn't often ask for much more than that.

They were nearly three miles along when Ab pointed ahead and to the left. A faint-lighted trail led up into a brushy cañon over there. Patterson looked, halted, swung down, and walked ahead, bent over, peering at the ground. There were tracks going up through the break in the hills and they were fresh. He went back, got astride, and without a word Ab turned his horse.

Past the first thorny wall of brush there was a good trail. It seemed to Patterson to have been selected out by someone, possibly for just such an emergency as now existed. His hopes soared when they came upon a head-hung saddled horse standing in ankle-high grass. The animal had clearly been ridden to the limit of its endurance. It paid no attention whatsoever when Patterson and Ab got down and approached it.

Ab, feeling the seat of the saddle, said: "Still warm, Patterson. I don't know how you did it, but you sure put us on the right track." Ab turned to trace out the uphill course of this trail and gradually began to shake his head. "If those two are riding double on the same tuckered animal, they can't escape. Not now."

The pair of them pushed on. The little trail went directly toward a sheer wall of obsidian rock, then, when it seemed it must end there, it abruptly turned due westward and sprang up the slope, making a snake-like curve rising out of the cañon. As they pushed on, following this dim trail, Ab said: "I've always heard renegades in these hills couldn't be found unless they wanted to be, but until tonight I never knew just how easy it'd be for fleein' men to get away in here."

The trail was wide enough for one horseman at a time, and, although it had obviously been maintained down below, probably as an accessible escape route, the farther Patterson led out along it, the brushier it became until where it eventually flattened out upon a chilly plateau and there was no brush. After that, he and Ab Folsom loped for a while, until the forest began coming down to them, then they slowed and went more cautiously again.

"Good bushwhackin' country," Ab observed softly, and hauled out his six-gun to carry it lightly in his lap, cocked. He suddenly uttered an oath. "There was a carbine in the boot on that done-in horse back below," he said, sounding disgusted with himself. "Why didn't I use my head and fetch it along?"

"Got any Winchester shells left?" asked Patterson, up ahead.

"No."

"Neither did the man who left it behind," said Patterson. "Otherwise, it wouldn't be back there. There's nothing more completely useless in this man's world, Ab, than an empty carbine. They're even too short to make a decent crutch."

A half hour later, deep in the trees that bordered their gloomy trail as it passed through a crevice in the hills, Patterson got down again because of the increased darkness in here, and went along on foot, leading his horse, watching for fresh shod horse tracks. They were there, one horse traveling slowly.

"Tracks are pretty deep," Patterson said. "He either weighs a ton or he's carrying double."

"No saddle horse weighs a ton," stated Ab, swinging his head from side to side as they went in among the trees. "So that means he's packin' double."

They were beginning to rise up out of the crevice cañon when, somewhere far ahead, a horse's whinny floated down to them. Patterson halted at once. Ab, farther back, slid to the ground, dropped his reins, and walked up beside Patterson, pointing up the yonder southward slope where that sound had come from.

"Skyline those cottonwoods up there," Ab said. "It's got to be a water hole of some kind. Otherwise, there'd be no cottonwoods growin' this high in the mountains. They'll be givin' the horse a breather up there. Patterson, maybe we'd better finish this on foot."

Patterson didn't think so. "Get astride, Ab."

They went slowly now. The ground underfoot was spongy; they would be leaving very clear tracks, but that didn't matter. What *did* matter was that they didn't make a sound.

The moon was drifting on down the sky. There was a paleness to the horizon where black upthrusts stood starkly darker than the night. Where those cottonwoods grew was near the distant top-out. Evidently, Patterson told himself, the trail boosted itself straight up from where he and Ab now were, crossed over the rim, and plunged on down the far side of the crest, continuing its southward run.

Patterson stopped when Ab hissed. They were now as close as they dared get on horseback. Tying the horses back in the trees, they went onward again, this time afoot and also no longer staying upon the trail. Patterson had his rifle. Ab had only his six-gun.

A falling star burned a long scratch across the underbelly of the sky, flaming out in its straight-down plunge. A night-owl, startled from its sentinel perch in a bull pine, flapped in an ungainly manner and made Ab jump a foot, and afterward choke over some excellently descriptive but not necessarily accurate names for this big bird.

Patterson could, by hunching down, catch the yonder cotton-woods against the skyline. In this way he was able to estimate his course, the distance yet to be covered, and get some idea of the terrain up there. It seemed that the shaggy old smooth-trunked trees were growing in a small dip where the background slope rose nearly straight up. The trail was visible in a ghostly way as it made its erratic way up to that spot.

Ab stepped up, bent his head, and whispered: "Maybe, if we split up and come onto them from the west and east, we could catch 'em in a cross-fire."

Patterson frowned. "No thanks," he growled. "I've used up all my luck for one night. If you were off to the west and I was to the east, you could shoot me as easy as them. Now shut up. We're getting too close for talk."

Ab subsided. They moved out again, got less than 100 yards from the cottonwoods, and heard a man's tired voice drag out some indistinguishable words. For a moment there was no response, then, when it came, Patterson looked around at Ab. That second voice was unmistakably Buck's. He said distinctly: "It's not important how they knew to follow Joe. It's only important they *did*, so now we're damned near afoot, the gang's dead or scattered, and, unless we get moving, they'll find us here, too."

The other voice spoke a little louder. It was Blackie up there with Buck. He said: "They won't stand a chance of findin' this trail until sunup. We're safe for another couple of hours. Besides, m'damned horse needs the rest."

Patterson reached inside his jacket, brought forth a tubular length of sewn leather, uncapped it under Ab's interested attention, drew forth his telescopic sight, screwed it into place atop his rifle barrel, and raised the gun. There wasn't actually enough light to see clearly by, but nevertheless Patterson got a good close-up of that little clearing with its cottonwoods, its spring, and its tall, lush grass. As he lowered the gun, he motioned for Ab to follow along, and started ahead a foot at a time. They were almost within rifle range.

Blackie said, sounding drowsy and comfortable: "Buck, if them two wasn't in on it, then who the hell was it that turned us back at the pass?"

"I don't know," growled the outlaw chieftain. "Forget it. That part's over and done with."

"Not to me it ain't," growled Blackie. "I'm going to hunt those two down if it's the last thing I ever do."

XVII

Patterson slowly raised his carbine, dropped his head low to squint through the telescopic sight, and at the same time he said in a high-pitched and carrying tone of voice: "Blackie, it just might be the last thing you ever do!"

At once someone up by the spring dropped and rolled over loose earth and ripped out a startled curse. But there was the sound of only that one man, and for a long time afterward that's all Patterson and Ab were permitted to hear.

Their approach had been successfully stealthy. Neither Buck nor Blackie apparently had had any idea at all they weren't alone up in this wild spot until Patterson had called to them.

Ab, not approving of Patterson's permitting their enemies to be alerted, stepped behind a tree and waited for the inevitable hail of lead. It didn't come; the night ran on, the stillness grew, and eventually Ab lost his scowl to begin looking instead a little uneasy. Obviously, if Buck and Blackie decided not to make their stand in among the cottonwoods, and decided instead to carry the fight to their attackers, they could squirm and crawl down out of their little hideaway, in which case the positions would be reversed. He slipped up where Patterson had his rifle resting in the lowest crotch of a tree while he knelt and watched through the telescopic sight. He said: "Patterson, we better move. They know about where you spoke from. They can belly-crawl around in this lousy darkness and get behind us, maybe."

Patterson raised up, motioned for Ab to look through his glass sight, and waited until the deputy had done this. Despite the gloom, there was barely enough moonlight and star shine to permit a viewer through that sight to see all the pertinent details up at the cottonwood spring. Ab wagged his head and gazed admiringly at the telescopic sight.

"Never saw anything quite like that thing," he whispered. "Hell, I could even make out the horse a hundred feet beyond the spring, up in its grassy place."

"How would they crawl down here without us spotting them, then?" Patterson asked.

Ab shrugged. "Reckon they couldn't," he admitted, and sank down upon the ground beside Patterson. "But they're sure awful quiet up there."

"They've got reason to be, Ab. We've got 'em bottled up like a covey of quail. They've got to do some palavering. They've got to talk this out. One horse, two men. The back trail cut off and the onward trail up over the rim exposed. They aren't in too good a position."

"All the same," returned Ab softly, "I'd like it better if they *did* somethin'. I get the creeps between the shoulder blades waitin' like this."

The moon continued to drop down and the sky began to darken gently. Where those cottonwood trees stood, there was a ghostly paleness from star shine reflected off the rearward slope, but elsewhere all around, including the gloomy little patch of trees where Patterson and Ab lay, the night thickened instead of brightened.

They had been watching and waiting nearly fifteen minutes before a man's voice sang across the little distance to them. It was Buck's voice; they had no difficulty ascertaining that after the first few words. Buck didn't slur his words, wasn't as roughly ungrammatical as Westerners usually were. He said: "Is that you, Patterson?"

"Yes, it's me."

"How many are with you?"

"Come on down and find out."

Buck was briefly silent, then he said: "Patterson, how did it end down there?"

"Joe's dead, Buck. So are about a half dozen others."

After another pause Buck said: "How did those cattlemen manage it?"

"Trailed Hickman. Waited until the two bands came together, then attacked."

"That sounds about right," asserted the outlaw chieftain, his voice conversationally casual, as though he and Patterson were discussing the weather or the price of beef. "And at the pass . . . when we tried to escape back into the hills . . . who was that in the rocks who turned us off?"

"Me, Buck. Me and Ab Folsom. Ab's a deputy sheriff from Devon. I'm an Association man from Denver."

Blackie interrupted here with a howl of wrath and savage curses. "I told you, Buck!" he exploded. "I told you I didn't see them two after the fight started! I told you they must've run on ahead to get into that pass and . . . !"

"Shut up!" snarled Buck. And after Blackie profanely subsided, Buck said: "Patterson, you figuring on taking us back?"

247

"Have to, Buck, that's part of my job."

"You took a big chance, riding into the Roost, you and Ab. I could've had you killed any time."

Patterson looked down where Ab was lying. He bent low and whispered: "He's just talking now. Watch close, Ab. I've got a feeling he's holding our attention while Blackie tries something."

"Patterson? You hear me, down there?"

"I hear you, Buck. Sure, you could've had us killed. But that's part of our jobs, taking long chances. This time it paid off. Your crew's finished and so are you. Why don't you go back the easy way?"

"Come on up here and get me, Patterson," the outlaw said. "No man likes being made a fool of. Come on up and give me a chance to even that up between us."

Patterson looked over where Ab was creeping away, heading around through the trees and northward in the direction he evidently expected Blackie to come. It struck Patterson that Ab was going in the right direction. It also struck him that Blackie's course might be only secondarily toward the lawman. What was of paramount importance to both sides now wasn't a shoot-out, particularly—it was saddle horses. As long as Ab kept between the horses and the outlaws, he would sooner or later encounter Blackie.

"What say, Patterson, you coming up or not?"

"I don't have to run you down, Buck. All I've got to do is keep you flat on your belly up there. Dunstan and the cattlemen will be along after dawn."

For a moment Buck was silent. The hills around and slopes were silent. Gloom descended in thick layers where straining men were anxious to hold, or to break this stalemate.

Patterson took a long survey of the uphill area through his glass sight. For a while he could make out no movement at all. He knew about where Ab was, but even so he couldn't detect his movement or even his shadow among the shaggy old dark-trunked trees. When he ultimately spied movement, he knew from the distance and the direction that it couldn't be Ab. That crawling man was too far up the yonder slope and he was crawling down, not up. This had to be either Blackie or Buck. To determine which Patterson called out.

"Buck, what's the sense of this? You can't get away and I don't particularly want to shoot you. Give it up and come on down here without your guns."

"Thanks!" called Buck, still up near the spring, in among the cottonwoods. "Thanks for the consideration, Patterson. To be frank as hell, I don't look forward to shooting you, either, but you know I can't give it up. Ten or twenty years in prison at my age would be the same as a death sentence. I think we'll have to end it right here."

Patterson looked through the sight again. He knew where Buck was. He also now understood who that was creeping stealthily down from the spring area: Blackie. But Ab was by now so far off there was no way for Patterson to warn him that he and Blackie were stalking along toward an unsuspected collision course. He decided to use his rifle and sank down for another search of that brushy patch where he'd seen Blackie crawling down.

Blackie was no longer anywhere in sight! Fear grew in Patterson. He somehow had to let Ab know he was being stalked, and he had to let him know fast, otherwise Ab and Blackie would be too close together for Patterson to risk shooting. The only way he could think of to accomplish this was to fire into the brush about where he thought the outlaw might be. Buck called over to him saying something about a stand-off. Patterson dropped down, swung his rifle, aimed, and squeezed off a shot. The vicious blast of that weapon, so entirely different from the deeper roar of a Winchester saddle gun, bounced off the slopes and went in waves of echoing sound back down over the rearward plain.

At once Buck fired toward Patterson's muzzle blast, which Patterson had expected. The bullet came close. Patterson whipped his barrel back around and squeezed off another shot in Buck's direction. This time the answering gunshot came from a new position. Buck was rolling clear after each shot. He was also doing something else; he was pinning Patterson down to give Blackie his chance at Ab.

Patterson understood the equality of this battle perfectly. He removed his rifle from the tree-limb, fired once over where he'd last seen Blackie, then swiftly raised the barrel and let fly with a shot up toward the spring. This little rapid maneuver caught Buck unprepared. Patterson's slug must have come uncomfortably close because, as Buck fired back, he was flinching, his bullet sang high overhead.

Over to the southwest where underbrush and trees met, Ab's six-gun roared, its deeper, throatier tone drowning out the other guns. Ahead of Buck through the underbrush another .45 roared right back. Ab and Blackie dueled it out shot for shot. Patterson and Buck traded lead, one shooting uphill, the other shooting downhill.

Someone let off a high scream over where Ab and Blackie were stubbornly fighting and one of those six-guns went silent. Patterson tried hard to determine which man over there had fired last, and couldn't decide. He held his own fire peering intently southwestward, waiting for one or the other of those two battlers to let go with a final shot. Neither of them did. He thought—hoped—that scream of a fatally hit fighter had come from Blackie, but he had no way of knowing about this.

Buck slammed a shot down into Patterson's belt of trees. He winced but did not bother to reply. He, instead, got up into a low crouch and started up where he'd last seen Ab fade from sight in the underbrush. It was silent again, all around. There was a faint scent in the air of burned gunpowder. Underfoot, where layers of needles lay, Patterson's booted feet sank spongily, making not a sound as he crept forward. He knew Buck would now be turning his attention to those other two battlers, also. Buck would perhaps even be anticipating Patterson's move to go to Ab's aid. He therefore had to prolong his approach by avoiding the fastest onward route, and stay in among the murky spit of forest.

He did not think Buck might also be coming down into that area where a deadly fight had been concluded. He did not have time to consider all the facts of what might be involved here.

Once, when he was about where he'd last seen Ab, he paused to bend close and look for tracks, for bent limbs in the underbrush, for some sign that would indicate where his partner had gone. If there were tracks, it was entirely too dark among the trees and underbrush to make them out. He assumed Ab had to have crawled straight toward the spring, and went in that direction. If he'd dared call out, or even make some telltale little sound himself, Ab would hear and steer him on in. But he couldn't take that chance.

It took time, picking up each foot and setting it down again before bringing up the other foot, yet there was no alternative to this kind of stealth unless he wished to bring gunfire down upon himself, more importantly, down upon Ab, too.

He was fifty feet from the beginning of the slope leading up to the spring when he came upon a broken sage limb. He was heading in the right direction! By straightening up a little and peering out where eerie star shine glowed upon the yonder slope, he could distinctly make out the place where Blackie had been when he'd first spotted him slipping down from the spring. It was here, while he temporarily paused to get his bearings, that he heard the faint, heavy stirring of a body in the northward underbrush. He whipped around with his rifle, swinging low and ready. No shot came. In fact, even that little languid sound of sluggish movement was not repeated. He stepped through, using his shoulders to push aside underbrush, came into a little clearing that had an open place leading westward from it straight up the yonder slope toward the cottonwoods, and there Ab lay, his body flat out, his gun five feet off, his eyes looking straight up at Patterson in a fixed and stricken way. 100 feet farther up that little moonlighted open pathway toward the spring lay Blackie, crumpled, face down, obviously beyond all earthly aid.

Patterson leaned his rifle into some wiry sage, got down on one knee, and reached forth to open Ab's coat. Scarlet stained his hands at once. Ab weakly licked his lips and tried to speak. The words didn't form correctly. Ab's voice trailed off into a slurred whisper, and he closed his eyes.

Patterson located the wound. One of Blackie's bullets, probably the last one he ever fired, had caught Ab high in the chest, high and to the left. It looked as though it might have nicked the top of the lung, but when Patterson bent low to see, there was no trace of blood upon Ab's lips, so perhaps the bullet hadn't struck the lung at all. The hole, where the lead had entered, was not much larger than a man's thumb, but where it had emerged under the shoulder blade out back, it had made a ragged, much larger wound. Ab would very shortly bleed to death unless he got aid, and fast.

Patterson got off Ab's brush jacket, slit the shirt with his knife, and, using the shirt, worked up a rough but efficient bandage. He had a hard time stopping the blood, which was warm and thinned down from Ab's exertions.

He removed his own jacket to make the deputy comfortable and Ab came around as Patterson was securing his crude bandage.

"I got him," Ab whispered, his upward gaze rational but

slightly glazed. "He might have got me worse if you hadn't dumped that slug in behind him. That's some rifle you got, Patterson. He jumped like a scairt rabbit when that bullet hit. Jumped right out into the open place. I didn't expect it an' my first slug went wild. He let me have it, then, knocked me down. Dang' near took my breath away. I rolled over. He was comin' for me to finish it. I drilled him plumb through the *cabeza*. His hat flew a hundred feet. He never knew what hit him. Is he still out there?"

"Yeah, he's still out in the clearing. He's not going any-where . . . ever again. You'd better quit talking and just lie still, Ab."

The deputy tried to see up the trail, but Patterson put a hand out holding him down. "He was good with a gun," Ab said. "I always had him pegged for a fast gun, Patterson. Say, you know somethin'? I don't feel any pain. Not very much anyway. That's odd, isn't it, hit hard like I am?"

"That's the shock," muttered Patterson, finishing with the bandaging, wondering whether to raise Ab up enough to put his jacket back on him or not, and finally decided not to. He left Ab's own jacket under him, between his bandaged back and the ground, and covered Ab over the front with his own jacket.

"Is this the big one?" Ab asked huskily. "Come on, Patterson, you don't have to favor my feelings none."

Patterson didn't answer at once. While he was choosing the words, a third voice answered up for him. This voice came from the brush off to the left. Its owner was invisible over there, but both Ab and Patterson recognized it at once.

"That depends on Patterson," Buck said to Ab. "It doesn't have to be the big one, Ab. If Patterson touches his gun, I'll kill him, and, if he dies, you'll lie here alone and bleed to death. It's all in Patterson's hands, Ab."

XVIII

Neither Ab nor Patterson moved. Buck had clearly used the lull in the battle occasioned by the wounding of Ab Folsom to slip down from the spring, locate the two partners by their soft conversation, and get in behind them with his gun. Buck had also made a very good appraisal, too. If Patterson attempted to go for his gun, to spring away, draw, and fire, his chances of getting Buck before Buck got him were slim indeed, and, if Patterson died up in this secluded place, he would also be dooming Ab Folsom to death, because Ab could not move, could not in fact help himself at all. He would quietly lie there and bleed to death. Perhaps, someday, riders might come upon his body, but he would by that time have been dead a very long time because ordinarily no one but stealthy outlaws rode these badlands.

Patterson said, without moving, without making any gesture toward his hip-holstered six-gun: "You called it about right, Buck. On the other hand, you've got me over your sights, so if you fire now, Ab dies anyway."

"No," the outlaw chieftain said softly. "It's too late in life for me to start shooting men in the back, Patterson. You can quit worrying on that score. All I want is to get away. You are all that now stands between me and that wish."

"Why didn't you do it, instead of sneaking down here, Buck? You could've been a mile off by now. I couldn't have stopped you. Not with Ab to care for."

Buck arose and walked out of the underbrush. He was holding his cocked carbine in his left hand, the barrel pointing earthward. His expression was drawn and gray and bone-tired. "You know better, Patterson," he said, stepping out in the star shine where both Ab and Patterson could plainly see him. "That horse up there is weak and tuckered. When your friends come up here, which they'll eventually do, you could leave Ab with them and come after me." Buck gestured toward that custom-made rifle with its telescopic sight. "With that gun, Patterson, you could pick me off from a mile away. I couldn't hope to outrun you."

Patterson slowly arose up off his haunches. He and Buck faced one another over an intervening distance of 100 feet. "Go on," Patterson said. "What's the rest of it, Buck?"

"Your word. That's all, Patterson. Your word you won't come after me. In exchange I give you your life, and by doing that I also give you Ab's life."

Ab weakly raised his head to gaze at Patterson. The bronzed, rangy outlaw was also watching Patterson. It was one of those situations not many men are ever placed in and therefore it becomes easy for them always to aver that no man should ever compromise with his principles. Life is like that sometimes.

Patterson shrugged. "Not much of a choice," he said to Buck. "But it only temporarily saves you. They'll keep looking for you. As long as you're wanted, the law'll keep looking."

"That's my concern, not yours," Buck said shortly. "A man lives his life day by day, Patterson. I've been living mine like that for a long time. But, as I told you once before, just once I'd like to try living it differently. I'd like to find something legitimate and be able to plan far ahead into the future. I can't even hope for that, though, until you give me the chance. Well, time's getting along. Dawn'll be here in another hour. What do you say, Patterson?"

Ab propped himself up and made a wry face at Patterson. "Forget me," he said. "Despite what he thinks, I can make it out of here."

Buck glanced at the deputy sheriff. "You've got guts enough to try it, lawman. But a strong heart's no very good substitute for a sound body. But I know what you're trying to do. Make Patterson's decision easier. I like that in you. But it doesn't help Patterson much. Not really."

A long moment of silence passed among them. Patterson looked at Buck and inclined his head. "You have my word. Go on, head out. And Buck . . . one word of advice . . . keep going. Keep going all the way to San Francisco. Don't ever come back. You give me your word on that and I'll give you mine there'll be no pursuit."

Buck raised his right hand and pushed it out. Patterson took it. The grip was hard and firm. They pumped each other's hands once, and stepped away. Buck turned and struck out back up the slope toward the cottonwoods where his recouped horse stood drowsing under a freshening sky that was paling off in the distant east.

Patterson and Ab watched the outlaw until he was lost to them in the yonder trees. Ab said: "Damned if I don't hope he makes it, Glenn. I don't know exactly why I hope that for him, but I do."

Patterson dropped down to one knee and placed a hand lightly upon Ab's chest. "Lie back and shut up. You've lost enough blood for one fight. As for him . . . well, it's not just me who's got to keep my promise. You were here, too, Ab, you heard it all."

Ab nodded. "Be a pretty low critter if I didn't feel that I owed him somethin' for my life, wouldn't I? Hell, Patterson, as far as I'm concerned he's gone on to greener pastures."

"I hope he finds them, Ab." Patterson lowered himself into a sitting posture.

Ab said: "Look in what's left of my shirt. There's m'tobacco sack in a pocket. How about twistin' me up a smoke?"

Patterson found the makings, dropped his head, and went to work. He had the cigarette finished when, far back up along the rim, a man's soft call drifted down. He twisted to look. So did Ab. Buck was skylined up there. He lifted one arm in a big wave, then pushed his mount on down the far side of the mountain top.

Patterson held the match for Ab. He said: "I wonder if he forgot something?" Ab pushed out a mouthful of smoke and quirked up one eyebrow. "His sister," Patterson stated.

Ab shook his head a little. "He didn't forget. A man doesn't forget something like that, Patterson. You'll figure out what to do about her."

"Will I?"

"Sure. Sellin' Hickman's ranch over there in the grass country would give his widow enough money to travel down to San Francisco . . . with her baby . . . in real style. It'd even tide her over until she could find her brother, and after that who knows? Sometimes fellers take in their sister's kids and raise 'em up to be real men. A lot better men than their pappy ever was."

Patterson gazed steadily at Ab for a long while, until, in fact, he heard the scratch of shod horses coming up through the pink-dawn light from the downward plain. Then he said: "All right, I'll do it for her. But you're going to have to lend a hand, Ab. I don't know a damned thing about selling ranches for widows."

"You get me out of here alive and I'll help you," said Ab. "I'll even do better'n that. I'll even help you get a job as a deputy sheriff under Will Conrad. It won't pay as much, probably, as being an Association man, but it sure lets a feller sleep a heap better at night." Ab killed his smoke and cocked his head. "You better go down on the trail and fetch Dunstan up here."

Patterson stood up, dusted off, and cast a close look downward. "Ab, what happened up here?" he softly asked.

Ab squinted. "I killed one, the other one got away. It was too dark to see him good enough to make an identification."

Patterson nodded, and walked down out of the trees. He had to go nearly a half mile because the cattlemen with Morgan Dunstan were coming along very cautiously in the faint light of the new day. They could distinctly catch the odor of burned powder, and, with daylight's help, could also make out the tracks where a fight had taken place. When they saw Patterson walking down toward them, though, they quickened their pace, for obviously, if there had still been enemies around, Patterson wouldn't be out in the open like that.

Morgan Dunstan was whisker-bristled, stiff, and sore. The men with him, all younger, all more accustomed to this rugged riding, dismounted without showing any of the weariness the older man showed. Dunstan saw the dried blood on Patterson and said sharply: "Are you hurt?"

"No, but Ab Folsom is. He's hard hit," replied Patterson. "We'll have to make a travois and be damned careful about how we get him down out of here."

Dunstan turned. "Some of you boys cut some poles and rig up a travois," he ordered, then faced forward again. "Where are they?" he asked, his meaning clear enough.

"One's dead," replied Patterson, impassively, "and one got away."

"Which direction, dammit. We'll split up. Half go back with Folsom. Half get on his trail."

"No. He's got too big a start. Anyway, he won't cause any more trouble. You can stake your ranch on that, Mister Dunstan."

The older man looked up along the southward rim where soft dawn light was tinting the forbidding dark peaks and sags. "You're probably right," he mused. "We got Hickman. He was the big gun among 'em evidently. This one that got away . . . he's probably so scairt he'll be runnin' a year from now. All right. Let's go get Ab and get back down out of here. I sent some of the boys on back with the bodies. That feller you left with us at the Roost . . . he escaped in the night."

Dunstan started to move past. Patterson said, dumbfounded:

"Escaped, that fat cook? Dunstan, how could a sniveling tub of lard like that get away with all you fellows watching him?"

Dunstan not only did not reply, but he kept right on striding along as though he hadn't heard. One of the other men sauntered up, caught Patterson's attention, and raffishly winked. This man said softly, with his grinning friends looking on: "Tell you how it was, friend. Ralph never went on none of the cattle raids with the other ones. Besides that, he was about as totally helpless as a growed man could be. So . . . when he went outside, a couple of the boys sort of steered him over where a loose horse was standing with its saddle already on, and then they sort of steered him on southward through the Roost to the trail."

Patterson slowly, gradually comprehended. These hard men, violent in battle and in most ways unrelenting, had made their correct judgment of Ralph; taken back to Willows, he undoubtedly would have been hung, or at the very least sentenced to possibly twenty years in prison. They'd had their revenge on the rustlers. They had no intention of seeing anyone who hadn't been in that fierce fight on the prairie step in and tell them what must be done with a useless cohort of the smashed rustling ring, so they'd sent Ralph on his way.

"You understand?" the raffish cowboy asked.

Patterson nodded. "I understand. You have no idea just how *well* I understand. Let's get to rigging out this travois for Deputy Folsom. And one more thing . . . there's a dead one up that yonder slope. He deserves a better burial than he's likely to get if we leave him here."

Three of the riders nodded and started on up toward the sun-drenched clearing where Blackie lay. The others started fashioning a travois for Ab. Patterson took that raffish man and went on up where Ab and Morgan Dunstan were quietly talking. Dunstan, it turned out, had brought along a bottle from the saloon down at the Roost. Ab's cheeks showed good color from that medicine. When Patterson came up, Ab looked up at him and slyly winked.

"Dunstan set the Roost on fire," he said. "That ought to discourage anyone from ever tryin' to start up another rustling organization in these lousy hills, Patterson."

"You better be quiet and get ready to suffer a little," Patterson said, bending to help lift the injured lawman.

They carried Ab gently out where the travois was being made fast to a gentle saddle animal. Two men were tightly stretching saddle blankets between the travois poles. Two other range riders had Patterson's and Ab's animals in tow. Morgan Dunstan waited until the men had eased Ab down upon his Indian pallet, then bent and tucked the whiskey bottle in beside the wounded man.

"If it gets too bad," he suggested, "try pullin' on that bottle. You'll probably hate yourself tomorrow, but for today it'll get you along well enough."

Ab smiled and rolled his eyes around until he saw Glenn Patterson. He slowly dropped one eyelid and lifted it again.

A cowboy got astride the horse ahead of Ab's travois, lifted the reins, and started off. The trail didn't get bad until they were making the switchback down the north slope, and down there a half dozen solicitous hands lifted Ab gently and carefully over the worst places. Far back, with the final posse man to leave the badlands, Blackie bumped along tied with his arms down one side of his saddle, his legs tied down the opposite side.

They got down upon the prairie northward bound with good warmth gradually rolling out over the land. From there on until they eventually struck the Willows trace, the land was level and smooth. Afterward, up closer to town, the way would be even better.

Patterson slouched along beside Ab's improvised, horse-drawn sling. He saw how the wounded man's steady, slitted gaze lay thoughtfully upon the receding hills far back. He could guess how Ab's thoughts were running. After a while he bent down and said in a tone too low for the others to hear: "You satisfied?"

Ab looked up and grinned. "Plumb satisfied, Glenn. Plumb satisfied. Even with this hole in me, I'm glad I decided to ride along with you. You're a pretty good man . . . for an Association man, that is."

ABOUT THE AUTHOR

Lauran Paine who, under his own name and various pseudonyms has written over 1,000 books, was born in Duluth, Minnesota. His family moved to California when he was at a young age and his apprenticeship as a Western writer came about through the years he spent in the livestock trade, rodeos, and even motion pictures where he served as an extra because of his expert horsemanship in several films starring movie cowboy Johnny Mack Brown. In the late 1930s, Paine trapped wild horses in northern Arizona and even, for a time, worked as a professional farrier. Paine came to know the Old West through the eyes of many who had been born in the previous century, and he learned that Western life had been very different from the way it was portrayed on the screen. "I knew men who had killed other men," he later recalled. "But they were the exceptions. Prior to and during the Depression, people were just too busy eking out an existence to indulge in Saturday-night brawls." He served in the U.S. Navy in the Second World War and began writing for Western pulp magazines following his discharge. It is interesting to note that all of his earliest novels (written under his own name and the pseudonym Mark Carrel) were published in the British market and he soon had as strong a following in that country as in the United States. Paine's Western fiction is characterized by strong plots, authenticity, an apparently effortless ability to construct situation and character, and a preference for building his stories upon a solid foundation of historical fact. *Adobe Empire* (1956), one of his best novels, is a fictionalized account of the last twenty years in the life of trader William Bent and, in an off-trail way, has a melancholy, bittersweet texture that is not easily forgotten. In later novels like *The White Bird* (Five Star Westerns, 1997) and *Cache Cañon* (Five Star Westerns, 1998), he showed that the special magic and power of his stories and characters had only matured along with his basic themes of changing times, changing attitudes, learning from experience, respecting Nature, and the yearning for a simpler, more moderate way of life. His next Five Star Western will be *Hurd's Crossing*.